1.99

ROBERT BURNS (1759–96). Scottish poet and songwriter, best remembered for 'Auld Lang Syne', which is sung all over the English-speaking world during New Year celebrations.

Robert Burns was born in Ayrshire, Scotland, one of seven children and the son of a cotter. He was given an excellent education by his father and from an early age read the Bible, the English Augustans and Shakespeare. He wrote verses while still at school and worked as a labourer and ploughman on the farm, which was struggling to survive. He suffered severe penury, and the privation and overwork of subsistence farming began the rheumatic heart disease which was to cause his premature death. His father died bankrupt in 1784, and Burns leased a farm at Mossgiel, which he referred to in the poetry he was by now writing profusely. His poems of this period include 'The Cotter's Saturday Night', 'To a Mouse', 'Holy Willie's Prayer' and 'The Holy Fair'. He was strongly influenced by the writing of Henry MacKenzie, particularly his novel *The Man of Feeling*, which Burns loved 'next to the Bible'. He met Jean Armour in 1785, whom he accepted as his wife three years later, after she had borne him two pairs of twins. He became embroiled with various other amatory attachments, particularly with Mary Campbell, who is mentioned in his poem 'To Mary in Heaven' and with whom he was planning to emigrate until her untimely death in 1786, reputedly in childbirth. In the same year his publisher in Kilmarnock published Burns's *Poems, Chiefly in the Scottish Dialect*, which was an instant success. His overwhelming popularity was revealed most strongly in the adulation shown by his fellow countrymen, but MacKenzie was also to praise him as 'a Heaven-taught ploughman'. Unfortunately this great acclaim went to Burns's head and led him into a life of dissipation and debauchery. His writing style changed as he was persuaded to emulate the sentimental fashion of the time, producing poems such as 'The Lament', 'Despondency' and 'Address to Edinburgh', yet his characteristic tone thankfully remained intact. His career developed and he was requested to collect some old Scottish songs for *The Scots Musical Museum*, which led him to writing songs himself, most famously 'Auld Lang Syne', 'O My Luve's Like a Red, Red Rose', 'Ye Banks and Braes' and 'Scots Wha Hae'. In 1787 he travelled in the Highlands and the Borders, collecting tunes and words. He viewed these contributions as his patriotic duty and so accepted no fee, although he continued to publish work of his own. Burns was offered a job as an Excise officer, and in 1791 he could eventually relinquish the farming life which had proved such a strain to him and move to Dumfries. In the same year he was to publish his last major work, the narrative poem 'Tam o'Shanter'. In 1795 he joined the Dumfries Volunteers against the French. Robert Burns died in 1796.

This classic collection includes all of Burns's best-loved poetry and songs, such as 'Auld Lang Syne', 'To a Mouse' and 'Holy Willie's Prayer'. His voice is as resonant today as when he was composing his work in the local Scottish dialect two centuries ago.

PENGUIN POPULAR CLASSICS

ROBERT BURNS
SELECTED POEMS

PENGUIN BOOKS

PENGUIN BOOKS

Published by the Penguin Group
Penguin Books Ltd, 27 Wrights Lane, London w8 5tz, England
Penguin Putnam Inc., 375 Hudson Street, New York, New York 10014, USA
Penguin Books Australia Ltd, Ringwood, Victoria, Australia
Penguin Books Canada Ltd, 10 Alcorn Avenue, Toronto, Ontario, Canada m4v 3b2
Penguin Books (NZ) Ltd, Private Bag 102902, NSMC, Auckland, New Zealand

Penguin Books Ltd, Registered Offices: Harmondsworth, Middlesex, England

This edition first published 1946
Published in Penguin Popular Classics 1996
5 7 9 10 8 6 4

Printed in England by Cox & Wyman Ltd, Reading, Berkshire

Contents.

POEMS, EPISTLES, &c.

SONGS AND BALLADS.

Poems, Epistles, &c.

TAM O' SHANTER.

When chapman billies leave the street,
And drouthy neibors neibors meet,
As market-days are wearing late,
An' folk begin to tak the gate;
While we sit bousing at the nappy,
An' getting fou and unco happy,
We think na on the lang Scots miles,
The mosses, waters, slaps, and styles,
That lie between us and our hame,
Where sits our sulky sullen dame,   10
Gathering her brows like gathering storm,
Nursing her wrath to keep it warm.

   This truth fand honest Tam o' Shanter,
As he frae Ayr ae night did canter—
(Auld Ayr, wham ne'er a town surpasses
For honest men and bonnie lasses).

   O Tam! hadst thou but been sae wise
As ta'en thy ain wife Kate's advice!
She tauld thee weel thou was a skellum,
A bletherin', blusterin', drunken blellum;   20
That frae November till October,
Ae market-day thou was na sober;
That ilka melder wi' the miller
Thou sat as lang as thou had siller;
That every naig was ca'd a shoe on,
The smith and thee gat roarin' fou on;

That at the Lord's house, even on Sunday,
Thou drank wi' Kirkton Jean till Monday.
She prophesied that, late or soon,
Thou would be found deep drown'd in Doon;   30
Or catch'd wi' warlocks in the mirk
By Alloway's auld haunted kirk.

   Ah, gentle dames! it gars me greet
To think how mony counsels sweet,
How mony lengthen'd sage advices,
The husband frae the wife despises!

   But to our tale: Ae market night,
Tam had got planted unco right,
Fast by an ingle, bleezing finely,
Wi' reaming swats, that drank divinely;   40
And at his elbow, Souter Johnny,
His ancient, trusty, drouthy crony;
Tam lo'ed him like a very brither;
They had been fou for weeks thegither.
The night drave on wi' sangs and clatter,
And aye the ale was growing better:
The landlady and Tam grew gracious,
Wi' favours secret, sweet, and precious;
The souter tauld his queerest stories;
The landlord's laugh was ready chorus: 50
The storm without might rair and rustle,
Tam did na mind the storm a whistle.

   Care, mad to see a man sae happy,
E'en drown'd himsel amang the nappy.
As bees flee hame wi' lades o' treasure,
The minutes wing'd their way wi' pleasure;
Kings may be blest, but Tam was glorious,
O'er a' the ills o' life victorious!

   But pleasures are like poppies spread—
You seize the flow'r, its bloom is shed;   60
Or like the snow falls in the river—
A moment white, then melts for ever;
Or like the borealis race,
That flit ere you can point their place;
Or like the rainbow's lovely form
Evanishing amid the storm.
Nae man can tether time nor tide;
The hour approaches Tam maun ride;

That hour, o' night's black arch the key-stane,
That dreary hour, he mounts his beast in;　　70
And sic a night he taks the road in,
As ne'er poor sinner was abroad in.
　　The wind blew as 'twad blawn its last;
The rattling show'rs rose on the blast;
The speedy gleams the darkness swallow'd;
Loud, deep, and lang, the thunder bellow'd:
That night, a child might understand,
The Deil had business on his hand.
　　Weel mounted on his gray mare, Meg,
A better never lifted leg,　　　　　　　80
Tam skelpit on thro' dub and mire,
Despising wind, and rain, and fire;
Whiles holding fast his gude blue bonnet;
Whiles crooning o'er some auld Scots sonnet;
Whiles glow'ring round wi' prudent cares,
Lest bogles catch him unawares.
Kirk-Alloway was drawing nigh,
Whare ghaists and houlets nightly cry.
　　By this time he was cross the ford,
Whore in the snaw the chapman smoor'd;　　90
And past the birks and meikle stane,
Where drunken Charlie brak 's neck-bane;
And thro' the whins, and by the cairn,
Where hunters fand the murder'd bairn;
And near the thorn, aboon the well,
Where Mungo's mither hang'd hersel.
Before him Doon pours all his floods;
The doubling storm roars thro' the woods;
The lightnings flash from pole to pole;
Near and more near the thunders roll:　　100
When, glimmering thro' the groaning trees,
Kirk-Alloway seem'd in a bleeze;
Thro' ilka bore the beams were glancing;
And loud resounded mirth and dancing.
　　Inspiring bold John Barleycorn!
What dangers thou canst make us scorn!
Wi' tippenny, we fear nae evil;
Wi' usquebae, we'll face the devil!
The swats sae ream'd in Tammie's noddle,
Fair play, he car'd na deils a boddle!　　110

But Maggie stood right sair astonish'd,
Till, by the heel and hand admonish'd,
She ventur'd forward on the light;
And, vow! Tam saw an unco sight!
Warlocks and witches in a dance!
Nae cotillon brent new frae France,
But hornpipes, jigs, strathspeys, and reels,
Put life and mettle in their heels.
A winnock-bunker in the east,
There sat auld Nick, in shape o' beast—   120
A touzie tyke, black, grim, and large!
To gie them music was his charge:
He screw'd the pipes and gart them skirl.
Till roof and rafters a' did dirl.
Coffins stood round like open presses,
That shaw'd the dead in their last dresses;
And by some devilish cantraip sleight
Each in its cauld hand held a light,
By which heroic Tam was able
To note upon the haly table   130
A murderer's banes in gibbet-airns;
Twa span-lang, wee, unchristen'd bairns;
A thief new-cutted frae the rape—
Wi' his last gasp his gab did gape;
Five tomahawks, wi' blude red rusted;
Five scymitars, wi' murder crusted;
A garter, which a babe had strangled;
A knife, a father's throat had mangled,
Whom his ain son o' life bereft—
The gray hairs yet stack to the heft;   140
Wi' mair of horrible and awfu',
Which even to name wad be unlawfu'.
   As Tammie glowr'd, amaz'd, and curious,
The mirth and fun grew fast and furious:
The piper loud and louder blew;
The dancers quick and quicker flew;
They reel'd, they set, they cross'd, they cleekit,
Till ilka carlin swat and reekit,
And coost her duddies to the wark,
And linkit at it in her sark!   150
   Now Tam, O Tam! had thae been queans,
A' plump and strapping in their teens;

Their sarks, instead o' creeshie flannen,
Been snaw-white seventeen hunder linen!
Thir breeks o' mine, my only pair,
That ance were plush, o' gude blue hair,
I wad hae gi'en them off my hurdies,
For ae blink o' the bonnie burdies!
But wither'd beldams, auld and droll,
Rigwoodie hags wad spean a foal,   160
Louping and flinging on a crummock,
I wonder didna turn thy stomach.
But Tam kent what was what fu' brawlie
There was ae winsome wench and walie
That night enlisted in the core,
Lang after kent on Carrick shore!
(For mony a beast to dead she shot,
And perish'd mony a bonnie boat,
And shook baith meikle corn and bear,
And kept the country-side in fear.)   170
Her cutty sark, o' Paisley harn,
That while a lassie she had worn,
In longitude tho' sorely scanty,
It was her best, and she was vauntie.
Ah! little kent thy reverend grannie
That sark she coft for her wee Nannie
Wi' twa pund Scots ('twas a' her riches)
Wad ever grac'd a dance of witches!
But here my muse 'her wing maun cour :
Sic flights are far beyond her pow'r—   180
To sing how Nannie lap and flang,
(A souple jade she was, and strang);
And how Tam stood, like ane bewitch'd,
And thought his very een enrich'd;
Even Satan glowr'd, and fidg'd fu' fain,
And hotch'd and blew wi' might and main:
Till first ae caper, syne anither,
Tam tint his reason a' thegither,
And roars out 'Weel done, Cutty-sark!'
And in an instant all was dark!   190
And scarcely had he Maggie rallied,
When out the hellish legion sallied.
As bees bizz out wi' angry fyke
When plundering herds assail their byke,

As open pussie's mortal foes
When pop! she starts before their nose,
As eager runs the market-crowd,
When 'Catch the thief!' resounds aloud.
So Maggie runs; the witches follow,
Wi' mony an eldritch skriech and hollow.   200
    Ah, Tam! ah, Tam! thou'll get thy fairin'!
In hell they'll roast thee like a herrin'!
In vain thy Kate awaits thy comin'!
Kate soon will be a woefu' woman!
Now do thy speedy utmost, Meg,
And win the key-stane o' the brig:
There at them thou thy tail may toss,
A running stream they darena cross.
But ere the key-stane she could make,
The fient a tail she had to shake!   210
For Nannie, far before the rest,
Hard upon noble Maggie prest,
And flew at Tam wi' furious ettle;
But little wist she Maggie's mettle!
Ae spring brought off her master hale,
But left behind her ain gray tail:
The carlin claught her by the rump,
And left poor Maggie scarce a stump.
    Now, wha this tale o' truth shall read,
Each man and mother's son, take heed;   220
Whene'er to drink you are inclin'd,
Or cutty-sarks rin in your mind,
Think! ye may buy the joys o'er dear;
Remember Tam o' Shanter's mare.

THE JOLLY BEGGARS.

When lyart leaves bestrow the yird,
Or, wavering like the baukie bird,
  Bedim cauld Boreas' blast ;
When hailstanes drive wi' bitter skyte,
And infant frosts begin to bite,
  In hoary cranreuch drest ;
Ae night at e'en a merry core
  O' randie gangrel bodies
In Poosie Nansie's held the splore,
  To drink their orra duddies.   10
    Wi' quaffing and laughing,
      They rantod and they sang ;
    Wi' jumping and thumping
    The very girdle rang.

First, niest the fire, in auld red rags,
Ane sat, weel brac'd wi' mealy bags,
  And knapsack a' in order ;
His doxy lay within his arm ;
Wi' usquebae and blankets warm.
  She blinket on her sodger ;   20
An' aye he gies the tosy drab
  The tither skelpin' kiss,
While she held up her greedy gab,
  Just like an aumous dish :
    Ilk smack still did crack still
      Just like a cadger's whip ;
    Then staggering, and swaggering,
    He roar'd this ditty up—

I am a son of Mars, who have been in many wars,
  And show my cuts and scars wherever I come ;   30
This here was for a wench, and that other in a trench,
  When welcoming the French at the sound of the drum.
                Lal de daudle, &c.

My 'prenticeship I pass'd where my leader breath'd his
          last,
    When the bloody die was cast on the heights of Abrám;
And I servèd out my trade when the gallant game was
          play'd,
    And the Moro low was laid at the sound of the drum.

I lastly was with Curtis, among the floating batt'ries,
    And there I left for witness an arm and a limb:
Yet let my country need me, with Elliot to head me, 40
    I'd clatter on my stumps at the sound of a drum.

And now tho' I must beg, with a wooden arm and leg,
    And many a tatter'd rag hanging over my bum,
I'm as happy with my wallet, my bottle, and my callet,
    As when I used in scarlet to follow a drum.

What tho' with hoary locks I must stand the winter
          shocks,
    Beneath the woods and rocks oftentimes for a home?
When the t'other bag I sell, and the t'other bottle tell,
    I could meet a troop of hell at the sound of the drum.

            He ended; and the kebars sheuk   50
                Aboon the chorus roar;
            While frighted rattons backward leuk,
                And seek the benmost bore.
            A fairy fiddler frae the neuk,
                He skirled out *Encore!*
            But up arose the martial chuck,
                And laid the loud uproar.

I once was a maid, tho' I cannot tell when,
And still my delight is in proper young men;
Some one of a troop of dragoons was my daddie,   60
No wonder I'm fond of a sodger laddie.
                              Sing, Lal de dal, &c.

The first of my loves was a swaggering blade,
To rattle the thundering drum was his trade;
His leg was so tight, and his cheek was so ruddy,
Transported I was with my sodger laddie.

But the godly old chaplain left him in the lurch;
The sword I forsook for the sake of the church;
He ventur'd the soul, and I riskèd the body,—
'Twas then I prov'd false to my sodger laddie. 70

Full soon I grew sick of my sanctified sot,
The regiment at large for a husband I got;
From the gilded spontoon to the fife I was ready,
I askèd no more but a sodger laddie.

But the peace it reduced me to beg in despair,
Till I met my old boy at a Cunningham fair;
His rags regimental they flutter'd so gaudy,
My heart it rejoiced at a sodger laddie.

And now I have liv'd—I know not how long,
And still I can join in a cup or a song; 80
But whilst with both hands I can hold the glass steady,
Here's to thee, my hero, my sodger laddie!

Poor Merry Andrew in the neuk
　Sat guzzling wi' a tinkler hizzie;
They mind't na wha the chorus touk,
　Between themselves they were sae busy.
　At length, wi' drink and courting dizzy,
He stoitered up an' made a face;
　Then turn'd, an' laid a smack on Grizzy,
Syne tun'd his pipes wi' grave grimace. 90

Sir Wisdom's a fool when he's fou,
　Sir Knave is a fool in a session;
He's there but a 'prentice I trow,
　But I am a fool by profession.

My grannie she bought me a beuk,
   And I held awa to the school;
I fear I my talent misteuk,
   But what will ye hae of a fool?

For drink I would venture my neck;
   A hizzie's the half o' my craft;   100
But what could ye other expect,
   Of ane that's avowedly daft?

I ance was tied up like a stirk,
   For civilly swearing and quaffing;
I ance was abused i' the kirk,
   For touzling a lass i' my daffin.

Poor Andrew that tumbles for sport,
   Let naebody name wi' a jeer;
There's even, I'm tauld, i' the Court,
   A tumbler ca'd the Premier.   110

Observ'd ye yon reverend lad
   Maks faces to tickle the mob?
He rails at our mountebank squad—
   It's rivalship just i' the job.

And now my conclusion I'll tell,
   For, faith! I'm confoundedly dry;
The chiel that's a fool for himsel',
   Gude Lord! he's far dafter than I.

Then niest outspak a raucle carlin,
Wha kent fu' weel to cleek the sterling,   120
For mony a pursie she had hookit,
And had in mony a well been dookit;
Her love had been a Highland laddie,
But weary fa' the waefu' woodie!
Wi' sighs and sobs, she thus began
To wail her braw John Highlandman:—

A Highland lad my love was born,
The Lawlan' laws he held in scorn ;
But he still was faithfu' to his clan,
My gallant braw John Highlandman.   130

CHORUS.

Sing hey, my braw John Highlandman !
Sing ho, my braw John Highlandman !
There 's no a lad in a' the lan'
Was match for my John Highlandman.

With his philibeg an' tartan plaid,
And gude claymore down by his side,
The ladies' hearts he did trepan,
My gallant braw John Highlandman.

We rangèd a' from Tweed to Spey,
And lived like lords 'and ladies gay ;   140
For a Lawlan' face he fearèd nane,
My gallant braw John Highlandman.

They banish'd him beyond the sea ;
But ere the bud was on the tree,
Adown my cheeks the pearls ran,
Embracing my John Highlandman.

But oh ! they catch'd him at the last,
And bound him in a dungeon fast ;
My curse upon them every one !
They've hang'd my braw John Highlandman. 150

And now a widow I must mourn
The pleasures that will ne'er return ;
No comfort but a hearty can,
When I think on John Highlandman.

A pigmy scraper wi' his fiddle,
Wha used at trysts and fairs to driddle,
Her strappin' limb and gaucy middle
      (He reach'd nae higher)
Had holed his heartie like a riddle,
      And blawn't on fire.   160

Wi' hand on haunch, and upward ee,
He croon'd his gamut, one, two, three,
Then, in an arioso key,
      The wee. Apollo
Set aff, wi' allegretto glee,
      His giga solo.

Let me ryke up to dight that tear,
And go wi' me and be my dear,
And then your every care and fear
  May whistle owre the lave o't.   170

CHORUS.

I am a fiddler to my trade,
And a' the tunes that e'er I play'd,
The sweetest still to wife or maid,
  Was whistle owre the lave o't.

At kirns and weddings we'se be there,
And oh! sae nicely 's we will fare;
We'll bouse about, till Daddie Care
  Sings whistle owre the lave o't.

Sae merrily 's the banes we'll pyke,
And sun oursels about the dyke,   180
And at our leisure, when ye like,
  We'll whistle owre the lave o't.

But bless me wi' your heav'n o' charms,
And while I kittle hair on thairms,
Hunger and cauld, and a' sic harms,
  May whistle owre the lave o't.

Her charms had struck a sturdy caird,
  As well as poor gut-scraper;
He taks the fiddler by the beard,
  And draws a roosty rapier— 190

He swoor, by a' was swearing worth,
  To spit him like a pliver,
Unless he would from that time forth
  Relinquish her for ever.

Wi' ghastly ee, poor tweedle-dee
  Upon his hunkers bended,
And pray'd for grace wi' ruefu' face,
  And sae the quarrel ended.

But tho' his little heart did grieve
  When round the tinkler prest her,
He feign'd to snirtle in his sleeve, 200
  When thus the caird address'd her :—

My bonnie lass, I work in brass,
  A tinkler is my station;
I've travell'd round all Christian ground
  In this my occupation;
I've ta'en the gold, I've been enroll'd
  In many a noble squadron;
But vain they search'd, when off I march'd
  To go and clout the cauldron. 210

Despise that shrimp, that wither'd imp,
  Wi' a' his noise and caperin';
And tak a share wi' those that bear
  The budget and the apron;
And, by that stoup, my faith and houp!
  And by that dear Kilbaigie,
If e'er ye want, or meet wi' scant,
  May I ne'er weet my craigie.

The caird prevail'd—th' unblushing fair
  In his embraces sunk,   220
Partly wi' love o'ercome sae sair,
  And partly she was drunk.
Sir Violino, with an air
  That show'd a man o' spunk,
Wish'd unison between the pair,
  And made the bottle clunk
          To their health that night.

But urchin Cupid shot a shaft
  That play'd a dame a shavie ;
The fiddler rak'd her fore and aft,   230
  Behint the chicken cavie.
Her lord, a wight of Homer's craft,
  Tho' limpin' wi' the spavie,
He hirpled up, and lap like daft,
  And shor'd them *Dainty Davie*
          O' boot that night.

He was a care-defying blade
  As ever Bacchus listed ;
Tho' Fortune sair upon him laid,
  His heart she ever miss'd it.   240
He had nae wish, but to be glad,
  Nor want but when he thirsted ;
He hated nought but to be sad,
  And thus the Muse suggested
          His sang that night.

I am a bard of no regard
  Wi' gentlefolks, and a' that ;
But Homer-like, the glowrin' byke,
  Frae town to town I draw that.

CHORUS.

For a' that, and a' that,
  And twice as meikle's a' that ;   250
I've lost but ane, I've twa behin',
  I've wife eneugh for a' that.

I never drank the Muses' stank,
  Castalia's burn, and a' that;
But there it streams, and richly reams!
  My Helicon I ca' that.

Great love I bear to a' the fair,
  Their humble slave, and a' that;
But lordly will, I hold it still   260
  A mortal sin to thraw that.

In raptures sweet this hour we meet
  Wi' mutual love, and a' that;
But for how lang the flee may stang,
  Let inclination law that.

Their tricks and craft hae put me daft,
  They've ta'en me in, and a' that;
But clear your decks, and *Here's the sex!*
  I like the jads for a' that.

    For a' that, and a' that,   270
      And twice as meikle 's a' that,
    My dearest bluid, to do them guid,
      They're welcome till't, for a' that.

So sung the bard—and Nansie's wa's
Shook with a thunder of applause,
  Re-echo'd from each mouth;
They toom'd their pocks, an' pawn'd their duds,
They scarcely left to co'er their fuds,
  To quench their lowin' drouth.
Then owre again the jovial thrang   280
  The poet did request
To lowse his pack, an' wale a sang,
  A ballad o' the best;
    He rising, rejoicing,
      Between his twa Deborahs,
    Looks round him, an' found them
      Impatient for the chorus.

See the smoking bowl before us,
  Mark our jovial ragged ring;
Round and round take up the chorus,   290
  And in raptures let us sing—

CHORUS.

A fig for those by law protected!
  Liberty's a glorious feast!
Courts for cowards were erected,
  Churches built to please the priest.

What is title? what is treasure?
  What is reputation's care?
If we lead a life of pleasure,
  'Tis no matter how or where!

With the ready trick and fable,   300
  Round we wander all the day;
And at night, in barn or stable,
  Hug our doxies on the hay.

Does the train-attended carriage
  Thro' the country lighter rove?
Does the sober bed of marriage
  Witness brighter scenes of love?

Life is all a variorum,
  We regard not how it goes;
Let them cant about decorum   310
  Who have characters to lose.

Here's to budgets, bags, and wallets!
  Here's to all the wandering train!
Here's our ragged brats and callets!
  One and all cry out *Amen!*

[THE SAILOR'S SONG.]

Tho' women's minds, like winter winds,
  May shift, an' turn, and a' that,
The noblest breast adores them maist—
  A consequence I draw that.

CHORUS.

  For a' that, and a' that,
    An' twice as meikle 's a' that;
  The bonnie lass that I lo'e best,
    She'll be my ain for a' that!

Great love I bear to a' the fair,
  Their humble slave and a' that;
But lordly will, I hold it still
  A mortal sin to thraw that.

But there is ane aboon the lave
  Has wit, an' sense, and a' that;
A bonnie lass, I like her best,
  An' wha a crime dare ca' that?

In rapture sweet this hour we meet
  Wi' mutual love, and a' that;
But for how lang the flee may stang,—
  Let inclination law that.

Their tricks an' craft hae put me daft;
  They've ta'en me in, and a' that;
But clear your decks, an' *Here's the sex!*
  I like the jads for a' that!

320

330

[THE CAIRD'S SECOND SONG.]

O merry hae I been teethin' a heckle,   340
   An' merry hae I been shapin' a spoon ;
O merry hae I been cloutin' a kettle,
   An' kissin' my Katie when a' was done.
O a' the lang day I ca' at my hammer,
   An' a' the lang day I whistle and sing,
A' the lang night I cuddle my kimmer,
   An' a' the lang night am as happy 's a King.

Bitter in dool I lickit my winnins,
   O' marrying Bess, to gie her a slave :
Bless'd be the hour she cool'd in her linens,   350
   And blythe be the bird that sings on her grave.
Come to my arms, my Katie, my Katie,
   O come to my arms, an' kiss me again !
Drucken or sober, here 's to thee, Katie !
   And bless'd be the day I did it again.

———•———

HALLOWEEN.

Upon that night, when fairies light
   On Cassilis Downans dance,
Or owre the lays, in splendid blaze,
   On sprightly coursers prance ;
Or for Colean the rout is ta'en,
   Beneath the moon's pale beams ;
There, up the Cove, to stray an' rove
   Amang the rocks and streams
            To sport that night ;

Amang the bonnie winding banks   10
  Where Doon rins wimplin' clear,
Where Bruce ance ruled the martial ranks
  An' shook his Carrick spear,
Some merry friendly country-folks
  Together did convene
To burn their nits, an' pou their stocks,
  An' haud their Halloween
                Fu' blythe that night:

The lasses feat, an' cleanly neat,
  Mair braw than when they're fine;   20
Their faces blythe fu' sweetly kythe
  Hearts leal, an' warm, an' kin':
The lads sae trig, wi' wooer-babs
  Weel knotted on their garten,
Some unco blate, an' some wi' gabs
  Gar lasses' hearts gang startin'
                Whyles fast at night.

Then, first an foremost, thro' the kail,
  Their stocks maun a' be sought ance:
They steek their een, an' grape an' wale   30
  For muckle anes an' straught anes.
Poor hav'rel Will fell aff the drift,
  An' wander'd thro' the bow-kail,
An' pou'd, for want o' better shift,
  A runt was like a sow-tail,
                Sae bow'd, that night.

Then, straught or crookèd, yird or nane,
  They roar an' cry a' throu'ther;
The very wee things toddlin' rin—
  Wi' stocks out-owre their shouther;   40
An' gif the custock's sweet or sour,
  Wi' joctelegs they taste them;
Syne coziely, aboon the door,
  Wi' cannie care they've plac'd them
                To lie that night.

The lasses staw frae 'mang them a'
　To pou their stalks o' corn ;
But Rab slips out, an' jinks about,
　Behint the muckle thorn :
He grippit Nelly hard an' fast ;　　　　　　　50
　Loud skirled a' the lasses ;
But her tap-pickle maist was lost,
　When kiutlin' i' the fause-house
　　　　　　Wi' him that night.

The auld guidwife's well-hoordit nits
　Are round an' round divided,
An' mony lads' an' lasses' fates
　Are there that night decided :
Some kindle, couthie, side by side,
　An' burn thegither trimly ;　　　　　　　60
Some start awa, wi' saucy pride,
　An' jump out-owre the chimlie
　　　　　　Fu' high that night.

Jean slips in twa, wi' tentie e'e ;
　Wha 'twas, she wadna tell ;
But this is Jock, an' this is me,
　She says in to hersel :
He bleez'd owre her, an' she owre him,
　As they wad never mair part ;
Till fuff ! he started up the lum,　　　　　　70
　An' Jean had e'en a sair heart
　　　　　　To see't that night.

Poor Willie, wi' his bow-kail runt,
　Was brunt wi' primsie Mallie,
An' Mary, nae doubt, took the drunt,
　To be compar'd to Willie :
Mall's nit lap out, wi' pridefu' fling,
　An' her ain fit it brunt it ;
While Willie lap, an' swoor by jing,
　'Twas just the way he wanted　　　　　　80
　　　　　　To be that night.

Nell had the fause-house in her min',
  She pits hersel an' Rob in;
In loving bleeze they sweetly join,
  Till white in ase they're sobbin:
Nell's heart was dancin' at the view:
  She whisper'd Rob to leuk for't:
Rob, stownlins, prie'd her bonnie mou',
  Fu' cozie in the neuk for't,
              Unseen that night.   90

But Merran sat behint their backs,
  Her thoughts on Andrew Bell;
She lea'es them gashin' at their cracks,
  An' slips out by hersel:
She thro' the yard the nearest taks,
  An' to the kiln she goes then,
An' darklins grapit for the bauks,
  And in the blue-clue throws then,
              Right fear'd that night.

An' aye she win't, an' aye she swat,   100
  I wat she made nae jaukin';
Till something held within the pat,
  Guid Lord! but she was quaukin'!
But whether 'twas the Deil himsel,
  Or whether 'twas a bauk-en',
Or whether it was Andrew Bell,
  She did na wait on talkin
              To spier that night.

Wee Jenny to her grannie says,
  'Will ye go wi' me, grannie?   110
I'll eat the apple at the glass,
  I gat frae uncle Johnie:'
She fuff't her pipe wi' sic a lunt,
  In wrath she was sae vap'rin,
She noticed na an aizle brunt
  Her braw new worset apron
              Out-thro' that night.

· Ye little skelpie-limmer's face!
  I daur you try sic sportin',
As seek the foul Thief ony place,   120
  For him to spae your fortune!
Nae doubt but ye may get a sight!
  Great cause ye hae to fear it;
For mony a ane has gotten a fright,
  An' lived an' died deleerit,
          On sic a night.

' Ae hairst afore the Sherra-moor,—
  I mind't as weel 's yestreen,
I was a gilpey then, I'm sure
  I was na past fyfteen: 130
The simmer had been cauld an' wat,
  An' stuff was unco green;
An' aye a rantin' kirn we gat,
  An' just on Halloween
          It fell that night.

Our stibble-rig was Rab M'Graen,
  A clever, sturdy fallow;
His sin gat Eppie Sim wi' wean,
  That liv'd in Achmacalla;
He gat hemp-seed, I mind it weel,   140
  An' he made unco light o't;
But mony a day was by himsel,
  He was sae sairly frighted
          That vera night.'

Then up gat fechtin' Jamie Fleck,
  An' he swoor by his conscience
That he could saw hemp-seed a peck;
  For it was a' but nonsense:
The auld guidman raught down the pock,
  An' out a handfu' gied him;   150
Syne bad him slip frae 'mang the folk,
  Sometime when nae ane see'd him,
          An' try't that night.

He marches thro' amang the stacks,
   Tho' he was something sturtin';
The graip he for a harrow taks,
   An' haurls at his curpin:
An' ev'ry now an' then, he says,
   'Hemp-seed! I saw thee,
An' her that is to be my lass   160
   Come after me an' draw thee
          As fast this night.'

He whistled up Lord Lennox' march,
   To keep his courage cheery;
Altho' his hair began to arch,
   He was sae fley'd an' eerie:
Till presently he hears a squeak,
   An' then a grane an' gruntle;
He by his shouther gae a keek,
   An' tumbl'd wi' a wintle   170
          Out-owre that night.

He roar'd a horrid murder-shout,
   In dreadfu' desperation!
An' young an' auld come rinnin' out,
   An' hear the sad narration:
He swoor 'twas hilchin Jean M'Craw,
   Or crouchie Merran Humphie,
Till stop! she trotted thro' them a';
   An' wha was it but grumphie
          Asteer that night!   184 180

Meg fain wad to the barn gane
   To winn three wechts o' naething;
But for to meet the Deil her lane,
   She pat but little faith in:
She gies the herd a pickle nits,
   And twa red-cheekit apples,
To watch, while for the barn she sets,
   In hopes to see Tam Kipples
          That very night.

She turns the key wi' cannie thraw,   190
  An' owre the threshold ventures ;
But first on Sawnie gies a ca',
  Syne bauldly in she enters ;
A ratton rattl'd up the wa',
  An' she cried 'Lord preserve her !'
An' ran thro' midden-hole an' a',
  An' pray'd wi' zeal an' fervour
            Fu' fast that night.

They hoy't out Will, wi' sair advice ;
  They hecht him some fine braw ane ;   200
It chanced the stack he faddom'd thrice
  Was timmer-propt for thrawin' :
He taks a swirlie auld moss-oak
  For some black gruesome Carlin ;
An' loot a winze, an' drew a stroke,
  Till skin in blypes cam haurlin'
            Aff's nieves that night.

A wanton widow Leezie was,
  As cantie as a kittlin ;
But och ! that night, amang the shaws,   210
  She gat a fearfu' settlin' !
She thro' the whins, an' by the cairn,
  An' owre the hill gaed scrievin' ;
Where three laird's lands met at a burn,
  To dip her left sark-sleeve in,
            Was bent that night.

Whyles owre a linn the burnie plays,
  As thro' the glen it wimpled ;
Whyles round a rocky scaur it strays ;
  Whyles in a wiel it dimpled ;   220
Whyles glitter'd to the nightly rays,
  Wi' bickering, dancing dazzle ;
Whyles cookit underneath the braes,
  Below the spreading hazel,
            Unseen that night.

Amang the brackens on the brae,
  Between her an' the moon,
The Deil, or else an outler quey,
  Gat up an' gae a croon:
Poor Leezie's heart maist lap the hool;   230
  Near lav'rock height she jumpit,
But miss'd a fit, an' in the pool
  Out-owre the lugs she plumpit,
            Wi' a plunge that night.

In order, on the clean hearth-stane,
  The luggies three are ranged;
And every time great care is ta'en,
  To see them duly changed:
Auld uncle John, wha wedlock's joys
  Sin' Mar's year did desire,   240
Because he gat the toom dish thrice,
  He heav'd them on the fire
            In wrath that night.

Wi' merry sangs, an' friendly cracks,
  I wat they did na weary;
And unco tales, an' funny jokes,—
  Their sports were cheap and cheery;
Till butter'd sow'ns, wi' fragrant lunt,
  Set a' their gabs a-steerin';
Syne, wi' a social glass o' strunt,   250
  They parted aff careerin'
            Fu' blythe that night.

THE COTTER'S SATURDAY NIGHT.

My lov'd, my honour'd, much respected friend!
  No mercenary bard his homage pays:
With honest pride I scorn each selfish end,
  My dearest meed a friend's esteem and praise:
To you I sing, in simple Scottish lays,
The lowly train in life's sequester'd scene;
  The native feelings strong, the guileless ways;
What Aiken in a cottage would have been—
Ah! tho' his worth unknown, far happier there, I ween.

November chill blaws loud wi' angry sough;   10
  The short'ning winter-day is near a close;
The miry beasts retreating frae the pleugh;
  The black'ning trains o' craws to their repose:
The toil-worn Cotter frae his labour goes,
This night his weekly moil is at an end,
  Collects his spades, his mattocks, and his hoes,
Hoping the morn in ease and rest to spend,
And weary, o'er the moor, his course does hameward bend.

At length his lonely cot appears in view,
  Beneath the shelter of an agèd tree;   20
Th' expectant wee-things, toddlin', stacher through
  To meet their Dad, wi' flichterin' noise an' glee.
His wee bit ingle, blinkin bonnilie,
His clean hearth-stane, his thrifty wifie's smile,
  The lisping infant prattling on his knee,
Does a' his weary kiaugh and care beguile,
An' makes him quite forget his labour an' his toil.

Belyve, the elder bairns come drapping in,
  At service out, amang the farmers roun';
Some ca' the pleugh, some herd, some tentie rin   30
  A cannie errand to a neibor town:

Their eldest hope, their Jenny, woman-grown,
In youthfu' bloom, love sparkling in her e'e,
  Comes hame, perhaps to shew a braw new gown,
Or deposite her sair-won penny-fee,
To help her parents dear, if they in hardship be.

With joy unfeign'd brothers and sisters meet,
  An' each for other's weelfare kindly spiers:
The social hours, swift-wing'd, unnoticed fleet;
  Each tells the uncos that he sees or hears;   40
  The parents, partial, eye their hopeful years;
Anticipation forward points the view.
  The mother, wi' her needle an' her sheers,
Gars auld claes look amaist as weel 's the new;
The father mixes a' wi' admonition due.

Their master's an' their mistress's command,
  The younkers a' are warnèd to obey;
An' mind their labours wi' an eydent hand,
  An' ne'er, tho' out o' sight, to jauk or play:
  'And O! be sure to fear the Lord alway,   50
An' mind your duty, duly, morn an' night!
  Lest in temptation's path ye gang astray,
Implore His counsel and assisting might:
They never sought in vain that sought the Lord aright!'

But hark! a rap comes gently to the door;
  Jenny, wha kens the meaning o' the same,
Tells how a neibor lad cam o'er the moor,
  To do some errands, and convoy her hame.
  The wily mother sees the conscious flame
Sparkle in Jenny's e'e, and flush her cheek;   60
  Wi' heart-struck anxious care, inquires his name,
While Jenny hafflins is afraid to speak;
Weel pleased the mother hears it's nae wild worthless rake.

Wi' kindly welcome, Jenny brings him ben;
  A strappin' youth; he takes the mother's eye;
Blythe Jenny sees the visit 's no ill ta'en;
  The father cracks of horses, pleughs, and kye.

The youngster's artless heart o'erflows wi' joy,
But blate and laithfu', scarce can weel behave ;
　The mother, wi' a woman's wiles, can spy　　　70
What makes the youth sae bashfu' an' sae grave ;
Weel-pleased to think her bairn's respected like the lave.

O happy love ! where love like this is found ;
　O heart-felt raptures ! bliss beyond compare !
I've pacèd much this weary mortal round,
　And sage experience bids me this declare—
　　' If Heaven a draught of heavenly pleasure spare,
One cordial in this melancholy vale,
　'Tis when a youthful, loving, modest pair
In other's arms breathe out the tender tale,　　80
Beneath the milk-white thorn that scents the evening gale.'

Is there, in human form, that bears a heart—
　A wretch, a villain, lost to love and truth—
That can, with studied, sly, ensnaring art,
　Betray sweet Jenny's unsuspecting youth ?
　Curse on his perjur'd arts, dissembling smooth !
Are honour, virtue, conscience, all exil'd ?
　Is there no pity, no relenting ruth,
Points to the parents fondling o'er their child ?
Then paints the ruin'd maid, and their distraction wild ?　90

But now the supper crowns their simple board,
　The halesome parritch, chief of Scotia's food :
The sowpe their only hawkie does afford,
　That 'yont the hallan snugly chows her cood ;
　The dame brings forth in complimental mood,
To grace the lad, her weel-hain'd kebbuck, fell ;
　And aft he's prest, and aft he ca's it good ;
The frugal wifie, garrulous, will tell
How 'twas a towmond auld sin' lint was i' the bell.

The cheerfu' supper done, wi' serious face　　100
　They round the ingle form a circle wide ;
The sire turns o'er, wi' patriarchal grace,
　The big ha'-bible, ance his father's pride :

His bonnet rev'rently is laid aside,
His lyart haffets wearing thin an' bare ;
   Those strains that once did sweet in Zion glide—
He wales a portion with judicious care,
And ' Let us worship God ! ' he says with solemn air.

They chant their artless notes in simple guise ;
   They tune their hearts, by far the noblest aim :   110
Perhaps Dundee's wild warbling measures rise,
   Or plaintive Martyrs, worthy of the name ;
   Or noble Elgin beets the heav'nward flame,
The sweetest far of Scotia's holy lays :
   Compared with these, Italian trills are tame ;
The tickled ears no heartfelt raptures raise ;
Nae unison hae they with our Creator's praise.

The priest-like father reads the sacred page,
   How Abram was the friend of God on high ;
Or Moses bade eternal warfare wage   120
   With Amalek's ungracious progeny ;
   Or how the royal bard did groaning lie
Beneath the stroke of Heaven's avenging ire ;
   Or Job's pathetic plaint, and wailing cry ;
Or rapt Isaiah's wild seraphic fire ;
Or other holy seers that tune the sacred lyre.

Perhaps the Christian volume is the theme,
   How guiltless blood for guilty man was shed ;
How He who bore in Heaven the second name
   Had not on earth whereon to lay His head ;   130
   How His first followers and servants sped ;
The precepts sage they wrote to many a land :
   How he, was lone in Patmos banishèd,
Saw in the sun a mighty angel stand,
And heard great Bab'lon's doom pronounced by Heaven's
   command.

Then kneeling down to Heaven's Eternal King
   The saint, the father, and the husband prays :
Hope ' springs exulting on triumphant wing '
   That thus they all shall meet in future days :

There ever bask in uncreated rays,   140
No more to sigh, or shed the bitter tear,
  Together hymning their Creator's praise,
In such society, yet still more dear ;
While circling Time moves round in an eternal sphere.

Compared with this, how poor Religion's pride,
  In all the pomp of method and of art,
When men display to congregations wide
  Devotion's every grace, except the heart !
  The Power, incensed, the pageant will desert,
The pompous strain, the sacerdotal stole ;   150
  But haply, in some cottage far apart,
May hear, well pleased, the language of the soul ;
And in His Book of Life the inmates poor enrol.

Then homeward all take off their several way ;
  The youngling cottagers retire to rest :
The parent-pair their secret homage pay,
  And proffer up to Heav'n the warm request,
  That He who stills the raven's clamorous nest,
And decks the lily fair in flowery pride,
  Would, in the way His wisdom sees the best,   160
For them and for their little ones provide ;
But chiefly in their hearts with grace divine preside.

From scenes like these old Scotia's grandeur springs,
  That makes her loved at home, revered abroad :
Princes and lords are but the breath of kings,
  'An honest man's the noblest work of God ;'
  And certes, in fair virtue's heavenly road,
The cottage leaves the palace far behind ;
  What is a lordling's pomp ? a cumbrous load,
Disguising oft the wretch of human kind,   170
Studied in arts of hell, in wickedness refin'd !

O Scotia ! my dear, my native soil !
  For whom my warmest wish to Heaven is sent !
Long may thy hardy sons of rustic toil
  Be blest with health, and peace, and sweet content !

And O may Heaven their simple lives prevent
From luxury's contagion, weak and vile;
  Then, howe'er crowns and coronets be rent,
A virtuous populace may rise the while, 179
And stand a wall of fire around their much-loved isle.

O Thou! who poured the patriotic tide
  That streamed thro' Wallace's undaunted heart,
Who dared to nobly stem tyrannic pride,
  Or nobly die—the second glorious part,
  (The patriot's God, peculiarly thou art,
His friend, inspirer, guardian, and reward!)
  O never, never, Scotia's realm desert;
But still the patriot, and the patriot-bard,
In bright succession raise, her ornament and guard!

———◆———

THE HOLY FAIR.

*A robe of seeming truth and trust
  Hid crafty observation;
And secret hung, with poison'd crust,
  The dirk of defamation:
A mask that like the gorget show'd,
  Dye-varying on the pigeon;
And for a mantle large and broad,
  He wrapt him in religion.*
           HYPOCRISY À LA MODE.

UPON a simmer Sunday morn,
  When Nature's face is fair,
I walkèd forth to view the corn,
  An' snuff the caller air.
The risin' sun, owre Galston muirs,
  Wi' glorious light was glintin';
The hares were hirplin' down the furrs,
  The lav'rocks they were chantin'
             Fu' sweet that day.

As lightsomely I glowr'd abroad,　　　　　10
　To see a scene sae gay,
Three hizzies, early at the road,
　Cam skelpin' up the way.
Twa had manteeles o' dolefu' black,
　But' ane wi' lyart lining;
The third, that gaed a wee a-back,
　Was in the fashion shining
　　　　　　　Fu' gay that day.

The twa appear'd like sisters twin,
　In feature, form, an' claes;　　　　　20
Their visage wither'd, lang an' thin,
　An' sour as ony slaes:
The third cam up, hap-stap-an'-lowp,
　As light as ony lambie,
An' wi' a curchie low did stoop,
　As soon as e'er she saw me,
　　　　　　　Fu' kind that day.

Wi' bonnet aff, quoth I, 'Sweet lass,
　I think ye seem to ken me;
I'm sure I've seen that bonnie face,　　　　30
　But yet I canna name ye.'
Quo' she, an' laughin' as she spak,
　An' taks me by the hands,
·Ye, for my sake, hae gi'en the feck
　Of a' the ten commands
　　　　　　　A screed some day.

'My name is Fun—your crony dear,
　The nearest friend ye hae;
An' this is Superstition here,
　An' that's Hypocrisy.　　　　　40
I'm gaun to Mauchline Holy Fair,
　To spend an hour in daffin':
Gin ye'll go there, yon runkled pair,
　We will get famous laughin'
　　　　　　　At them this day.'

Quoth I, 'Wi' a' my heart, I'll do't;
   I'll get my Sunday's sark on,
An' meet you on the holy spot;
   Faith, we'se hae fine remarkin'!'
Then I gaed hame at crowdie-time,   50
   An' soon I made me ready;
For roads were clad, frae side to side,
   Wi' mony a wearie bodie
                 In droves that day.

Here farmers gash in ridin' graith
   Gaed hoddin' by their cotters;
There swankies young in braw braid-claith
   Are springin' owre the gutters.
The lasses, skelpin' barefit, thrang,
   In silks an' scarlets glitter,   60
Wi' sweet-milk cheese, in mony a whang,
   An' farls bak'd wi' butter,
                 Fu' crump that day.

When by the plate we set our nose,
   Weel heapèd up wi' ha'pence,
A greedy glow'r Black Bonnet throws,
   An' we maun draw our tippence.
Then in we go to see the show:
   On ev'ry side they're gath'rin';
Some carryin' deals, some chairs an' stools,   70
   An' some are busy bleth'rin'
                 Right loud that day.

Here stands a shed to fend the show'rs,
   An' screen our country gentry;
There racer Jess an' twa-three whores
   Are blinkin' at the entry.
Here sits a raw o' tittlin' jades,
   Wi' heavin' breasts an' bare neck,
An' there a batch o' wabster lads,
   Blackguardin' frae Kilmarnock   80
                 For fun this day.

Here some are thinkin' on their sins,
  An' some upo' their claes;
Ane curses feet that fyl'd his shins,
  Anither sighs an' prays:
On this hand sits a chosen swatch,
  Wi' screw'd up, grace-proud faces;
On that a set o' chaps, at watch,
  Thrang winkin' on the lasses
                  To chairs that day.   90

O happy is that man an' blest!
  Nae wonder that it pride him!
Wha's ain dear lass, that he likes best,
  Comes clinkin' down beside him!
Wi' arm repos'd on the chair-back
  He sweetly does compose him;
Which, by degrees, slips round her neck,
  An's loof upon her bosom,
                  Unkenn'd that day.

Now a' the congregation o'er   100
  Is silent expectation;
For Moodie speels the holy door,
  Wi' tidings o' damnation.
Should Hornie, as in ancient days,
  'Mang sons o' God present him,
The very sight o' Moodie's face
  To's ain het hame had sent him
                  Wi' fright that day.

Hear how he clears the points o' faith
  Wi' rattlin' an' wi' thumpin'!   110
Now meekly calm, now wild in wrath,
  He's stampin' an' he's jumpin'!
His lengthen'd chin, his turned-up snout,
  His eldritch squeal an' gestures,
O how they fire the heart devout,
  Like cantharidian plaisters,
                  On sic a day!

But, hark! the tent has chang'd its voice;
   There's peace an' rest nae langer;
For a' the real judges rise,   120
   They canna sit for anger.
Smith opens out his cauld harangues,
   On practice and on morals;
An' aff the godly pour in thrangs
   To gie the jars an' barrels
                A lift that day.

What signifies his barren shine
   Of moral pow'rs an' reason?
His English style an' gesture fine
   Are a' clean out o' season.   130
Like Socrates or Antonine,
   Or some auld pagan Heathen,
The moral man he does define,
   But ne'er a word o' faith in
                That's right that day.

In guid time comes an antidote
   Against sic poison'd nostrum;
For Peebles, frae the water-fit,
   Ascends the holy rostrum:
See, up he's got the word o' God,   140
   An' meek an' mim has view'd it,
While Common Sense has ta'en the road,
   An' aff, an' up the Cowgate
                Fast, fast, that day.

Wee Miller, neist, the Guard relieves,
   An' Orthodoxy raibles,
Tho' in his heart he weel believes,
   An' thinks it auld wives' fables:
But, faith! the birkie wants a Manse,
   So cannilie he hums them;   150
Altho' his carnal wit an' sense
   Like hafflins-wise o'ercomes him
                At times that day.

Now, butt an' ben, the Change-house fills,
 Wi' yill-caup Commentators ;
Here 's crying out for bakes an' gills,
 An' there the pint-stowp clatters ;
While thick an' thrang, an' loud an' lang,
 Wi' logic, an' wi' Scripture,
They raise a din, that in the end   160
 Is like to breed a rupture
     O' wrath that day.

Leeze me on drink ! it gi'es us mair
 Than either school or college :
It kindles wit, it waukens lair,
 It pangs us fou o' knowledge.
Be't whisky gill, or penny wheep,
 Or ony stronger potion,
It never fails, on drinkin' deep,
 To kittle up our notion   170
     By night or day.

The lads an' lasses, blythely bent
 To mind baith saul an' body,
Sit round the table, weel content,
 An' steer about the toddy.
On this ane's dress, an' that ane's leuk,
 They're makin observations ;
While some are cosy i' the neuk,
 An' formin' assignations
    To meet some day. 180

But now the Lord's ain trumpet touts,
 Till a' the hills are rairin',
An' echoes back return the shouts ;
 Black Russel is na sparin' :
His piercing words, like Highlan' swords,
 Divide the joints an' marrow ;
His talk o' Hell, where devils dwell,
 Our very 'sauls does harrow '
    Wi' fright that day !

A vast, unbottom'd, boundless pit,   190
  Fill'd fou o' lowin' brunstane,
Wha's ragin' flame, an' scorchin' heat,
  Wad melt the hardest whun-stane!
The half-asleep start up wi' fear
  An' think they hear it roarin',
When presently it does appear
  'Twas but some neebor snorin'
           Asleep that day.

'Twad be owre lang a tale to tell
  How mony stories past,   200
An' how they crowded to the yill,
  When they were a' dismist;
How drink gaed round, in cogs an' caups,
  Amang the furms and benches;
An' cheese an' bread, frae women's laps,
  Was dealt about in lunches,
           An' dawds that day.

In comes a gawsie, gash guidwife,
  An' sits down by the fire,
Syne draws her kebbuck an' her knife;   210
  The lasses they are shyer.
The auld guidmen, about the grace,
  Frae side to side they bother,
Till some ane by his bonnet lays,
  An' gi'es them't like a tether,
           Fu' lang that day.

Waesucks! for him that gets nae lass,
  Or lasses that hae naething!
Sma' need has he to say a grace,
  Or melvie his braw claithing!   220
O wives, be mindfu', ance yoursel
  How bonnie lads ye wanted,
An' dinna for a kebbuck-heel
  Let lasses be affronted
           On sic a day!

Now Clinkumbell, wi' rattlin' tow,
  Begins to jow an' croon ;
Some swagger hame the best they dow,
  Some wait the afternoon.
At slaps the billies halt a blink,   230
  Till lasses strip their shoon :
Wi' faith an' hope, an' love an' drink,
  They're a' in famous tune
                 For crack that day.

How mony hearts this day converts
  O' sinners and o' lasses !
Their hearts o' stane, gin night, are gane
  As saft as ony flesh is.
There's some are fou o' love divine,
  There's some are fou o' brandy ;   240
An' mony jobs that day begin,
  May end in houghmagandie
                 Some ither day.

———◆———

THE TWA DOGS.

'Twas in that place o' Scotland's Isle,
That bears the name o' auld King Coil,
Upon a bonnie day in June,
When wearin' through the afternoon,
Twa dogs, that werena thrang at hame,
Forgather'd ance upon a time.

  The first I'll name, they ca'd him Caesar,
Was keepit for his Honour's pleasure ;
His hair, his size, his mouth, his lugs,
Show'd he was nane o' Scotland's dogs,   10
But whalpit some place far abroad,
Where sailors gang to fish for cod.
  His lockèd, letter'd, braw brass collar,
Shew'd him the gentleman and scholar ;

But though he was o' high degree,
The fient a pride, nae pride had he ;
But wad hae spent ane hour caressin'
E'en wi' a tinkler-gipsy's messan :
At kirk or market, mill or smiddie,
Nae tawted tyke, though e'er sae duddie,   20
But he wad stand as glad to see him,
An' stroan'd on stanes an' hillocks wi' him.

The tither was a ploughman's collie,
A rhyming, ranting, raving billie ;
Wha for his friend and comrade had him,
And in his freaks had Luath ca'd him,
After some dog in Highland sang,
Was made lang syne—Lord knows how lang.

He was a gash an' faithfu' tyke,
As ever lap a sheugh or dyke ;   30
His honest, sonsie, bawsent face
Aye gat him friends in ilka place.
His breast was white, his tousie back
Weel clad wi' coat o' glossy black ;
His gawsie tail, wi' upward curl,
Hung o'er his hurdies wi' a swirl.

Nae doubt but they were fain o' ither,
And unco pack and thick thegither ;
Wi' social nose whyles snuff'd and snowkit ;
Whyles mice and moudieworts they howkit ;   40
Whyles scour'd awa in lang excursion,
And worried ither in diversion ;
Until wi' daffin' weary grown,
Upon a knowe they sat them down,
And there began a lang digression
About the lords of the creation.

CAESAR.

I've aften wonder'd, honest Luath,
What sort o' life poor dogs like you have ;
An' when the gentry's life I saw,
What way poor bodies liv'd ava.   50

Our Laird gets in his rackèd rents,
His coals, his kain, and a' his stents;
He rises when he likes himsel';
His flunkies answer at the bell:
He ca's his coach; he ca's his horse;
He draws a bonny silken purse
As lang's my tail, where, through the steeks,
The yellow-letter'd Geordie keeks.

Frae morn to e'en it's nought but toiling
At baking, roasting, frying, boiling;   60
And though the gentry first are stechin',
Yet e'en the ha' folk fill their pechan
Wi' sauce, ragouts, and sic like trashtrie,
That's little short o' downright wastrie.
Our whipper-in, wee blastit wonner!
Poor worthless elf! it eats a dinner
Better than ony tenant man
His Honour has in a' the lan';
An' what poor cot-folk pit their painch in,
I own it's past my comprehension.   70

LUATH.

Trowth, Caesar, whyles they're fash'd eneugh;
A cottar howkin' in a sheugh,
Wi' dirty stanes biggin' a dyke,
Baring a quarry, and sic like;
Himsel', a wife, he thus sustains,
A smytrie o' wee duddy weans,
And nought but his han'-darg to keep
Them right and tight in thack and rape.

And when they meet wi' sair disasters,
Like loss o' health, or want o' masters,   80
Ye maist wad think, a wee touch langer
And they maun starve o' cauld and hunger;
But how it comes I never kent yet,
They're maistly wonderfu' contented;
An' buirdly chiels and clever hizzies
Are bred in sic a way as this is.

CAESAR.

But then, to see how ye're negleckit,
How huff'd, and cuff'd, and disrespeckit,

Lord, man! our gentry care sae little
For delvers, ditchers and sic cattle;　90
They gang as saucy by poor folk
As I wad by a stinking brock.

I've noticed, on our Laird's court-day,
An' mony a time my heart's been wae,
Poor tenant bodies, scant o' cash,
How they maun thole a factor's snash;
He'll stamp and threaten, curse and swear,
He'll apprehend them, poind their gear:
While they maun stan', wi' aspect humble,
An' hear it a', an' fear an' tremble!　100
I see how folk live that hae riches;
But surely poor folk maun be wretches!

LUATH.

They're no' sae wretched's ane wad think,
Though constantly on poortith's brink:
They're sae accustom'd wi' the sight,
The view o't gi'es them little fright.

Then chance and fortune are sae guided,
They're aye in less or mair provided;
An' though fatigued wi' close employment,
A blink o' rest's a sweet enjoyment.　110

The dearest comfort o' their lives,
Their grushie weans an' faithfu' wives;
The prattling things are just their pride,
That sweetens a' their fireside.

And whyles twalpenny-worth o' nappy
Can mak the bodies unco happy;
They lay aside their private cares
To mind the Kirk and State affairs:
They'll talk o' patronage and priests,
Wi' kindling fury in their breasts;　120
Or tell what new taxation's comin',
And ferlie at the folk in Lon'on.

As bleak-faced Hallowmas returns
They get the jovial rantin' kirns,
When rural life o' every station
Unite in common recreation;
Love blinks, Wit slaps, and social Mirth
Forgets there's Care upo' the earth.

That merry day the year begins
They bar the door on frosty win's ;   130
The nappy reeks wi' mantling ream,
And sheds a heart-inspiring steam ;
The luntin' pipe and sneeshin'-mill
Are handed round wi' right gude-will ;
The canty auld folk crackin' crouse,
The young anes ranting through the house—
My heart has been sae fain to see them
That I for joy hae barkit wi' them.

Still it 's owre true that ye hae said,
Sic game is now owre aften play'd.   140
There 's mony a creditable stock
O' decent, honest, fawsont folk,
Are riven out baith root and branch
Some rascal's pridefu' greed to quench,
Wha thinks to knit himsel the faster
In favour wi' some gentle master,
Wha, aiblins, thrang a-parliamentin',
For Britain's gude his saul indentin—

CAESAR.

Haith, lad, ye little ken about it ;
For Britain's gude !—guid faith ! I doubt it !   150
Say rather, gaun as Premiers lead him,
And saying ay or no 's they bid him !
At operas and plays parading,
Mortgaging, gambling, masquerading.
Or maybe, in a frolic daft,
To Hague or Calais taks a waft,
To make a tour, an' tak a whirl,
To learn *bon ton* an' see the worl'.
There, at Vienna, or Versailles,
He rives his father's auld entails ;   160
Or by Madrid he takes the rout,
To thrum guitars and fecht wi' nowt ;
Or down Italian vista startles,
Whore-hunting amang groves o' myrtles ;
Then bouses drumly German water,
To make himsel' look fair and fatter,
And clear the consequential sorrows,
Love-gifts of Carnival signoras.

For Britain's gude!—for her destruction!
Wi' dissipation, feud, and faction!　　　170

LUATH.

Hech man! dear sirs! is that the gate
They waste sae mony a braw estate?
Are we sae foughten and harass'd
For gear to gang that gate at last?
O would they stay aback frae courts,
An' please themselves wi' country sports,
It wad for every ane be better,
The laird, the tenant, an' the cotter!
For thae frank, rantin', ramblin' billies,
Fient haet o' them's ill-hearted fellows:　　　180
Except for breakin' o' their timmer,
Or speaking lightly o' their limmer,
Or shootin' o' a hare or moor-cock,
The ne'er-a-bit they're ill to poor folk.
But will ye tell me, Master Caesar?
Sure great folk's life's a life o' pleasure.;
Nae cauld nor hunger e'er can steer them,
The very thought o't needna fear them.

CAESAR.

Lord, man, were ye but whyles where I am,
The gentles ye wad ne'er envý 'em,　　　190
It's true, they needna starve or sweat,
Thro' winter's cauld or simmer's heat;
They've nae sair wark to craze their banes,
An' fill auld age wi' grips an' granes:
But human bodies are sic fools,
For a' their colleges and schools,
That when nae real ills perplex them,
They make enow themselves to vex them,
An' aye the less they hae to sturt them,
In like proportion less will hurt them.　　　200
A country fellow at the pleugh,
His acres till'd, he's right eneugh;
A country lassie at her wheel,
Her dizzens done, she's unco weel;
But gentlemen, an' ladies warst,
Wi' ev'ndown want o' wark are curst.

They loiter, lounging, lank, and lazy;
Though de'il haet ails them, yet uneasy;
Their days insipid, dull and tasteless;
Their nights unquiet, lang, and restless.   210
And e'en their sports, their balls, and races,
Their galloping through public places;
There's sic parade, sic pomp and art,
The joy can scarcely reach the heart.
The men cast out in party matches,
Then sowther a' in deep debauches:
Ae night they're mad wi' drink and whoring,
Neist day their life is past enduring.
The ladies arm-in-arm, in clusters,
As great and gracious a' as sisters;   220
But hear their absent thoughts o' ither,
They're a' run de'ils and jades thegither.
Whyles, owre the wee bit cup and platie,
They sip the scandal-potion pretty;
Or lee-lang nights, wi' crabbit leuks,
Pore owre the devil's picture beuks;
Stake on a chance a farmer's stack-yard,
And cheat like ony unhang'd blackguard.

There's some exception, man and woman;
But this is gentry's life in common.   230

By this the sun was out o' sight,
And darker gloamin brought the night;
The bum-clock humm'd wi' lazy drone,
The kye stood rowtin' i' the loan;
When up they gat and shook their lugs,
Rejoiced they werena men but dogs;
And each took aff his several way,
Resolved to meet some ither day.

—••—

THE BRIGS OF AYR.

THE simple Bard, rough at the rustic plough,
Learning his tuneful trade from every bough;
The chanting linnet, or the mellow thrush,
Hailing the setting sun, sweet, in the green thorn bush;
The soaring lark, the perching red-breast shrill,
Or deep-ton'd plovers gray, wild-whistling o'er the hill;
Shall he, nurst in the peasant's lowly shed,
To hardy independence bravely bred,
By early poverty to hardship steel'd,
And train'd to arms in stern Misfortune's field,—   10
Shall he be guilty of their hireling crimes,
The servile, mercenary Swiss of rhymes?
Or labour hard the panegyric close,
With all the venal soul of dedicating prose?
No! though his artless strains he rudely sings,
And throws his hand uncouthly o'er the strings,
He glows with all the spirit of the Bard,
Fame, honest fame, his great, his dear reward.
Still, if some patron's generous care he trace,
Skill'd in the secret to bestow with grace;   20
When Ballantyne befriends his humble name
And hands the rustic stranger up to fame,
With heartfelt throes his grateful bosom swells,
The godlike bliss, to give, alone excels.

'Twas when the stacks get on their winter-hap,
And thack and rape secure the toil-won crap;
Potatoe-bings are snuggèd up frae skaith
O' coming Winter's biting, frosty breath;
The bees, rejoicing o'er their summer toils,
Unnumber'd buds an' flowers' delicious spoils,   30
Seal'd up with frugal care in massive waxen piles,
Are doom'd by Man, that tyrant o'er the weak,
The death o' devils, smoor'd wi' brimstone reek:
The thund'ring guns are heard on ev'ry side,
The wounded coveys, reeling, scatter wide;

The feather'd field-mates, bound by Nature's tie,
Sires, mothers, children, in one carnage lie:
(What warm, poetic heart, but inly bleeds,
And execrates man's savage, ruthless deeds!)
Nae mair the flow'r in field or meadow springs;   40
Nae mair the grove with airy concert rings,
Except perhaps the Robin's whistling glee,
Proud o' the height o' some bit half-lang tree:
The hoary morns precede the sunny days,
Mild, calm, serene, wide spreads the noontide blaze,
While thick the gossamour waves wanton in the rays.

'Twas in that season when a simple Bard,
Unknown and poor, simplicity's reward,
Ae night, within the ancient brugh of Ayr,
By whim inspir'd, or haply prest wi' care,   50
He left his bed and took his wayward route,
And down by Simpson's wheel'd the left about:
(Whether impell'd by all-directing Fate,
To witness what I after shall narrate;
Or whether, rapt in meditation high,
He wander'd out he knew not where nor why:)
The drowsy Dungeon clock had number'd two,
And Wallace Tower had sworn the fact was true:
The tide-swoln Firth, wi' sullen-sounding roar,
Through the still night dash'd hoarse along the shore: 60
All else was hush'd as Nature's closèd e'e;
The silent moon shone high o'er tow'r and tree:
The chilly frost, beneath the silver beam,
Crept, gently-crusting, owre the glittering stream—
   When, lo! on either hand the list'ning Bard,
The clanging sough of whistling wings is heard;
Two dusky forms dart thro' the midnight air,
Swift as the gos drives on the wheeling hare;
Ane on th' Auld Brig his airy shape uprears,
The ither flutters o'er the rising piers: 70
Our warlock Rhymer instantly descried
The Sprites that owre the Brigs of Ayr preside.
(That Bards are second-sighted is nae joke,
And ken the lingo of the sp'ritual folk;
Fays, Spunkies, Kelpies, a', they can explain them,
And ev'n the very deils they brawly ken them.)

Auld Brig appear'd o' ancient Pictish race,
The very wrinkles Gothic in his face;
He seem'd as he wi' Time had warstl'd lang,
Yet, teughly doure, he bade an unco bang.   80
New Brig was buskit, in a braw new coat,
That he, at Lon'on, frae ane Adams got;
In's hand five taper staves as smooth's a bead,
Wi' virls an' whirlygigums at the head.
The Goth was stalking round with anxious search,
Spying the time-worn flaws in ev'ry arch;
It chanc'd his new-come neebor took his e'e,
And e'en a vex'd and angry heart had he!
Wi' thieveless sneer to see his modish mien,
He, down the water, gies him this guid-een:—   90

AULD BRIG.

I doubtna, frien', ye'll think ye're nae sheep-shank.
Ance ye were streekit owre frae bank to bank!
But gin ye be a brig as auld as me—
Tho', faith! that date, I doubt, ye'll never see—
There'll be, if that day come, I'll wad a boddle,
Some fewer whigmaleeries in your noddle.

NEW BRIG.

Auld Vandal! ye but show your little mense,
Just much about it wi' your scanty sense;
Will your poor narrow foot-path of a street,
Where twa wheel-barrows tremble when they meet,   100
Your ruin'd formless bulk o' stane and lime,
Compare wi' bonnie brigs o' modern time?
There's men of taste wou'd tak the Ducat stream,
Tho' they should cast the very sark and swim,
Ere they would grate their feelings wi' the view
O' sic an ugly Gothic hulk as you.

AULD BRIG.

Conceited gowk! puff'd up wi' windy pride!
This mony a year I've stood the flood an' tide;
And tho' wi' crazy eild I'm sair forfairn,
I'll be a brig, when ye're a shapeless cairn!   110

As yet ye little ken about the matter,
But twa-three winters will inform ye better.
When heavy, dark, continued, a'-day rains,
Wi' deepening deluges o'erflow the plains;
When from the hills where springs the brawling Coil,
Or stately Lugar's mossy fountains boil,
Or where the Greenock winds his moorland course,
Or haunted Garpal draws his feeble source,
Arous'd by blust'ring winds an' spotting thowes,
In mony a torrent down the snaw-broo rowes;   120
While crashing ice, borne on the roaring spate,
Sweeps dams, an' mills, an' brigs, a' to the gate;
And from Glenbuck, down to the Ratton-key,
Auld Ayr is just one lengthen'd, tumbling sea;
Then down ye'll hurl, deil nor ye never rise!
And dash the gumlie jaups up to the pouring skies!
A lesson sadly teaching, to your cost,
That architecture's noble art is lost!

NEW BRIG.

Fine architecture, trowth, I needs must say't o't,
The Lord be thankit that we've tint the gate o't!   130
Gaunt, ghastly, ghaist-alluring edifices,
Hanging with threat'ning jut, like precipices;
O'er-arching, mouldy, gloom-inspiring coves,
Supporting roofs, fantastic, stony groves;
Windows and doors in nameless sculptures drest,
With order, symmetry, or taste unblest;
Forms like some bedlam Statuary's dream,
The craz'd creations of misguided whim;
Forms might be worshipp'd on the bended knee,
And still the second dread command be free,   140
Their likeness is not found on earth, in air, or sea!
Mansions that would disgrace the building taste
Of any mason reptile, bird, or beast;
Fit only for a doited monkish race,
Or frosty maids forsworn the dear embrace,
Or cuifs of later times wha held the notion
That sullen gloom was sterling, true devotion;
Fancies that our guid Brugh denies protection,
And soon may they expire, unblest with resurrection!

AULD BRIG.

O ye, my dear-remember'd, ancient yealings,   150
Were ye but here to share my wounded feelings!
Ye worthy Proveses, an' mony a Bailie,
Wha in the paths o' righteousness did toil aye;
Ye dainty Deacons, an' ye douce Conveeners,
To whom our moderns are but causey-cleaners!
Ye godly Councils wha hae blest this town;
Ye godly Brethren o' the sacred gown,
Wha meekly gie your hurdies to the smiters;
And (what would now be strange) ye godly Writers:
A' ye douce folk I've borne aboon the broo,   160
Were ye but here, what would ye say or do!
How would your spirits groan in deep vexation,
To see each melancholy alteration;
And agonizing, curse the time and place
When ye begat the base degen'rate race!
Nae langer rev'rend men, their country's glory,
In plain braid Scots hold forth a plain braid story;
Nae langer thrifty citizens, an' douce,
Meet owre a pint, or in the Council-house;
But staumrel, corky-headed, graceless Gentry,   170
The herryment and ruin of the country;
Men, three-parts made by tailors and by barbers,
Wha waste your weel-hain'd gear on damn'd new brigs and
     harbours!

NEW BRIG.

Now haud you there! for faith ye've said enough,
And muckle mair than ye can mak to through:
As for your Priesthood, I shall say but little,
Corbies and Clergy are a shot right kittle;
But, under favour o' your langer beard,
Abuse o' Magistrates might weel be spar'd;
To liken them to your auld-warld squad,   180
I must needs say, comparisons are odd.
In Ayr, wag-wits nae mair can have a handle
To mouth 'a Citizen,' a term o' scandal;
Nae mair the Council waddles down the street,
In all the pomp of ignorant conceit;

Men wha grew wise priggin' owre hops an' raisins,
Or gather'd liberal views in bonds and seisins.
If haply Knowledge, on a random tramp,
Had shor'd them wi' a glimmer of his lamp,
And would to Common-sense for once betray'd them,   190
Plain dull Stupidity stept kindly in to aid them.

WHAT farther clishmaclaver might been said,
What bloody wars, if Sprites had blood to shed,
No man can tell; but all before their sight
A fairy train appear'd in order bright;
Adown the glittering stream they featly danc'd;
Bright to the moon their various dresses glanc'd:
They footed o'er the watery glass so neat,
The infant ice scarce bent beneath their feet;
While arts of Minstrelsy among them rung,   200
And soul-ennobling Bards heroic ditties sung.
O had M'Lauchlan, thairm-inspiring sage,
Been there to hear this heavenly band engage,
When thro' his dear strathspeys they bore with Highland rage,
Or when they struck old Scotia's melting airs,
The lover's raptur'd joys or bleeding cares,
How would his Highland lug been nobler fired,
And ev'n his matchless hand with finer touch inspired!
No guess could tell what instrument appear'd,
But all the soul of Music's self was heard;   210
Harmonious concert rung in every part,
While simple melody pour'd moving on the heart.
   The Genius of the Stream in front appears,
A venerable Chief, advanced in years;
His hoary head with water-lilies crown'd,
His manly leg with garter-tangle bound.
Next came the loveliest pair in all the ring,
Sweet Female Beauty hand in hand with Spring;
Then, crown'd with flow'ry hay, came Rural Joy,
And Summer, with his fervid-beaming eye;   220
All-cheering Plenty, with her flowing horn,
Led yellow Autumn wreath'd with nodding corn;
Then Winter's time-bleach'd locks did hoary show,
By Hospitality with cloudless brow;
Next follow'd Courage with his martial stride,
From where the Feal wild-woody coverts hide;

Benevolence, with mild benignant air,
A female form, came from the towers of Stair:
Learning and Worth in equal measures trode
From simple Catrine, their long-loved abode;   230
Last, white-robed Peace, crown'd with a hazel wreath,
To rustic Agriculture did bequeath
The broken iron instruments of death:
At sight of whom our Sprites forgat their kindling wrath.

THE VISION.

DUAN FIRST.

The sun had closed the winter day,
The curlers quat their roarin' play,
An' hunger'd maukin taen her way
  To kail-yards green,
While faithless snaws ilk step betray
  Where she has been.

The thresher's weary flingin'-tree
The lee-lang day had tirèd me;
And when the day had clos'd his e'e,
  Far i' the west,   10
Ben i' the spence, right pensivelie,
  I gaed to rest.

There lanely by the ingle-cheek
I sat and eyed the spewing reek,
That fill'd, wi' hoast-provoking smeek,
  The auld clay biggin';
An' heard the restless rattons squeak
  About the riggin'.

All in this mottie misty clime,
I backward mused on wasted time,   20
How I had spent my youthfu' prime,
  An' done nae-thing,
But stringin' blethers up in rhyme,
  For fools to sing.

Had I to guid advice but harkit,
I might, by this, hae led a market,
Or strutted in a bank, and clarkit
      My cash-account:
While here, half-mad, half-fed, half-sarkit,
      Is a' th' amount.   30

I started, mutt'ring 'blockhead! coof!'
And heaved on high my waukit loof,
To swear by a' yon starry roof,
      Or some rash aith,
That I, henceforth, would be rhyme-proof
      Till my last breath—

When click! the string the snick did draw;
An' jee! the door gaed to the wa';
And by my ingle-lowe I saw,
      Now bleezin' bright,
A tight outlandish hizzie, braw,
      Come full in sight.   40

Ye need na doubt I held my whisht;
The infant aith, half-form'd, was crusht;
I glowr'd as eerie 's I'd been dusht
      In some wild glen;
When sweet, like modest worth, she blusht,
      An' steppèd ben.

Green, slender, leaf-clad holly-boughs
Were twisted, gracefu', round her brows;
I took her for some Scottish Muse
      By that same token;   50
And come to stop these reckless vows,
      Would soon been broken.

A hare-brain'd, sentimental trace,
Was strongly markèd in her face;
A wildly-witty rustic grace
      Shone full upon her;
Her eye, ev'n turn'd on empty space,
      Beam'd keen with honour.   60

Down flow'd her robe, a tartan sheen,
Till half a leg was scrimply seen;
An' such a leg! my bonnie Jean
      Could only peer it;
Sae straught, sae taper, tight, and clean,
      Nane else came near it.

Her mantle large, of greenish hue,
My gazing wonder chiefly drew;
Deep lights and shades, bold-mingling, threw
      A lustre grand;   70
And seem'd to my astonish'd view
      A well-known land.

Here rivers in the sea were lost;
There mountains to the skies were tost:
Here tumbling billows mark'd the coast
      With surging foam;
There, distant shone Art's lofty boast,
      The lordly dome.

Here Doon pour'd down his far-fetch'd floods;
There well-fed Irwine stately thuds;   80
Auld hermit Ayr staw thro' his woods,
      On to the shore;
And many a lesser torrent scuds,
      With seeming roar.

Low in a sandy valley spread,
An ancient borough rear'd her head;
Still, as in Scottish story read,
      She boasts a race,
To ev'ry nobler virtue bred,
      And polish'd grace.   90

By stately tower or palace fair,
Or ruins pendent in the air,
Bold stems of heroes, here and there,
      I could discern;
Some seem'd to muse, some seem'd to dare,
      With feature stern.

My heart did glowing transport feel,
To see a race heroic wheel,
And brandish round, the deep-dyed steel
          In sturdy blows;   100
While back-recoiling seem'd to reel
          Their Suthron foes.

His Country's Saviour, mark him well!
Bold Richardton's heroic swell;
The Chief—on Sark who glorious fell,
          In high command;
And he whom ruthless fates expel
          His native land.

There, where a sceptred Pictish shade
Stalk'd round his ashes lowly laid,   110
I mark'd a martial race, pourtray'd
          In colours strong;
Bold, soldier-featur'd, undismay'd
          They strode along.

Thro' many a wild romantic grove,
Near many a hermit-fancied cove
(Fit haunts for Friendship or for Love
          In musing mood)
An agèd Judge, I saw him rove
          Dispensing good.   120

With deep-struck reverential awe
The learned Sire and Son I saw;
To Nature's God and Nature's law
          They gave their lore;
This, all its source and end to draw,
          That, to adore.

Brydon's brave ward I well could spy,
Beneath old Scotia's smiling eye.;
Who call'd on Fame, low standing by,
          To hand him on,   130
Where many a patriot name on high,
          And hero shone.

DUAN SECOND.

WITH musing-deep astonish'd stare,
I view'd the heavenly-seeming Fair;
A whisp'ring throb did witness bear
      Of kindred sweet,
When with an elder Sister's air
      She did me greet.

'All hail! my own inspired bard!
In me thy native Muse regard!   140
Nor longer mourn thy fate is hard,
      Thus poorly low;
I come to give thee such reward
      As we bestow.

'Know the great Genius of this land
Has many a light aërial band,
Who, all beneath his high command,
      Harmoniously,
As arts or arms they understand,
      Their labours ply.   150

'They Scotia's race among them share:
Some fire the soldier on to dare;
Some rouse the patriot up to bare
      Corruption's heart:
Some teach the bard, a darling care,
      The tuneful art.

''Mong swelling floods of reeking gore,
They, ardent, kindling spirits pour;
Or, 'mid the venal senate's roar,
      They, sightless, stand,   160
To mend the honest patriot lore,
      And grace the hand.

'And when the bard, or hoary sage,
Charm or instruct the future age,
They bind the wild poetic rage
      In energy,
Or point the inconclusive page
      Full on the eye.

'Hence Fullarton, the brave and young;
Hence Dempster's zeal-inspirèd tongue;   170
Hence sweet harmonious Beattie sung
        His Minstrel lays,
Or tore, with noble ardour stung,
        The sceptic's bays.

'To lower orders are assign'd
The humbler ranks of human-kind,
The rustic bard, the lab'ring hind,
        The artisan;
All choose, as various they're inclin'd,
        The various man.   180

'When yellow waves the heavy grain,
The threat'ning storm some strongly rein;
Some teach to meliorate the plain
        With tillage-skill;
And some instruct the shepherd-train,
        Blythe o'er the hill.

'Some hint the lover's harmless wile;
Some grace the maiden's artless smile;
Some soothe the lab'rer's weary toil
        For humble gains,   190
And make his cottage-scenes beguile
        His cares and pains.

'Some, bounded to a district-space,
Explore at large man's infant race,
To mark the embryotic trace
        Of rustic bard;
And careful note each op'ning grace,
        A guide and guard.

'Of these am I—Coila my name;
And this district as mine I claim,   200
Where once the Campbells, chiefs of fame,
        Held ruling pow'r:
I mark'd thy embryo-tuneful flame,
        Thy natal hour.

'With future hope I oft would gaze,
Fond, on thy little early ways,
Thy rudely-caroll'd, chiming phrase,
      In uncouth rhymes,—
Fired at the simple artless lays
      Of other times.   210

'I saw thee seek the sounding shore,
Delighted with the dashing roar;
Or when the North his fleecy store
      Drove thro' the sky,
I saw grim Nature's visage hoar
      Struck thy young eye.

'Or when the deep green-mantled Earth
Warm-cherish'd ev'ry flow'ret's birth,.
And joy and music pouring forth
      In ev'ry grove,   220
I saw thee eye the gen'ral mirth
      With boundless love.

'When ripen'd fields and azure skies
Call'd forth the reapers' rustling noise,
I saw thee leave their ev'ning joys,
      And lonely stalk,
To vent thy bosom's swelling rise
      In pensive walk.

'When youthful love, warm-blushing strong,
Keen-shivering shot thy nerves along,   230
Those accents, grateful to thy tongue,
      Th' adorèd Name,
I taught thee how to pour in song,
      To soothe thy flame.

'I saw thy pulse's maddening play
Wild send thee pleasure's devious way,
Misled by fancy's meteor ray,
      By passion driven;
But yet the light that led astray
      Was light from Heaven.   240

'I taught thy manners-painting strains,
The loves, the ways of simple swains,
Till now, o'er all my wide domains
   Thy fame extends;
And some, the pride of Coila's plains,
   Become thy friends.

'Thou canst not learn, nor can I show,
To paint with Thomson's landscape-glow;
Or wake the bosom-melting throe
   With Shenstone's art;   250
Or pour with Gray the moving flow
   Warm on the heart.

'Yet all beneath th' unrivall'd rose
The lowly daisy sweetly blows;
Tho' large the forest's monarch throws
   His army shade,
Yet green the juicy hawthorn grows
   Adown the glade.

'Then never murmur nor repine;
Strive in thy humble sphere to shine;   260
And trust me, not Potosi's mine,
   Nor king's regard,
Can give a bliss o'ermatching thine,
   A rustic Bard.

'To give my counsels all in one,
Thy tuneful flame still careful fan;
Preserve the dignity of Man,
   With Soul erect;
And trust the Universal Plan
   Will all protect.   270

'And wear thou this': She solemn said,
And bound the holly round my head:
The polish'd leaves and berries red
   Did rustling play;
And, like a passing thought, she fled
   In light away.

THE DEATH AND DYING WORDS OF POOR
MAILIE, THE AUTHOR'S ONLY PET YOWE.

As Mailie, an' her lambs thegither,
Was ae day nibbling on the tether,
Upon her cloot she coost a hitch,
An' owre she warsled in the ditch;
There, groaning, dying, she did lie,
When Hughoc he cam doytin by.
　　Wi' glowrin' een, an' lifted han's,
Poor Hughoc like a statue stan's;
He saw her days were near-hand ended,
But, wae's my heart! he could na mend it!　　10
He gapèd wide, but naething spak;
At length poor Mailie silence brak:—

'O thou, whase lamentable face
Appears to mourn my woefu' case!
My dying words attentive hear,
An' bear them to my Master dear.
　　'Tell him, if e'er again he keep
As muckle gear as buy a sheep,—
O bid him never tie them mair
Wi' wicked strings o' hemp or hair!　　20
But ca' them out to park or hill,
An' let them wander at their will;
So may his flock increase, an' grow
To scores o' lambs, an' packs o' woo'!
　　'Tell him he was a Master kin',
An' aye was guid to me an' mine;
An' now my dying charge I gie him,
My helpless lambs, I trust them wi' him.
　　'O bid him save their harmless lives
Frae dogs, an' tods, an' butchers' knives!　　30
But gie them guid cow-milk their fill,
Till they be fit to fend themsel:
An' tent them duly, e'en an' morn,
Wi' teats o' hay an' ripps o' corn.

'An' may they never learn the gates
Of ither vile wanrestfu' pets—
·To slink thro' slaps, an' reave an' steal,
At stacks o' pease, or stocks o' kail.
So may they, like their great forbears,
For mony a year come thro' the shears ;   40
So wives will gie them bits o' bread,
   An' bairns greet for them when they're dead.
   'My poor tup-lamb, my son an' heir,
O bid him breed him up wi' care !
An', if he live to be a beast,
To pit some havins in his breast !
An' warn him, what I winna name,
To stay content wi' yowes at hame ;
An' no to rin an' wear his cloots,
Like ither menseless graceless brutes.   50
   'An' neist my yowie, silly thing,
Gude keep thee frae a tether string !
O may thou ne'er forgather up
Wi' ony blastit moorland tup ;
But ay keep mind to moop an' mell,
   Wi' sheep o' credit like thysel !
   'And now, my bairns, wi' my last breath
I lea'e my blessin wi' you baith ;
An' when you think upo' your mither,
Mind to be kind to ane anither.   60
   'Now, honest Hughoc, dinna fail
To tell my master a' my tale ;
An' bid him burn this cursed tether ;
An', for thy pains, thou'se get my blether.'

   This said, poor Mailie turn'd her head,
An' closed her een amang the dead !

—————•◦•—————

POOR MAILIE'S ELEGY.

Lament in rhyme, lament in prose,
Wi' saut tears tricklin' down your nose;
Our bardie's fate is at a close,
                    Past a' remead;
The last sad cape-stane of his woes—
                    Poor Mailie's dead!

It's no the loss o' warl's gear
That could sae bitter draw the tear,
Or mak our bardie, dowie, wear
                    The mourning weed: 10
He's lost a friend and neibor dear
                    In Mailie dead.

Thro' a' the toun she trotted by him;
A lang half-mile she could descry him;
Wi' kindly bleat, when she did spy him,
                    She ran wi' speed:
A friend mair faithfu' ne'er cam nigh him
                    Than Mailie dead.

I wat she was a sheep o' sense,
An' could behave hersel wi' mense;   20
I'll say't, she never brak a fence
                    Thro' thievish greed.
Our bardie, lanely, keeps the spence
                    Sin' Mailie's dead.

Or, if he wanders up the howe,
Her living image in her yowe
Comes bleating to him, owre the knowe,
                    For bits o' bread,
An' down the briny pearls rowe
                    For Mailie dead.   30

She was nae get o' moorland tups,
Wi' tawted ket, an' hairy hips;
For her forbears were brought in ships
                    Frae yont the Tweed:
A bonnier fleesh ne'er cross'd the clips
                    Than Mailie's, dead.

Wae worth the man wha first did shape
That vile wanchancie thing—a rape !
It maks guid fellows girn an' gape,
   Wi' chokin' dread ;   40
An' Robin's bonnet wave wi' crape
   For Mailie dead.

O a' ye bards on bonnie Doon !
An' wha on Ayr your chanters tune !
Come, join the melancholious croon
   O' Robin's reed ;
His heart will never get aboon
   His Mailie dead !

———•••———

DEATH AND DOCTOR HORNBOOK.

SOME books are lies frae end to end,
And some great lies were never penn'd :
Ev'n ministers, they hae been kenn'd,
   In holy rapture,
A rousing whid at times to vend,
   And nail't wi' Scripture.

But this that I am gaun to tell,
Which lately on a night befell,
Is just as true 's the Deil 's in hell
   Or Dublin city :   10
That e'er he nearer comes oursel
   'S a muckle pity.

The Clachan yill had made me canty,
I wasna fou, but just had plenty ;
I stacher'd whyles, but yet took tent aye
   To free the ditches ;
An' hillocks, stanes, an' bushes kent aye
   Frae ghaists an' witches.

The rising moon began to glowre
The distant Cumnock hills out-owre :   20
To count her horns, wi' a' my pow'r,
               I set mysel ;
But whether she had three or four
               I cou'd na tell.

I was come round about the hill,
And todlin' down on Willie's mill,
Setting my staff, wi' a' my skill,
               To keep me sicker ;
Tho' leeward whyles, against my will,
               I took a bicker.   30

I there wi' Something did forgather,
That pat me in an eerie swither ;
An awfu' scythe, out-owre ae shouther,
               Clear-dangling, hang ;
A three-tae'd leister on the ither
               Lay large an' lang.

Its stature seem'd lang Scotch ells twa,
The queerest shape that e'er I saw,
For fient a wame it had ava ;
               And then its shanks,   40
They were as thin, as sharp an' sma'
               As cheeks o' branks.

' Guid-een,' quo' I ; 'Friend ! hae ye been mawin,
When ither folk are busy sawin ? '
It seem'd to mak. a kind o' stan',
               But naething spak ;
At length says I, 'Friend, wh'are ye gaun ?
               Will ye go back ? '

It spak right howe—'My name is Death,
But be na fley'd.'—Quoth I, 'Guid faith,   50
Ye're maybe come to stap my breath ;
               But tent me, billie :
I red ye weel, tak care o' skaith,
               See, there's a gully ! '

'Gudeman,' quo' he, 'put up your whittle,
I'm no design'd to try its mettle;
But if I did—I wad be kittle
          To be mislear'd—
I wad na mind it, no that spittle
          Out-owre my beard.'   60

'Weel, weel!' says I, 'a bargain be't;
Come, gies your hand, an' sae we're gree't;
We'll ease our shanks an' tak a seat—
          Come, gies your news;
This while ye hae been mony a gate,
          At mony a house.'

'Ay, ay!' quo' he, an' shook his head,
'It's e'en a lang lang time indeed
Sin' I began to nick the thread,
          An' choke the breath: 70
Folk maun do something for their bread,
          An' sae maun Death.

'Sax thousand years are near-hand fled,
Sin' I was to the butching bred;
An' mony a scheme in vain's been laid
          To stap or scaur me;
Till ane Hornbook's ta'en up the trade,
          An' faith! he'll waur me.

'Ye ken Jock Hornbook i' the clachan—
Deil mak his king's-hood in a spleuchan!   80
He's grown sae well acquaint wi' Buchan
          An' ither chaps,
The weans haud out their fingers laughin',
          And pouk my hips.

'See, here's a scythe, and there's a dart—
They hae pierc'd mony a gallant heart;
But Doctor Hornbook, wi' his art
          And cursed skill,
Has made them baith no worth a fart!
          Damn'd haet they'll kill. 90

' 'Twas but yestreen, nae farther gane,
I threw a noble throw at ane—
Wi' less, I'm sure, I've hundreds slain—
   But deil may care!
It just play'd dirl on the bane,
   But did nae mair.

' Hornbook was by wi' ready art,
And had sae fortified the part
That, when I lookèd to my dart,
   It was sae blunt, 100
Fient haet o't wad hae pierc'd the heart
   O' a kail-runt.

' I drew my scythe in sic a fury
I near-hand cowpit wi' my hurry,
But yet the bauld Apothecary
   Withstood the shock;
I might as weel hae tried a quarry
   O' hard whin rock.

' E'en them he canna get attended,
Altho' their face he ne'er had kenn'd it, 110
Just sh— in a kail-blade, and send it,
   As soon 's he smells 't,
Baith their disease, and what will mend it,
   At once he tells 't.

' And then a' doctor's saws and whittles,
Of a' dimensions, shapes, an' mettles,
A' kinds o' boxes, mugs, an' bottles,
   He 's sure to hae;
Their Latin names as fast he rattles
   As A B C. 120

' Calces o' fossils, earths, and trees;
True sal-marinum o' the seas;
The farina of beans and pease,
   He has 't in plenty;
Aqua-fortis, what you please,
   He can content ye.

'Forbye some new uncommon weapons, —
Urinus spiritus of capons ;
Or mite-horn shavings, filings, scrapings,
        Distill'd per se ;   130
Sal-alkali o' midge-tail clippings,
        And mony mae.'

'Wae's me for Johnny Ged's Hole now,'
Quoth I, 'if that thae news be true !
His braw calf-ward where gowans grew
        Sae white and bonnie,
Nae doubt they'll rive it wi' the plew ;
        They'll ruin Johnie !'

The creature grain'd an eldritch laugh,
And says 'Ye needna yoke the pleugh,   140
Kirk-yards will soon be till'd eneugh,
        Tak ye nae fear ;
They'll a' be trench'd wi' mony a sheugh
        In twa-three year.

'Where I kill'd ane, a fair strae-death,
By loss o' blood or want o' breath,
This night I'm free to tak my aith
        That Hornbook's skill
Has clad a score i' their last claith,
        By drap and pill.   150

'An honest wabster to his trade,
Whase wife's twa nieves were scarce weel-bred,
Gat tippence-worth to mend her head
        When it was sair ;
The wife slade cannie to her bed,
        But ne'er spak mair.

'A country laird had ta'en the batts,
Or some curmurring in his guts,
His only son for Hornbook sets,
        An' pays him well :   160
The lad, for twa guid gimmer-pets,
        Was laird himsel.

'A bonnie lass, ye kenn'd her name,
Some ill-brewn drink had hov'd her wame ;
She trusts hersel, to hide the shame,
                    In Hornbook's care ;
Horn sent her aff to her lang hame,
                    To hide it there.

'That's just a swatch o' Hornbook's way ;
Thus goes he on from day to day,   170
Thus does he poison, kill, an' slay,
                    An's weel pay'd for 't ;
Yet stops me o' my lawfu' prey
                    Wi' his damn'd dirt.

'But, hark ! I'll tell you of a plot,
Tho' dinna ye be speaking o't ;
I'll nail the self-conceited sot
                    As dead's a herrin' :
Niest time we meet, I'll wad a groat,
                    He gets his fairin' !'   180

But, just as he began to tell,
The auld kirk-hammer strak the bell
Some wee short hour ayont the twal,
                    Which rais'd us baith :
I took the way that pleas'd mysel,
                    And sae did Death.

A DREAM.

Guid-mornin' to your Majesty !
    May heaven augment your blisses
On ev'ry new birth-day ye see—
    A humble poet wishes !
My bardship here, at your levee,
    On sic a day as this is,
Is sure an uncouth sight to see
    Amang thae birth-day dresses
                    Sae fine this day.

I see ye're complimented thrang,   10
   By mony a lord an' lady ;
'God save the King ! ' 's a cuckoo sang
   That's unco easy said aye ;
The poets, too, a venal gang,
   Wi' rhymes well-turn'd an' ready,
Wad gar you trow ye ne'er do wrang,
   But aye unerring steady,
              On sic a day.

For me, before a monarch's face—
   Ev'n there I winna flatter ;   20
For neither pension, post, nor place,
   Am I your humble debtor :
So nae reflection on your Grace,
   Your kingship to bespatter ;
There's mony waur been o' the race,
   And aiblins ane been better
              Than you this day.

'Tis very true, my sovereign King,
   My skill may weel be doubted ;
But Facts are chiels that winna ding,   30
   An' downa be disputed :
Your royal nest, beneath your wing,
   Is e'en right reft an' clouted,
An' now the third part of the string,
   An' less, will gang about it,
              Than did ae day.

Far be't frae me that I aspire
   To blame your legislation,
Or say ye wisdom want, or fire,
   To rule this mighty nation ;   40
But faith ! I muckle doubt, my Sire,
   Ye've trusted ministration
To chaps wha in a barn or byre
   Wad better fill'd their station
              Than courts yon day.

And now ye've gien auld Britain peace
  Her broken shins to plaister,
Your sair taxation does her fleece
  Till she has scarce a tester.
For me, thank God! my life's a lease,   50
  Nae bargain wearing faster,
Or faith! I fear that with the geese
  I shortly boost to pasture
              I' the craft some day.

I'm no mistrusting Willie Pitt
  When taxes he enlarges
(An' Will's a true guid fallow's get,
  A name not envy spairges)
That he intends to pay your debt,
  An' lessen a' your charges;   60
But God's sake! let nae saving fit
  Abridge your bonnie barges
              An' boats this day.

Adieu, my Liege! may freedom geck
  Beneath your high protection;
An' may ye rax Corruption's neck,
  And gie her for dissection!
But since I'm here, I'll no neglect,
  In loyal true affection,
To pay your Queen, with due respect,   70
  My fealty an' subjection
              This great Birth-day.

Hail, Majesty most Excellent!
  While nobles strive to please ye,
Will ye accept a compliment
  A simple poet gies ye?
Thae bonny bairntime Heav'n has lent,
  Still higher may they heeze ye
In bliss, till fate some day is sent
  For ever to release ye   80
              Frae care that day.

For you, young Potentate o' Wales,
  I tell your Highness fairly,
Down pleasure's stream wi' swelling sails
  I'm tauld ye're driving rarely;
But some day ye may gnaw your nails,
  An' curse your folly sairly,
That ere ye brak Diana's pales,
  Or rattled dice wi' Charlie,
         By night or day.   90

Yet aft a ragged cowt's been known
  To mak a noble aiver;
So ye may doucely fill a throne,
  For a' their clish-ma-claver;
There, him at Agincourt wha shone,
  Few better were or braver;
And yet, wi' funny queer Sir John,
  He was an unco shaver
         For mony a day.

For you, right rev'rend Osnaburg,   100
  Nane sets the lawn-sleeve sweeter,
Altho' a ribban' at your lug
  Wad been a dress completer:
As ye disown yon paughty dog
  That bears the keys of Peter,
Then swith! an' get a wife to hug,
  Or trouth! ye'll stain the mitre
         Some luckless day.

Young royal Tarry Breeks, I learn
  Ye've lately come athwart her—   110
A glorious galley, stem and stern,
  Weel rigg'd for Venus' barter;
But first hang out, that she'll discern
  Your hymeneal charter;
Then heave aboard your grapple airn,
  An' large upon her quarter
         Come full that day.

Ye, lastly, bonnie blossoms a',
  Ye royal lasses dainty,
Heav'n mak you guid as weel as braw,   120
  An' gie you lads a-plenty:
But sneer na British boys awa',
  For kings are unco scant aye;
An' German gentles are but sma',
  They're better just than want aye
          On ony day.

God bless you a'! Consider now
  Ye're unco muckle dautit;
But, e'er the course o' life be through,
  It may be bitter sautit: 130
An' I hae seen their coggie fou
  That yet hae tarrow't at it;
But or the day was done, I trow,
  The laggen they hae clautit
          Fu' clean that day.

ADDRESS TO THE DEIL.

O THOU! whatever title suit thee,
Auld Hornie, Satan, Nick, or Clootie,
Wha in yon cavern grim an' sootie,
          Clos'd under hatches,
Spairges about the brunstane cootie,
          To scaud poor wretches!

Hear me, auld Hangie, for a wee,
An' let poor damnèd bodies be;
I'm sure sma' pleasure it can gie,
          Ev'n to a deil,   10
To skelp an' scaud poor dogs like me,
          An' hear us squeal!

Great is thy pow'r, an' great thy fame;
Far kenn'd an' noted is thy name;
An', tho' yon lowin heugh's thy hame,
  Thou travels far;
An' faith! thou's neither lag nor lame,
  Nor blate nor scaur.

Whyles rangin' like a roarin' lion
For prey, a' holes an' corners tryin';   20
Whyles on the strong-wing'd tempest flyin',
  Tirlin' the kirks;
Whyles, in the human bosom pryin',
  Unseen thou lurks.

I've heard my reverend grannie say,
In lanely glens ye like to stray;
Or, where auld ruin'd castles gray
  Nod to the moon,
Ye fright the nightly wand'rer's way,
  Wi' eldritch croon.   30

When twilight did my grannie summon
To say her pray'rs, douce, honest woman!
Aft yont the dyke she's heard you bummin',
  Wi' eerie drone;
Or, rustlin', thro' the boortrees comin',
  Wi' heavy groan.

Ae dreary windy winter night
The stars shot down wi' sklentin' light,
Wi' you mysel I gat a fright
  Ayont the lough;   40
Ye like a rash-buss stood in sight
  Wi' waving sough.

The cudgel in my nieve did shake,
Each bristled hair stood like a stake,
When wi' an eldritch stoor 'quaick, quaick,'
  Amang the springs,
Awa ye squatter'd like a drake
  On whistlin' wings.

Let warlocks grim an' wither'd hags
Tell how wi' you on ragweed nags   50
They skim the muirs, an' dizzy crags
      Wi' wicked speed ;
And in kirk-yards renew their leagues
      Owre howkit dead.

Thence country wives, wi' toil an' pain,
May plunge an' plunge the kirn in vain ;
For oh! the yellow treasure's taen
      By witchin' skill ;
An' dawtit twal-pint Hawkie's gane
      As yell's the bill.   60

Thence mystic knots mak great abuse
On young guidmen, fond, keen, an' crouse ;
When the best wark-lume i' the house,
      By cantrip wit,
Is instant made no worth a louse,
      Just at the bit.

When thowes dissolve the snawy hoord,
An' float the jinglin' icy-boord,
Then water-kelpies haunt the foord,
      By your direction,   70
An' 'nighted trav'llers are allur'd
      To their destruction.

An' aft your moss-traversing spunkies
Decoy the wight that late an' drunk is :
The bleezin, curst, mischievous monkies
      Delude his eyes,
Till in some miry slough he sunk is,
      Ne'er mair to rise.

When masons' mystic word an' grip
In storms an' tempests raise you up,   80
Some cock or cat your rage maun stop,
      Or, strange to tell !
The youngest brither ye wad whip
      Aff straught to hell.

Lang syne, in Eden's bonnie yard,
When youthfu' lovers first were pair'd,
And all the soul of love they shar'd,
   The raptur'd hour,
Sweet on the fragrant flow'ry swaird,
   In shady bow'r;   90

Then you, ye auld snick-drawing dog!
Ye cam to Paradise incog.
An' play'd on man a cursed brogue,
   (Black be you fa'!)
An' gied the infant warld a shog,
   'Maist ruin'd a'.

D'ye mind that day, when in a bizz,
Wi' reekit duds, an' reestit gizz,
Ye did present your smoutie phiz
   'Mang better folk,   100
An' sklented on the man of Uz
   Your spitefu' joke?

An' how ye gat him i' your thrall,
An' brak him out o' house an' hal',
While scabs an' blotches did him gall
   Wi' bitter claw,
An' lows'd his ill-tongu'd wicked scawl,
   Was warst ava?

But a' your doings to rehearse,
Your wily snares an' fechtin' fierce, 110
Sin' that day Michael did you pierce,
   Down to this time,
Wad ding a' Lallan tongue, or Erse,
   In prose or rhyme.

An' now, auld Cloots, I ken ye're thinkin',
A certain Bardie's rantin', drinkin',
Some luckless hour will send him linkin',
   To your black pit;
But faith! he'll turn a corner jinkin',
   An' cheat you yet.   120

But fare you weel, auld Nickie-ben!
O wad ye tak a thought an' men'!
Ye aiblins might—I dinna ken—
      Still hae a stake:
I'm wae to think upo' yon den,
        Ev'n for your sake!

——••——

THE ORDINATION.

KILMARNOCK wabsters, fidge and claw,
  An' pour your creeshie nations;
An' ye wha leather rax an' draw,
  Of a' denominations;
Swith to the Laigh Kirk, ane an' a',
  An' there tak up your stations;
Then aff to Begbie's in a raw,
  An' pour divine libations
          For joy this day.

Curst Common-sense, that imp o' hell,
  Cam in wi' Maggie Lauder;
But Oliphant aft made her yell,
  An' Russel sair misca'd her;
This day Mackinlay takes the flail,
  An' he 's the boy will blaud her!
He'll clap a shangan on her tail,
  An' set the bairns to daud her
          Wi' dirt this day.

Mak haste an' turn king David owre,
  An' lilt wi' holy clangor;
O' double verse come gie us four,
  An' skirl up the Bangor:
This day the Kirk kicks up a stoure,
  Nae mair the knaves shall wrang her,
For Heresy is in her pow'r,
  And gloriously she'll whang her
          Wi' pith this day.

Come, let a proper text be read,
 An' touch it aff wi' vigour,
How graceless Ham leugh at his dad,   30
 Which made Canaan a nigger ;
Or Phineas drove the murdering blade,
 Wi' whore-abhorring rigour ;
Or Zipporah, the scauldin jad,
 Was like a bluidy tiger
       I' th' inn that day.

There try his mettle on the creed,
 And bind him down, wi' caution
That stipend is a carnal weed
 He takes but for the fashion ;   40
An' gie him o'er the flock,—to feed,
 And punish each transgression ;
Especial, rams that cross the breed—
 Gie them sufficient threshin',
       Spare them nae day.

Now, auld Kilmarnock, cock thy tail,
 An' toss thy horns fu' canty ;
Nae mair thou 'lt rowte out-owre the dale,
 Because thy pasture 's scanty ;
For lapfu's large o' gospel kail   50
 Shall fill thy crib in plenty,
An' runts o' grace the pick an' wale,
 No gi'en by way o' dainty,
       But ilka day.

Nae mair by Babel streams we'll weep,
 To think upon our Zion ;
And hing our fiddles up to sleep,
 Like baby-clouts a-dryin' :
Come, screw the pegs wi' tunefu' cheep,
 And o'er the thairms be tryin' ;   60
O rare ! to see our elbucks wheep,
 And a' like lamb-tails flyin'
       Fu' fast this day !

Lang patronage, wi' rod o' airn,
  Has shor'd the Kirk's undoin',
As lately Fenwick, sair forfairn,
  Has proven to its ruin :
Our patron, honest man ! Glencairn,
  He saw mischief was brewin' :
An' like a godly elect bairn,   70
  He 's wal'd us out a true ane,
              And sound this day.

Now Robertson, harangue nae mair,
  But steek your gab for ever ;
Or try the wicked town of Ayr,
  For there they'll think you clever ;
Or, nae reflection on your lear,
  Ye may commence a shaver ;
Or to the Netherton repair,
  And turn a carpet-weaver   80
              Aff-hand this day.

Mu'trie and you were just a match,
  We never had sic twa drones ;
Auld Hornie did the Laigh Kirk watch,
  Just like a winkin' baudrons ;
And aye he catch'd the tither wretch,
  To fry them in his caudrons ;
But now his Honour maun detach,
  Wi' a' his brimstone squadrons,
              Fast, fast this day.   90

See, see auld Orthodoxy's faes
  She 's swingein' thro' the city ;
Hark how the nine-tail'd cat she plays !
  I vow it 's unco pretty !
There Learning, with his Greekish face,
  Grunts out some Latin ditty ;
And Common-sense is gaun, she says,
  To mak to Jamie Beattie
              Her plaint this day.

But there's Morality himsel,   100
    Embracing all opinions;
Hear how he gies the tither yell,
    Between his twa companions;
See how she peels the skin an' fell,
    As ane were peelin onions!
— Now there, they're packèd aff to hell,
    And banish'd our dominions
                    Henceforth this day.

O happy day! rejoice, rejoice!
    Come bouse about the porter!   110
Morality's demure decoys
    Shall here nae mair find quarter:
Mackinlay, Russel, are the boys
    That heresy can torture;
They'll gie her on a rape a hoyse,
    And cowe her measure shorter
                    By th' head some day.

Come, bring the tither mutchkin in,
    And here's, for a conclusion,
To every New Light mother's son   120
    From this time forth, Confusion!
If mair they deave us wi' their din,
    Or patronage intrusion,
We'll light a spunk, and, ev'ry skin,
    We'll rin them aff in fusion
                    Like oil, some day.

THE AUTHOR'S EARNEST CRY AND PRAYER

TO THE SCOTCH REPRESENTATIVES IN THE HOUSE OF COMMONS.

Ye Irish lords, ye knights an' squires,
Wha represent our brughs an' shires,
An' doucely manage our affairs
    In Parliament,
To you a simple poet's prayers
    Are humbly sent.

Alas! my roupit muse is hearse;
Your Honours' heart wi' grief 'twad pierce
To see her sitten on her arse
    Low i' the dust,   10
An' screechin' out prosaic verse,
    An' like to brust!

Tell them wha hae the chief direction,
Scotland an' me's in great affliction,
E'er sin' they laid that curst restriction
    On aqua vitæ;
An' rouse them up to strong conviction,
    An' move their pity.

Stand forth, an' tell yon Premier youth
The honest, open, naked truth: 20
Tell him o' mine an' Scotland's drouth,
    His servants humble:
The muckle devil blaw ye south,
    If ye dissemble!

Does ony great man glunch an' gloom?
Speak out, an' never fash your thumb!
Let posts an' pensions sink or soom
    Wi' them wha grant them;
If honestly they canna come,
    Far better want them.   30

In gath'rin' votes you were na slack;
Now stand as tightly by your tack;
Ne'er claw your lug, an' fidge your back,
        An' hum an' haw;
But raise your arm, an' tell your crack
        Before them a'.

Paint Scotland greetin 'owre her thrissle;
Her mutchkin stoup as toom's a whissle:
An' damn'd Excisemen in a bussle,
        Seizin a stell,   40
Triumphant crushin't like a mussle
        Or limpet shell.

Then on the tither hand present her,
A blackguard smuggler, right behint her,
An' cheek-for-chow, a chuffie vintner,
        Colleaguing join,
Pickin' her pouch as bare as Winter
        Of a' kind coin.

Is there, that bears the name o' Scot,
But feels his heart's bluid rising hot,   50
To see his poor auld mither's pot
        Thus dung in staves,
An' plunder'd o' her hindmost groat
        By gallows knaves?

Alas! I'm but a nameless wight,
Trode i' the mire out o' sight!
But could I like. Montgomeries fight,
        Or gab like Boswell,
There's some sark-necks I wad draw tight,
        An' tie some hose well.   60

God bless your Honours, can ye see 't,
The kind, auld, cantie carlin greet,
An' no get warmly to your feet
        An' gar them hear it?
An' tell them wi' a patriot-heat,
        Ye winna bear it?

Some o' you nicely ken the laws
To round the period an' pause,
An' with rhetoric clause on clause
            To mak harangues ;   70
Then echo thro' Saint Stephen's wa's
            Auld Scotland's wrangs.

Dempster, a true blue Scot I'se warran' ;
Thee, aith-detesting, chaste Kilkerran ;
An' that glib-gabbèd Highland Baron,
            The Laird o' Graham ;
An' ane, a chap that 's damn'd auldfarran,
            Dundas his name ;

Erskine, a spunkie Norland billie ;
True Campbells, Frederik an' Ilay ;   80
An' Livingston, the bauld Sir Willie ;
            An' mony ithers,
Whom auld Demosthenes or Tully
            Might own for brithers.

Arouse, my boys ! exert your mettle
To get auld Scotland back her kettle ;
Or faith ! I'll wad my new pleugh-pettle,
            Ye'll see 't or lang,
She'll teach you, wi' a reekin whittle,
            Anither sang.   90

This while she 's been in crankous mood ;
Her lost Militia fir'd her bluid
(Deil nor they never mair do guid
            Play'd her that pliskie !)
An' now she 's like to rin red-wud
            About her whisky.

An' Lord, if ance they pit her till 't,
Her tartan petticoat she'll kilt,
An', durk an' pistol at her belt,
            She'll tak the streets,   100
An' rin her whittle to the hilt
            I' th' first she meets !

For God sake, sirs ! then speak her fair,
An' straik her cannie wi' the hair,
An' to the muckle house repair
　　　　　Wi' instant speed
An' strive, wi' a' your wit and lear,
　　　　　To get remead.

Yon ill-tongu'd tinkler, Charlie Fox,
May taunt you wi' his jeers an' mocks ;　　110
But gie him 't het, my hearty cocks !
　　　　　E'en cowe the cadie,
An' send him to his dicing-box
　　　　　An' sportin' lady.

Tell yon guid bluid o' auld Boconnock's
I'll be his debt twa mashlum bannocks,
An' drink his health in auld Nanse Tinnock's
　　　　　Nine times a-week,
If he some scheme, like tea an' winnocks,
　　　　　Wad kindly seek.　　120

Could he some commutation broach,
I'll pledge my aith in guid braid Scotch,
He need na fear their foul reproach
　　　　　Nor erudition,
Yon mixtie-maxtie queer hotch-potch,
　　　　　The Coalition.

Auld Scotland has a raucle tongue ;
She's just a devil wi' a rung ;
An' if she promise auld or young
　　　　　To tak their part,　　130
Tho' by the neck she should be strung,
　　　　　She'll no desert.

An' now, ye chosen Five-and-Forty,
May still your Mither's heart support ye ;
Then, though a minister grow dorty,
　　　　　An' kick your place,
Ye'll snap your fingers, poor an' hearty,
　　　　　Before his face.

God bless your Honours a' your days
Wi' sowps o' kail an' brats o' claes,   140
In spite o' a' the thievish kaes
        That haunt St. Jamie's!
Your humble poet sings an' prays,
        While Rab his name is.

Postscript.

Let half-starv'd slaves in warmer skies
See future wines rich-clust'ring rise;
Their lot auld Scotland ne'er envies,
        But, blythe an' frisky,
She eyes her free-born martial boys
        Tak aff their whisky.   150

What tho' their Phœbus kinder warms,
While fragrance blooms an' beauty charms,
When wretches range in famish'd swarms
        The scented groves,
Or, hounded forth, dishonour arms
        In hungry droves.

Their gun's a burdon on their shouther;
They downa bide the stink o' powther;
Their bauldest thought's a hank'ring swither
        To stan' or rin,   160
Till skelp! a shot—they're aff, a' throu'ther,
        To save their skin.

But bring a Scotsman frae his hill,
Clap in his cheek a Highland gill,
Say 'Such is royal George's will,
        An' there's the foe!'
He has nae thought but how to kill
        Twa at a blow.

Nae cauld faint-hearted doubtings tease him;
Death comes, wi' fearless eye he sees him;   170
Wi' bluidy hand a welcome gies him;
        An', when he fa's,
His latest draught o' breathin' lea'es him
        In faint huzzas.

Sages their solemn een may steek,
An' raise a philosophic reek,
An' physically causes seek
         In clime an' season ;
But tell me whisky's name in Greek,
         I'll tell the reason.   180

Scotland, my auld respected Mither !
Tho' whyles ye moistify your leather,
Till where ye sit, on craps o' heather,
         Ye tine your dam—
Freedom and Whisky gang thegither !
         Tak aff your dram !

ADDRESS TO THE UNCO GUID, OR THE
RIGIDLY RIGHTEOUS.

My son, these maxims make a rule,
*   And lump them aye thegither :*
The rigid righteous is a fool,
*   The rigid wise anither :*
The cleanest corn that e'er was dight,
*   May hae some pyles o' caff in ;*
So ne'er a fellow-creature slight
*   For random fits o' daffin.*
         SOLOMON (Eccles. vii. 16).

O YE wha are sae guid yoursel,
   Sae pious and sae holy,
Ye've nought to do but mark and tell
   Your neibour's fauts and folly !
Whase life is like a weel-gaun mill,
   Supplied wi' store o' water :
The heapèd happer's ebbing still,
   And still the clap plays clatter !

Hear me, ye venerable core,
  As counsel for poor mortals,   10
That frequent pass douce Wisdom's door.
  For glaikit Folly's portals;
I, for their thoughtless careless sakes,
  Would here propone defences,—
Their donsie tricks, their black mistakes,
  Their failings and mischances.

Ye see your state wi' their's compar'd,
  And shudder at the niffer;
But cast a moment's fair regard—
  What maks the mighty differ?   20
Discount what scant occasion gave,
  That purity ye pride in,
And (what's aft mair than a' the lave)
  Your better art o' hidin'.

Think, when your castigated pulse
  Gies now and then a wallop,
What ragings must his veins convulse,
  That still eternal gallop!
Wi' wind and tide fair i' your tail,
  Right on ye scud your sea-way;   30
But in the teeth o' baith to sail,
  It maks an unco leeway.

See Social life and Glee sit down,
  All joyous and unthinking,
Till, quite transmogrified, they're grown
  Debauchery and Drinking:
O would they stay to calculate
  Th' eternal consequences;
Or your more dreaded hell to state,
  Damnation of expenses!   40

Ye high, exalted, virtuous Dames,
  Tied up in godly laces,
Before ye gie poor Frailty names,
  Suppose a change o' cases;

A dear lov'd lad, convenience snug,
   A treacherous inclination—
But, let me whisper i' your lug,
   Ye're aiblins nae temptation.

Then gently scan your brother man,
   Still gentler sister woman;   50
Tho' they may gang a kennin wrang,
   To step aside is human.
One point must still be greatly dark,
   The moving why they do it;
And just as lamely can ye mark
   How far perhaps they rue it.

Who made the heart, 'tis He alone
   Decidedly can try us;
He knows each chord, its various tone,
   Each spring, its various bias.   60
Then at the balance let's be mute,
   We never can adjust it;
What's done we partly may compute,
   But know not what's resisted.

HOLY WILLIE'S PRAYER.

O Thou, wha in the Heavens dost dwell,
Wha, as it pleases best thysel',
Sends ane to heaven and ten to hell,
      A' for thy glory,
And no for ony guid or ill
      They've done afore thee!

I bless and praise thy matchless might,
Whan thousands thou hast left in night,
That I am here afore thy sight,
      For gifts an' grace   10
A burnin' an' a shinin' light,
      To a' this place.

What was I, or my generation,
That I should get sic exaltation?
I, wha deserve most just damnation,
      For broken laws,
Sax thousand years 'fore my creation,
        Thro' Adam's cause.

When frae my mither's womb I fell,
Thou might hae plungèd me in hell,   20
To gnash my gums, to weep and wail,
      In burnin' lakes,
Where damnèd devils roar and yell,
        Chain'd to their stakes;

Yet I am here a chosen sample,
To show thy grace is great and ample;
I'm here a pillar in thy temple,
      Strong as a rock,
A guide, a buckler, an example
        To a' thy flock.   30

O Lord, thou kens what zeal I bear,
When drinkers drink, and swearers swear,
And singin' there and dancin' here,
      Wi' great an' sma':
For I am keepit by thy fear
        Free frae them a'.

But yet, O Lord! confess I must
At times I'm fash'd wi' fleshy lust;
An' sometimes too, in warldly trust,
      Vile self gets in;   40
But thou remembers we are dust,
        Defil'd in sin.

O Lord! yestreen, thou kens, wi' Meg—
Thy pardon I sincerely beg;
O! may 't ne'er be a livin' plague
      To my dishonour,
An' I'll ne'er lift a lawless leg
        Again upon her.

Besides I farther maun allow,
Wi' Lizzie's lass, three times I trow—   50
But, Lord, that Friday I was fou,
   When I cam near her,
Or else thou kens thy servant true
   Wad never steer her.

May be thou lets this fleshly thorn
Beset thy servant e'en and morn
Lest he owre high and proud should turn,
   That he's sae gifted;
If sae, thy hand maun e'en be borne,
   Until thou lift it.   60

Lord, bless thy chosen in this place,
For here thou hast a chosen race;
But God confound their stubborn face,
   And blast their name,
Wha bring thy elders to disgrace
   An' public shame.

Lord, mind Gawn Hamilton's deserts,
He drinks, an' swears, an' plays at cartes,
Yet has sae mony takin' arts
   Wi' grit an' sma',   70
Frae God's ain priest the people's hearts
   He steals awa'.

An' when we chasten'd him therefor,
Thou kens how he bred sic a splore
As set the warld in a roar
   O' laughin' at us;
Curse thou his basket and his store,
   Kail and potatoes.

Lord, hear my earnest cry an' pray'r,
Against that presbyt'ry o' Ayr;   80
Thy strong right hand, Lord, make it bare
   Upo' their heads;
Lord, weigh it down, and dinna spare,
   For their misdeeds.

O Lord my God, that glib-tongu'd Aiken,
My very heart and soul are quakin',
To think how we stood sweatin', shakin',
      An' piss'd wi' dread,
While he, wi' hingin' lips and snakin',
      Held up his head.   90

Lord, in the day of vengeance try him;
Lord, visit them wha did employ him,
And pass not in thy mercy by them,
      Nor hear their pray'r:
But, for thy people's sake, destroy them,
      And dinna spare.

But, Lord, remember me and mine
Wi' mercies temp'ral and divine,
That I for gear and grace may shine
      Excell'd by nane,   100
And a' the glory shall be thine,
      Amen, Amen!

EPISTLE TO A YOUNG FRIEND.

I LANG hae thought, my youthfu' friend,
  A something to have sent you,
Tho' it should serve nae ither end
  Than just a kind memento;
But how the subject theme may gang,
  Let time and chance determine;
Perhaps it may turn out a sang,
  Perhaps turn out a sermon.

Ye'll try the world soon, my lad,
  And, Andrew dear, believe me,   10
Ye'll find mankind an unco squad,
  And muckle they may grieve ye:

For care and trouble set your thought,
  Ev'n when your end 's attained ;
And a' your views may come to nought,
  Where ev'ry nerve is strained.

I'll no say men are villains a' ;
  The real harden'd wicked,
Wha hae nae check but human law,
  Are to a few restricked :   20
But oh ! mankind are unco weak,
  An' little to be trusted ;
If self the wavering balance shake,
  It 's rarely right adjusted !

Yet they wha fa' in fortune's strife,
  Their fate we shouldna censure ;
For still th' important end of life
  They equally may answer.
A man may hae an honest heart,
  Tho' poortith hourly stare him ;   30
A man may tak a neibor's part,
  Yet hae nae cash to spare him.

Aye free, aff han', your story tell,
  When wi' a bosom crony ;
But still keep something to yoursel
  Ye scarcely tell to ony.
Conceal yoursel as weel 's ye can
  Frae critical dissection ;
But keek thro' ev'ry other man
  Wi' sharpen'd sly inspection.   40

The sacred lowe o' weel-plac'd love,
  Luxuriantly indulge it ;
But never tempt th' illicit rove,
  Tho' naething should divulge it :
I wave the quantum o' the sin,
  The hazard of concealing ;
But oh ! it hardens a' within,
  And petrifies the feeling !

To catch dame Fortune's golden smile,
  Assiduous wait upon her;   50
And gather gear by ev'ry wile
  That's justified by honour;
Not for to hide it in a hedge,
  Nor for a train attendant;
But for the glorious privilege
  Of being independent.

The fear o' hell's a hangman's whip
  To haud the wretch in order;
But where ye feel your honour grip,
  Let that aye be your border: 60
Its slightest touches, instant pause—
  Debar a' side pretences;
And resolutely keep its laws,
  Uncaring consequences.

The great Creator to revere
  Must sure become the creature;
But still the preaching cant forbear,
  And ev'n the rigid feature:
Yet ne'er with wits profane to range
  Be complaisance extended;   70
An atheist laugh's a poor exchange
  For Deity offended.

When ranting round in pleasure's ring,
  Religion may be blinded;
Or, if she gie a random sting,
  It may be little minded;
But when on life we're tempest-driv'n,
  A conscience but a canker—
A correspondence fix'd wi' Heav'n
  Is sure a noble anchor.   80

Adieu, dear amiable youth!
  Your heart can ne'er be wanting!
May prudence, fortitude, and truth
  Erect your brow undaunting.

In ploughman phrase, God send you speed
    Still daily to grow wiser;
And may ye better reck the rede
    Than ever did th' adviser!

———•———

TAM SAMSON'S ELEGY.

Has auld Kilmarnock seen the deil?
Or great Mackinlay thrawn his heel?
Or Robertson again grown weel,
            To preach an' read?
'Na, waur than a'!' cries ilka chiel,
            'Tam Samson's dead!'

Kilmarnock lang may grunt an' grane,
An' sigh, an' sab, an' greet her lane,
An' cleed her bairns, man, wife, an' wean,
            In mourning weed;   10
To death, she's dearly paid the kane,—
            Tam Samson's dead!

The Brethren o' the mystic level
May hing their head in woefu' bevel,
While by their nose the tears will revel,
            Like ony bead;
Death's gien the Lodge an unco devel,—
            Tam Samson's dead!

When Winter muffles up his cloak,
And binds the mire like a rock;   20
When to the loughs the curlers flock
            Wi' gleesome speed,
Wha will they station at the cock?
            Tam Samson's dead!

He was the king o' a' the core
To guard, or draw, or wick a bore,
Or up the rink like Jehu roar
      In time o' need ;
But now he lags on Death's hogscore,—
      Tam Samson 's dead !   30

Now safe the stately sawmont sail,
And trouts bedropp'd wi' crimson hail,
And eels weel kent for souple tail,
      And geds for greed,
Since dark in Death's fish-creel we wail
      Tam Samson dead !

Rejoice, ye birring paitricks a' ;
Ye cootie moorcocks, crousely craw ;
Ye maukins, cock your fud fu' braw,
      Withouten dread ;   40
Your mortal fae is now awa',—
      Tam Samson 's dead !

That woefu' morn be ever mourn'd
Saw him in shootin graith adorn'd,
While pointers round impatient burn'd,
      Frae couples freed ;
But oh ! he gaed and ne'er return'd !
      Tam Samson 's dead !

In vain auld age his body batters ;
In vain the gout his ancles fetters ;
In vain the burns cam down like waters,   50
      An acre braid !
Now ev'ry auld wife, greetin', clatters
      'Tam Samson 's dead !'

Owre mony a weary hag he limpit,
An' aye the tither shot he thumpit,
Till coward Death behind him jumpit
      Wi' deadly feide ;
Now he proclaims, wi' tout o' trumpet,
      'Tam Samson 's dead !'   60

When at his heart he felt the dagger,
He reel'd his wonted bottle-swagger,
But yet he drew the mortal trigger
              Wi' weel-aim'd heed;
'Lord, five!' he cried, an' owre did stagger;
           Tam Samson 's dead!

Ilk hoary hunter mourn'd a brither;
Ilk sportsman youth bemoan'd a father;
Yon auld grey stane, amang the heather,
             Marks out his head,   70
Where Burns has wrote, in rhyming blether,
           'Tam Samson 's dead!'

There low he lies in lasting rest;
Perhaps upon his mould'ring breast
Some spitfu' muirfowl bigs her nest,
             To hatch and breed;
Alas! nae mair he'll them molest!
           Tam Samson 's dead!

When August winds the heather wave,
And sportsmen wander by yon grave,   80
Three volleys let his memory crave
             O' pouther an' lead,
Till Echo answer frae her cave
           'Tam Samson 's dead!'

Heaven rest his saul, where'er he be!
Is th' wish o' mony mae than me:
He had twa faults, or maybe three,
             Yet what remead?
Ae social honest man want we:
           Tam Samson 's dead!   90

THE EPITAPH.

TAM SAMSON'S weel-worn clay here lies:
  Ye canting zealots, spare him!
If honest worth in heaven rise,
  Ye'll mend ere ye win near him.

Per Contra.

Go, Fame, an' canter like a filly
Thro' a' the streets an' neuks o' Killie,
Tell ev'ry social honest billie
      To cease his grievin',
For yet, unskaith'd by Death's gleg gullie,
      Tam Samson's livin'!   100

A WINTER NIGHT.

When biting Boreas, fell and doure,
Sharp shivers thro' the leafless bow'r;
When Phœbus gies a short-liv'd glow'r,
      Far south the lift,
Dim-dark'ning thro' the flaky show'r
      Or whirling drift;

Ae night the storm the steeples rocked,
Poor Labour sweet in sleep was locked,
While burns, wi' snawy wreaths up-choked,
      Wild-eddying swirl,   10
Or, thro' the mining outlet bocked,
      Down headlong hurl;

List'ning the doors an' winnocks rattle
I thought me on the ourie cattle,
Or silly sheep, wha bide this brattle
      O' winter war,
And thro' the drift, deep-lairing, sprattle
      Beneath a scar.

Ilk happing bird, wee, helpless thing!
That, in the merry months o' spring,   20
Delighted me to hear thee sing,
      What comes o' thee?
Where wilt thou cow'r thy chittering wing,
      An' close thy e'e?

Ev'n you, on murd'ring errands toil'd,
Lone from your savage homes exil'd,—
The blood-stained roost and sheep-cote spoil'd
   My heart forgets,
While pitiless the tempest wild
   Sore on you beats.   30

Now Phœbe, in her midnight reign,
Dark muffl'd, view'd the dreary plain ;
Still crowding thoughts, a pensive train,
   Rose in my soul,
When on my ear this plaintive strain,
   Slow, solemn, stole :—

' Blow, blow, ye winds, with heavier gust !
And freeze, thou bitter-biting frost !
Descend, ye chilly smothering snows !
Not all your rage, as now united, shows   40
 More hard unkindness unrelenting,
 Vengeful malice unrepenting,
Than heav'n-illumin'd man on brother man bestows !
 See stern Oppression's iron grip,
 Or mad Ambition's gory hand,
Sending, like blood-hounds from the slip,
 Woe, want, and murder o'er a land !
Ev'n in the peaceful rural vale,
Truth, weeping, tells the mournful tale
How pamper'd Luxury, Flatt'ry by her side,   50
 The parasite empoisoning her ear,
 With all the servile wretches in the rear,
Looks o'er proud property, extended wide ;
 And eyes the simple rustic hind,
 Whose toil upholds the glitt'ring show,
A creature of another kind,
Some coarser substance, unrefin'd,
Plac'd for her lordly use thus far, thus vile, below.

Where, where is Love's fond, tender throe,
With lordly Honour's lofty brow,   60
 The pow'rs you proudly own ?
Is there, beneath Love's noble name,
Can harbour, daɪk, the selfish aim
 To bless himself alone ?

Mark maiden-innocence a prey
  To love-pretending snares ;
This boasted honour turns away,
Shunning soft pity's rising sway,
Regardless of the tears, and unavailing pray'rs !
  Perhaps this hour, in mis'ry's squalid nest,   70
  She strains your infant to her joyless breast,
And with a mother's fears shrinks at the rocking blast !

Oh ye ! who, sunk in beds of down,
Feel not a want but what yourselves create,
Think, for a moment, on his wretched fate,
  Whom friends and fortune quite disown !
Ill satisfied keen nature's clam'rous call,
  Stretch'd on his straw he lays himself to sleep,
While thro' the ragged roof and chinky wall,
Chill o'er his slumbers piles the drifty heap !   80
Think on the dungeon's grim confine,
Where guilt and poor misfortune pine !
Guilt, erring man, relenting view !
But shall thy legal rage pursue
  The wretch, already crushèd low,
  By cruel fortune's undeservèd blow ?
Affliction's sons are brothers in distress ;
A brother to relieve, how exquisite the bliss !'

I heard nae mair ; for Chanticleer
  Shook off the pouthery snaw,   90
And hail'd the morning with a cheer,
  A cottage-rousing craw.

But deep this truth impress'd my mind—
  Thro' all His works abroad,
The heart benevolent and kind
  The most resembles God.

—◦◦—

SCOTCH DRINK.

Gie him strong drink, until he wink,
That's sinking in despair;
An' liquor guid to fire his bluid,
That's prest wi' grief an' care;
There let him bouse, an' deep carouse,
Wi' bumpers flowing o'er,
Till he forgets his loves or debts,
An' minds his griefs no more.
SOLOMON (Proverbs xxxi. 6, 7).

LET other Poets raise a fracas
'Bout vines, an' wines, an' drunken Bacchus,
An' crabbèd names an' stories wrack us,
   An' grate our lug;
I sing the juice Scotch bear can mak us,
  In glass or jug.

O thou, my Muse! guid auld Scotch Drink,
Whether thro' wimplin worms thou jink,
Or, richly brown, ream owre the brink,
   In glorious faem,   10
Inspire me, till I lisp an' wink,
   To sing thy name!

Let husky wheat the haughs adorn,
An' aits set up their awnie horn,
An' pease an' beans at een or morn,
   Perfume the plain;
Leeze me on, thee, John Barleycorn,
   Thou King o' grain!

On thee aft Scotland chows her cood,
In souple scones, the wale o' food!   20
Or tumblin' in the boiling flood
   Wi' kail an' beef;
But when thou pours thy strong heart's blood,
   There thou shines chief.

Food fills the wame, an' keeps us livin';
Tho' life 's a gift no worth receivin',
When heavy-dragg'd wi' pine an' grievin';
          But, oil'd by thee,
The wheels o' life gae down-hill, scrievin'
          Wi' rattlin' glee.   30

Thou clears the head o' doited Lear:
Thou cheers the heart o' drooping Care;
Thou strings the nerves o' Labour sair,
          At 's weary toil:
Thou even brightens dark Despair
          Wi' gloomy smile.

Aft, clad in massy siller weed,
Wi' gentles thou erects thy head;
Yet humbly kind, in time o' need,
          The poor man's wine,   40
His wee drap parritch, or his bread,
          Thou kitchens fine.

Thou art the life o' public haunts;
But thee, what were our fairs and rants?
Ev'n godly meetings o' the saunts,
          By thee inspir'd,
When gaping they besiege the tents,
          Are doubly fir'd.

That merry night we get the corn in!
O sweetly then thou reams the horn in!   50
Or reekin' on a New-Year mornin'
          In cog or bicker,
An' just a wee drap sp'ritual burn in,
          An' gusty sucker!

When Vulcan gies his bellows breath,
An' ploughmen gather wi' their graith,
O rare to see thee fizz an' freath
          I' th' luggèd caup!
Then Burnewin comes on like death
          At ev'ry chaup.   60

Nae mercy, then, for airn or steel;
The brawnie, banie, ploughman chiel,
Brings hard owrehip, wi' sturdy wheel,
   The strong forehammer,
Till block an' studdie ring an' reel
   Wi' dinsome clamour.

When skirlin' weanies see the light,
Thou maks the gossips clatter bright
How fumblin' cuifs their dearies slight—
   Wae worth the name!   70
Nae Howdie gets a social night,
   Or plack frae them.

When neibors anger at a plea,
An' just as wud as wud can be,
How easy can the barley-bree
   Cement the quarrel!
It's aye the cheapest lawyer's fee
   To taste the barrel.

Alake! that e'er my Muse has reason
To wyte her countrymen wi' treason;   80
But mony daily weet their weasan'
   Wi' liquors nice,
An' hardly, in a winter's season,
   E'er spier her price.

Wae worth that brandy, burning trash!
Fell source o' mony a pain an' brash!
Twins mony a poor, doylt, drucken hash,
   O' half his days;
An' sends, beside, auld Scotland's cash
   To her warst faes.   90

Ye Scots, wha wish auld Scotland well,
Ye chief, to you my tale I tell,
Poor plackless devils like mysel'!
   It sets you ill,
Wi' bitter, dearthfu' wines to mell,
   Or foreign gill.

May gravels round his blather wrench,
An' gouts torment him, inch by inch,
Wha twists his gruntle wi' a glunch
    O' sour disdain,   100
Out owre a glass o' whisky punch
    Wi' honest men !

O Whisky ! soul o' plays an' pranks !
Accept a bardie's gratefu' thanks !
When wanting thee, what tuneless cranks
    Are my poor verses !
Thou comes—they rattle i' their ranks
    At ither's arses !

Thee, Ferintosh ! O sadly lost !
Scotland, lament frae coast to coast ! 110
Now colic-grips an' barkin' hoast
    May kill us a' ;
For loyal Forbes' charter'd boast
    Is ta'en awa !

Thae curst horse-leeches o' th' Excise,
Wha mak the whisky stells their prize—
Haud up thy hand, deil ! Ance—twice—thrice !
    There, seize the blinkers !
An' bake them up in brunstane pies
    For poor damn'd drinkers. 120

Fortune ! if thou 'll but gie me still
Hale breeks, a bannock, and a gill,
An' rowth o' rhyme to rave at will,
    Tak' a' the rest,
An' deal'd about as thy blind skill
    Directs thee best.

ELEGY ON CAPT. MATTHEW HENDERSON,

A GENTLEMAN WHO HELD THE PATENT FOR HIS HONOURS
IMMEDIATELY FROM ALMIGHTY GOD.

O DEATH! thou tyrant fell and bloody!
The meikle devil wi' a woodie
Haurl thee hame to his black smiddie
    O'er hurcheon hides,
And like stock-fish come o'er his studdie
    Wi' thy auld sides!

He 's gane, he 's gane! he 's frae us torn,
The ae best fellow e'er was born!
Thee, Matthew, Nature's sel' shall mourn
    By wood and wild,   10
Where, haply, Pity strays forlorn,
    Frae man exil'd.

Ye hills, near neibors o' the starns,
That proudly cock your cresting cairns!
Ye cliffs, the haunts of sailing earns,
    Where echo slumbers!
Come join, ye Nature's sturdiest bairns,
    My wailing numbers!

Mourn, ilka grove the cushat kens!
Ye haz'lly shaws and briery dens!   20
Ye burnies, wimplin' down your glens,
    Wi' toddlin din,
Or foaming strang wi' hasty stens
    Frae lin to lin.

Mourn, little harebells o'er the lea;
Ye stately foxgloves fair to see;
Ye woodbines hanging bonnilie,
    In scented bow'rs;
Ye roses on your thorny tree,
    The first o' flow'rs.   30

At dawn when ev'ry grassy blade
Droops with a diamond at his head,
At ev'n when beans their fragrance shed
     I' th' rustling gale,
Ye maukins, whiddin' thro' the glade,
     Come join my wail.

Mourn, ye wee songsters o' the wood ;
Ye grouse that crap the heather bud;
Ye curlews calling thro' a clud ;
     Ye whistling plover ;   40
And mourn, ye whirring paitrick brood—
     He's gane for ever !

Mourn, sooty coots, and speckled teals ;
Ye fisher herons, watching eels ;
Ye duck and drake, wi' airy wheels
     Circling the lake ;
Ye bitterns, till the quagmire reels,
     Rair for his sake.

Mourn, clamouring craiks at close o' day,
'Mang fields o' flowering clover gay ;   50
And, when ye wing your annual way
     Frae our cauld shore,
Tell thae far warlds wha lies in clay,
     Wham we deplore.

Ye houlets, frae your ivy bow'r
In some auld tree, or eldritch tow'r,
What time the moon wi' silent glowr
     Sets up her horn,
Wail thro' the dreary midnight hour
     Till waukrife morn !   60

O rivers, forests, hills, and plains !
Oft have ye heard my canty strains ;
But now, what else for me remains
     But tales of woe ?
And frae my een the drapping rains
     Maun ever flow.

Mourn, Spring, thou darling of the year!
Ilk cowslip cup shall kep a tear:
Thou, Simmer, while each corny spear
  Shoots up its head,   70
Thy gay green flow'ry tresses shear
  For him that's dead!

Thou, Autumn, wi' thy yellow hair,
In grief thy sallow mantle tear!
Thou, Winter, hurling thro' the air
  The roaring blast,
Wide o'er the naked world declare
  The worth we've lost!

Mourn him, thou sun, great source of light!
Mourn, empress of the silent night!   80
And you, ye twinkling starnies bright,
  My Matthew mourn!
For through your orbs he's ta'en his flight,
  Ne'er to return.

O Henderson! the man! the brother!
And art thou gone, and gone for ever?
And hast thou crost that unknown river,
  Life's dreary bound?
Like thee, where shall I find another,
  The world around?   90

Go to your sculptur'd tombs, ye great,
In a' the tinsel trash o' state!
But by thy honest turf I'll wait,
  Thou man of worth!
And weep the ae best fellow's fate
  E'er lay in earth.

THE EPITAPH.

Stop, passenger! my story's brief,
 And truth I shall relate, man;
I tell nae common tale o' grief,
 For Matthew was a great man.   100

If thou uncommon merit hast,
  Yet spurn'd at fortune's door, man;
A look of pity hither cast,
  For Matthew was a poor man.

If thou a noble sodger art,
  That passest by this grave, man,
There moulders here a gallant heart;
  For Matthew was a brave man.

If thou on men, their works and ways,
  Canst throw uncommon light, man; 110
Here lies wha weel had won thy praise,
  For Matthew was a bright man.

If thou at friendship's sacred ca'
  Wad life itself resign, man;
The sympathetic tear maun fa',
  For Matthew was a kind man.

If thou art staunch without a stain,
  Like the unchanging blue, man;
This was a kinsman o' thy ain,
  For Matthew was a true man. 120

If thou hast wit, and fun, and fire,
  And ne'er guid wine did fear, man;
This was thy billie, dam, and sire,
  For Matthew was a queer man.

If ony whiggish whingein' sot,
  To blame poor Matthew dare, man;
May dool and sorrow be his lot,
  For Matthew was a rare man.

But now his radiant course is run,
  For Matthew's was a bright one; 130
His soul was like the glorious sun,
  A matchless, Heav'nly Light, man.

THE AULD FARMER'S NEW-YEAR MORNING
SALUTATION TO HIS AULD MARE, MAGGIE,

ON GIVING HER THE ACCUSTOMED RIPP OF CORN TO
HANSEL IN THE NEW YEAR.

A GUID New-Year I wish thee, Maggie!
Hae, there's a ripp to thy auld baggie:
Tho' thou's howe-backit now, an' knaggie,
   I've seen the day,
Thou could hae gane like ony staggie
   Out-owre the lay.

Tho' now thou's dowie, stiff, an' crazy,
An' thy auld hide's as white's a daisie,
I've seen thee dappled, sleek an' glaizie,
   A bonnie gray: 10
He should been tight that daur't to raize thee,
   Ance in a day.

Thou ance was i' the foremost rank,
A filly buirdly, steeve, an' swank,
An' set weel down a shapely shank,
   As e'er tread yird;
An' could hae flown out-owre a stank,
   Like ony bird.

It's now some nine-an'-twenty year,
Sin' thou was my guid-father's meere; 20
He gied me thee, o' tocher clear,
   An' fifty mark;
Tho' it was sma', 'twas weel-won gear,
   An' thou was stark.

When first I gaed to woo my Jenny,
Ye then was trottin' wi' your minnie:
Tho' ye was trickie, slee, an' funnie,
   Ye ne'er was donsie;
But hamely, tawie, quiet, an' cannie,
   An' unco sonsie. 30

That day ye pranc'd wi' muckle pride
When ye bure hame my bonnie bride ;
An' sweet an' gracefu' she did ride,
   Wi' maiden air !
Kyle Stewart I could braggèd wide
   For sic a pair.

Tho' now ye dow but hoyte and hobble,
An' wintle like a saumont-coble,
That day ye was a jinker noble
   For heels an' win' !   40
An' ran them till they a' did wobble
   Far, far behin'.

When thou an' I were young and skeigh,
An' stable-meals at fairs were driegh,
How thou wad prance, an' snore, an' skriegh
   An' tak the road !
Town's-bodies ran, and stood abeigh,
   An' ca't thee mad.

When thou was corn't, an' I was mellow,
We took the road aye like a swallow :   50
At brooses thou had ne'er a fellow
   For pith an' speed ;
But ev'ry tail thou pay't them hollow,
   Where'er thou gaed.

The sma', droop-rumpled, hunter cattle,
Might aiblins waur'd thee for a brattle ;
But sax Scotch miles, thou tried their mettle,
   An' gart them whaizle :
Nae whip nor spur, but just a wattle
   O' saugh or hazel.   60

Thou was a noble fittie-lan',
As e'er in tug or tow was drawn !
Aft thee an' I, in aucht hours' gaun,
   On guid March-weather,
Hae turn'd sax rood beside our han',
   For days thegither.

Thou never braindg't, an' fetch't, an' fliskit,
But thy auld tail thou wad hae whiskit,
An' spread abreed thy weel-fill'd brisket,
   Wi' pith an' pow'r,   70
Till spritty knowes wad rair't and riskit,
   An' slypet owre.

When frosts lay lang, an' snaws were deep,
An' threaten'd labour back to keep,
I gied thy cog a wee bit heap
   Aboon the timmer ;
I kenn'd my Maggie wad na sleep
   For that, or simmer.

In cart or car thou never reestit ;
The steyest brae thou wad hae faced it ; 80
Thou never lap, an' stenned, and breastit,
   Then stood to blaw ;
But, just thy step a wee thing hastit,
   Thou snoov't awa.

My pleugh is now thy bairn-time a',
Four gallant brutes as e'er did draw;
Forbye sax mae I've sell't awa
   That thou hast nurst :
They drew me thretteen pund an' twa,
   The very warst.   90

Mony a sair darg we twa hae·wrought,
An' wi' the weary warl' fought !
An' mony an anxious day I thought
   We wad be beat !
Yet here to crazy age we're brought,
   Wi' something yet.

And think na, my auld trusty servan',
That now perhaps thou's less deservin',
An' thy auld days may end in starvin' ;
   For my last fou,   100
A heapit stimpart I'll reserve ane
   Laid by for you.

We've worn to crazy years thegither;
We'll toyte about wi' ane anither;
Wi' tentie care I'll flit thy tether
        To some hain'd rig,
Where ye may nobly rax your leather,
        Wi' sma' fatigue.

TO A MOUSE, ON TURNING HER UP IN HER NEST WITH THE PLOUGH, NOVEMBER, 1785.

WEE, sleekit, cow'rin', tim'rous beastie,
O what a panic's in thy breastie!
Thou need na start awa sae hasty,
        Wi' bickering brattle!
I wad be laith to rin an' chase thee
        Wi' murd'ring pattle!

I'm truly sorry man's dominion
Has broken Nature's social union,
An' justifies that ill opinion
        Which makes thee startle   10
At me, thy poor earth-born companion,
        An' fellow-mortal!

I doubt na, whiles, but thou may thieve;
What then? poor beastie, thou maun live!
A daimen-icker in a thrave
        'S a sma' request:
I'll get a blessin' wi' the lave,
        And never miss 't!

Thy wee bit housie, too, in ruin!
Its silly wa's the win's are strewin'!   20
An' naething, now, to big a new ane,
        O' foggage green!
An' bleak December's winds ensuin',
        Baith snell an' keen!

Thou saw the fields laid bare and waste,
An' weary winter comin' fast,
An' cozie here, beneath the blast,
   Thou thought to dwell,
Till crash! the cruel coulter past
   Out-thro' thy cell.   30

That wee bit heap o' leaves an' stibble
Has cost thee mony a weary nibble!
Now thou's turn'd out, for a' thy trouble,
   But house or hald,
To thole the winter's sleety dribble,
   An' cranreuch cauld!

But, Mousie, thou art no thy lane,
In proving foresight may be vain:
The best laid schemes o' mice an' men
   Gang aft a-gley,   40
An' lea'e us nought but grief an' pain
   For promis'd joy.

Still thou art blest compar'd wi' me!
The present only toucheth thee:
But oh! I backward cast my e'e
   On prospects drear!
An' forward tho' I canna see,
   I guess an' fear!

————◆◆————

MAN WAS MADE TO MOURN.

WHEN chill November's surly blast
 Made fields and forests bare,
One ev'ning as I wander'd forth
 Along the banks of Ayr,
I spied a man, whose agèd step
 Seem'd weary, worn with care;
His face was furrow'd o'er with years,
 And hoary was his hair.

'Young stranger, whither wand'rest thou?'
　Began the rev'rend sage;   10
'Does thirst of wealth thy step constrain,
　Or youthful pleasure's rage?
Or, haply, prest with cares and woes,
　Too soon thou hast began
To wander forth with me to mourn
　The miseries of man.

'The sun that overhangs yon moors,
　Out-spreading far and wide,
Where hundreds labour to support
　A haughty lordling's pride—   20
I've seen yon weary winter-sun
　Twice forty times return,
And ev'ry time has added proofs
　That man was made to mourn.

'O man! while in thy early years,
　How prodigal of time!
Mis-spending all thy precious hours,
　Thy glorious youthful prime!
Alternate follies take the sway;
　Licentious passions burn;   30
Which tenfold force give nature's law,
　That man was made to mourn.

'Look not alone on youthful prime,
　Or manhood's active might;
Man then is useful to his kind,
　Supported is his right;
But see him on the edge of life,
　With cares and sorrows worn,
Then age and want, oh! ill-match'd pair!
　Show man was made to mourn.   40

'A few seem favourites of fate,
　In pleasure's lap carest;
Yet think not all the rich and great
　Are likewise truly blest.

But oh ! what crowds in ev'ry land
  All wretched and forlorn,
Thro' weary life this lesson learn—
  That man was made to mourn.

'Many and sharp the num'rous ills
  Inwoven with our frame !   50
More pointed still we make ourselves
  Regret, remorse, and shame !
And man, whose heaven-erected face
  The smiles of love adorn—
Man's inhumanity to man
  Makes countless thousands mourn !

'See yonder poor o'erlabour'd wight,
  So abject, mean, and vile,
Who begs a brother of the earth
  To give him leave to toil ;   60
And see his lordly fellow-worm
  The poor petition spurn,
Unmindful tho' a weeping wife
  And helpless offspring mourn.

'If I'm design'd yon lordling's slave,—
  By nature's law design'd,—
Why was an independent wish
  E'er planted in my mind ?
If not, why am I subject to
  His cruelty, or scorn ?   70
Or why has man the will and pow'r
  To make his fellow mourn ?

'Yet let not this too much, my son,
  Disturb thy youthful breast ;
This partial view of human-kind
  Is surely not the last !
The poor oppressèd honest man,
  Had never sure been born,
Had there not been some recompense
  To comfort those that mourn !   80

'O Death, the poor man's dearest friend,
  The kindest and the best!
Welcome the hour my agèd limbs
  Are laid with thee at rest!
The great, the wealthy, fear thy blow.
  From pomp and pleasure torn;
But oh! a blest relief to those
  That weary-laden mourn.'

TO A MOUNTAIN DAISY,

ON TURNING ONE DOWN WITH THE PLOUGH, IN APRIL, 1786.

Wee modest crimson-tippèd flow'r,
Thou 's met me in an evil hour;
For I maun crush amang the stoure
        Thy slender stem:
To spare thee now is past my pow'r,
        Thou bonnie gem.

Alas! it 's no thy neibor sweet,
The bonnie lark, companion meet,
Bending thee 'mang the dewy weet
        Wi' spreckl'd breast,   10
When upward springing, blythe to greet
        The purpling east.

Cauld blew the bitter-biting north
Upon thy early humble birth;
Yet cheerfully thou glinted forth
        Amid the storm,
Scarce rear'd above the parent-earth
        Thy tender form.

The flaunting flow'rs our gardens yield
High shelt'ring woods and wa's maun shield,   20
But thou, beneath the random bield
        O' clod or stane,
Adorns the histie stibble-field,
        Unseen, alane.

There, in thy scanty mantle clad,
Thy snawy bosom sun-ward spread,
Thou lifts thy unassuming head
   In humble guise;
But now the share uptears thy bed,
   And low thou lies!   30

Such is the fate of artless maid,
Sweet flow'ret of the rural shade,
By love's simplicity betray'd,
   And guileless trust,
Till she like thee, all soil'd, is laid
   Low i' the dust.

Such is the fate of simple bard,
On life's rough ocean luckless starr'd:
Unskilful he to note the card
   Of prudent lore,   40
Till billows rage, and gales blow hard,
   And whelm him o'er!

Such fate to suffering worth is giv'n,
Who long with wants and woes has striv'n,
By human pride or cunning driv'n
   To mis'ry's brink,
Till wrench'd of ev'ry stay but Heav'n,
   He, ruin'd, sink!

Ev'n thou who mourn'st the Daisy's fate,
That fate is thine—no distant date; 50
Stern Ruin's ploughshare drives elate
   Full on thy bloom,
Till crush'd beneath the furrow's weight
   Shall be thy doom!

TO RUIN.

ALL hail! inexorable lord,
At whose destruction-breathing word
  The mightiest empires fall!
Thy cruel woe-delighted train,
The ministers of grief and pain,
  A sullen welcome, all!
With stern-resolv'd despairing eye,
  I see each aimèd dart;
For one has cut my dearest tie,
  And quivers in my heart.   10
    Then low'ring, and pouring,
      The storm no more I dread,
    Tho' thick'ning and black'ning
      Round my devoted head.

And, thou grim pow'r, by life abhorr'd,
While life a pleasure can afford,
  Oh! hear a wretch's pray'r!
No more I shrink appall'd, afraid;
I court, I beg thy friendly aid,
  To close this scene of care!   20
When shall my soul, in silent peace,
  Resign life's joyless day?
My weary heart its throbbings cease,
  Cold-mould'ring in the clay?
    No fear more, no tear more,
      To stain my lifeless face,
    Enclaspèd, and graspèd
      Within thy cold embrace!

ON A SCOTCH BARD, GONE TO THE
WEST INDIES.

A' ye wha live by sowps o' drink,
A' ye wha live by crambo-clink,
A' ye wha live an' never think,
   Come mourn wi' me!
Our billie 's gi'en us a' a jink,
    An' owre the sea.

Lament him, a' ye rantin core,
Wha dearly like a random-splore ;
Nae mair he'll join the merry roar,
   In social key ;   10
For now he 's taen anither shore,
    An' owre the sea !

The bonnie lasses weel may wiss him,
And in their dear petitions place him ;
The widows, wives, an' a' may bless him,
   Wi' tearfu' e'e ;
For weel I wat they'll sairly miss him
    That 's owre the sea !

O Fortune, they hae room to grumble !
Hadst thou taen aff some drowsy bummle, 20
Wha can do nought but fyke an' fumble,
   'Twad been nae plea ;
But he was gleg as ony wumble,
    That 's owre the sea !

Auld cantie Kyle may weepers wear,
An' stain them wi' the saut saut tear:
'Twill mak her poor auld heart, I fear,
   In flinders flee ;
He was her Laureat mony a year,
    That 's owre the sea !   30

He saw misfortune's cauld nor-west
Lang mustering up a bitter blast;
A jillet brak his heart at last—
      Ill may she be!
So took a berth afore the mast,
      An' owre the sea.

To tremble under Fortune's cummock
On scarce a bellyfu' o' drummock,
Wi' his proud independent stomach,
      Could ill agree;
So row'd his hurdies in a hammock,
      An' owre the sea.   40

He ne'er was gi'en to great misguidin',
Yet coin his pouches wad na bide in;
Wi' him it ne'er was under hidin',
      He dealt it free:
The Muse was a' that he took pride in,
      That 's owre the sea.

Jamaica bodies, use him weel,
An' hap him in a cozie biel;
Ye'll find him aye a dainty chiel,
      And fu' o' glee;
He wad na wrang'd the vera deil,
      That 's owre the sea.   50

Fareweel, my rhyme-composing billie!
Your native soil was right ill-willie;
But may ye flourish like a lily,
      Now bonnilie!
I'll toast ye in my hindmost gillie,
      Tho' owre the sea!   60

ADDRESS TO EDINBURGH.

EDINA ! Scotia's darling seat,
   All hail thy palaces and tow'rs,
Where once beneath a monarch's feet
   Sat Legislation's sov'reign pow'rs.
   From marking wildly-scatter'd flow'rs,
As on the banks of Ayr I stray'd,
   And singing lone the ling'ring hours,
I shelter in thy honour'd shade.

Here Wealth still swells the golden tide,
   As busy trade his labours plies ;   10
There Architecture's noble pride
   Bids elegance and splendour rise ;
   Here Justice, from her native skies,
High wields her balance and her rod ;
   There Learning, with his eagle eyes,
Seeks Science in her coy abode.

Thy sons, Edina, social, kind,
   With open arms the stranger hail ;
Their views enlarg'd, their lib'ral mind,
   Above the narrow rural vale ;   20
   Attentive still to sorrow's wail,
Or modest merit's silent claim :
   And never may their sources fail !
And never envy blot their name !

Thy daughters bright thy walks adorn,
   Gay as the gilded summer sky,
Sweet as the dewy milk-white thorn,
   Dear as the raptur'd thrill of joy.
   Fair Burnet strikes th' adoring eye,
Heaven's beauties on my fancy shine ;   30
   I see the Sire of Love on high,
And own his work indeed divine !

There watching high the least alarms,
   Thy rough rude fortress gleams afar ;
Like some bold veteran, gray in arms,
   And mark'd with many a seamy scar :
   The pond'rous wall and massy bar,
Grim-rising o'er the rugged rock,
   Have oft withstood assailing war,
And oft repell'd th' invader's shock.   40

With awe-struck thought, and pitying tears,
   I view that noble stately dome,
Where Scotia's kings of other years,
   Fam'd heroes, had their royal home ;
   Alas, how chang'd the times to come !
Their royal name low in tho dust,
   Their hapless race wild-wand'ring roam ;
Tho' rigid law cries out 'twas just !

Wild beats my heart to trace your steps,
   Whose ancestors, in days of yore,   50
Thro' hostile ranks and ruin'd gaps
   Old Scotia's bloody lion bore.
   Ev'n I who sing in rustic lore,
Haply my sires have left their shed,
   And faced grim danger's loudest roar,
Bold-following where your fathers led !

Edina ! Scotia's darling seat,
   All hail thy palaces and tow'rs,
Where once beneath a monarch's feet
   Sat Legislation's sov'reign pow'rs !   60
   From marking wildly-scatter'd flow'rs,
As on the banks of Ayr I stray'd,
   And singing lone the ling'ring hours,
I shelter in thy honour'd shade.

LAMENT FOR JAMES, EARL OF GLENCAIRN.

THE wind blew hollow frae the hills ;
  By fits the sun's departing beam
Look'd on the fading yellow woods
  That waved o'er Lugar's winding stream.
Beneath a craigy steep, a bard,
  Laden with years and meikle pain,
In loud lament bewail'd his lord,
  Whom death had all untimely taen.

He lean'd him to an ancient aik,
  Whose trunk was mould'ring down with years ; 10
His locks were bleachèd white wi' time,
  His hoary cheek was wet wi' tears ;
And as he touch'd his trembling harp,
  And as he tun'd his doleful sang,
The winds, lamenting thro' their caves,
  To echo bore the notes alang.

'Ye scatter'd birds that faintly sing,
  The reliques of the vernal quire !
Ye woods that shed on a' the winds
  The honours of the agèd year !   20
A few short months, and glad and gay,
  Again ye'll charm the ear and e'e ;
But nocht in all revolving time
  Can gladness bring again to me.

'I am a bending agèd tree,
  That long has stood the wind and rain ,
But now has come a cruel blast,
  And my last hold of earth is gane :
Nae leaf o' mine shall greet the spring,
  Nae simmer sun exalt my bloom ;   30
But I maun lie before the storm,
  And others plant them in my room.

'I've seen so many changefu' years,
　　On earth I am a stranger grown ;
I wander in the ways of men,
　　Alike unknowing and unknown :
Unheard, unpitied, unreliev'd,
　　I bear alane my lade o' care,
For silent, low, on beds of dust,
　　Lie a' that would my sorrows share.   40

'And last (the sum of a' my griefs !)
　　My noble master lies in clay ;
The flow'r amang our barons bold,
　　His country's pride, his country's stay :
In weary being now I pine
　　For a' the life of life is dead,
And hope has left my agèd ken,
　　On forward wing for ever fled.

'Awake thy last sad voice, my harp !
　　The voice of woe and wild despair ;   50
Awake, resound thy latest lay,
　　Then sleep in silence evermair !
And thou, my last, best, only, friend,
　　That fillest an untimely tomb,
Accept this tribute from the bard
　　Thou brought from fortune's mirkest gloom.

'In poverty's low barren vale,
　　Thick mists obscure involv'd me round ;
Though oft I turn'd the wistful eye,
　　No ray of fame was to be found :   60
Thou found'st me, like the morning sun
　　That melts the fogs in limpid air ;
The friendless bard and rustic song
　　Became alike thy fostering care.

'O why has worth so short a date
　　While villains ripen grey with time ?
Must thou, the noble, gen'rous, great,
　　Fall in bold manhood's hardy prime ?

Why did I live to see that day,
  A day to me so full of woe?
O had I met the mortal shaft   70
  Which laid my benefactor low!

'The bridegroom may forget the bride
  Was made his wedded wife yestreen;
The monarch may forget the crown
  That on his head an hour has been;
The mother may forget the child
  That smiles sae sweetly on her knee;
But I'll remember thee, Glencairn,
  And a' that thou hast done for me!'   80

———•———

LAMENT OF MARY QUEEN OF SCOTS, ON THE
APPROACH OF SPRING.

Now Nature hangs her mantle green
  On every blooming tree,
And spreads her sheets o' daisies white
  Out-owre the grassy lea;
Now Phoebus cheers the crystal streams,
  And glads the azure skies;
But nought can glad the weary wight
  That fast in durance lies.

Now laverocks wake the merry morn,
  Aloft on dewy wing;   10
The merle, in his noontide bow'r,
  Makes woodland echoes ring;
The mavis mild wi' many a note,
  Sings drowsy day to rest:
In love and freedom they rejoice,
  Wi' care nor thrall opprest.

Now blooms the lily by the bank,
  The primrose down the brae;
The hawthorn's budding in the glen,
  And milk-white is the slae :   20
The meanest hind in fair Scotland
  May rove their sweets amang;
But I, the Queen of a' Scotland,
  Maun lie in prison strang.

I was the Queen o' bonnie France,
  Where happy I hae been;
Fu' lightly rase I in the morn,
  As blythe lay down at e'en :
And I'm the sov'reign of Scotland,
  And mony a traitor there;   30
Yet here I lie in foreign bands,
  And never-ending care.

But as for thee, thou false woman,
  My sister and my fae,
Grim vengeance yet shall whet a sword
  That thro' thy soul shall gae !
The weeping blood in woman's breast
  Was never known to thee;
Nor th' balm that draps on wounds of woe
  Frae woman's pitying e'e.   40

My son! my son! may kinder stars
  Upon thy fortune shine;
And may those pleasures gild thy reign,
  That ne'er wad blink on mine.
God keep thee frae thy mother's faes,
  Or turn their hearts to thee;
And where thou meet'st thy mother's friend,
  Remember him for me !

Oh! soon to me may summer-suns
  Nae mair light up the morn !   50
Nae mair to me the autumn winds
  Wave o'er the yellow corn !

And, in the narrow house o' death,
  Let winter round me rave;
And the next flow'rs that deck the spring
  Bloom on my peaceful grave!

———••———

THE TWA HERDS.

O A' ye pious godly flocks,
Weel fed on pastures orthodox,
Wha now will keep you frae the fox,
        Or worrying tykes?
Or wha will tent the waifs and crocks,
        About the dykes?

The twa best herds in a' the wast
That e'er gae gospel horn a blast
These five-and-twenty summers past,
        O dool to tell!   10
Hae had a bitter black out-cast
        Atween themsel.

O Moodie, man, and wordy Russel,
How could you raise so vile a bustle?
Ye'll see how new-light herds will whistle
        And think it fine!
The Lord's cause ne'er gat sic a twistle,
        Sin' I hae min'.

O sirs, whae'er wad hae expeckit
Your duty ye wad sae negleckit   20
Ye wha were ne'er by lairds respeckit
        To wear the plaid,
But by the brutes themselves eleckit
        To be their guide.

What flock wi' Moodie's flock could rank,
Sae hale and hearty every shank?
Nae poison'd soor Arminian stank
  He let them taste ;
Frae Calvin's well, aye clear, they drank—
  O' sic a feast!   30

The thummart, wil'-cat, brock and tod,
Weel kenn'd his voice thro' a' the wood ;
He smell'd their ilka hole and road
  Baith out and in,
And weel he lik'd to shed their bluid
  And sell their skin.

What herd like Russel tell'd his tale ?
His voice was heard thro' muir and dale ;
He kenn'd the Lord's sheep, ilka tail,
  O'er a' the height,   40
And saw gin they were sick or hale
  At the first sight.

He fine a mangy sheep could scrub,
Or nobly fling the gospel club,
And new-light herds could nicely drub
  Or pay their skin,
Could shake them owre the burning dub,
  Or heave them in.

Sic twa—O! do I live to see't ?
Sic famous twa should disagreet,   50
An' names like 'villain,' 'hypocrite,'
  Ilk ither gi'en,
While new-light herds wi' laughin' spite
  Say neither's leein'!

A' ye wha tent the gospel fauld—
There's Duncan deep, and Peebles shaul—
But chiefly thou, apostle Auld !
  We trust in thee,
That thou wilt work them, hot and cauld,
  Till they agree.   60

Consider, sirs, how we're beset!
There's scarce a new herd that we get,
But comes frae 'mang that cursed set
      I winna name:
I hope frae heaven to see them yet
      In fiery flame.

Dalrymple has been lang our fae,
M'Gill has wrought us meikle wae,
And that curs'd rascal ca'd M'Quhae,
      And baith the Shaws,   70
That aft hae made us black and blae
      Wi' vengefu' paws.

Auld Wodrow lang has hatch'd mischief:
We thought aye death wad bring relief,
But he has gotten, to our grief,
      Ane to succeed him,
A chiel wha'll soundly buff our beef,
      I meikle dread him.

And mony a ane that I could tell,
Wha fain would openly rebel;   80
Forby turn-coats amang oursel—
      There's Smith for ane;
I doubt he's but a grey nick quill,
      And that ye'll fin'

O a' ye flocks, owre a' the hills,
By mosses, meadows, moors, and fells,
Come join your counsels and your skills
      To cowe the lairds,
And get the brutes the power themsels
      To choose their herds.   90

Then Orthodoxy yet may prance,
And Learning in a woody dance,
And that fell cur ca'd Common Sense,
      That bites sae sair,
Be banish'd owre the seas to France;
      Let him bark there.

Then Shaw's and D'rymple's eloquence,
M'Gill's close nervous excellence,
M'Quhae's pathetic manly sense,
      And guid M'Math,   100
Wi' Smith, wha thro' the heart can glance,
      May a' pack aff!

ON THE LATE CAPTAIN GROSE'S PEREGRINA-
TIONS THRO' SCOTLAND.

COLLECTING THE ANTIQUITIES OF THAT KINGDOM.

HEAR, Land o' Cakes, and brither Scots,
Frae Maidenkirk to Johnny Groats;—
If there's a hole in a' your coats,
      I rede you tent it:
A chield's amang you taking notes,
      And, faith, he'll prent it.

If in your bounds ye chance to light
Upon a fine, fat, fodgel wight,
O' stature short, but genius bright,
      That's he, mark weel!   10
And wow! he has an unco sleight
      O' cauk and keel.

By some auld houlet-haunted biggin,
Or kirk deserted by its riggin'
It's ten to ane ye'll find him snug in
      Some eldritch part,
Wi' deils, they say, Lord save's! colleaguin'
      At some black art.

Ilk ghaist that haunts auld ha' or cham'er,
Ye gipsy-gang that deal in glamour,   20
And you, deep read in hell's black grammar,
         Warlocks and witches—
Ye'll quake at his conjuring hammer,
         Ye midnight bitches !

It 's tauld he was a sodger bred,
And ane wad rather fa'n than fled ;
But now he 's quat the spurtle-blade
         And dog-skin wallet,
And taen the—Antiquarian trade
         I think they call it.   30

He has a fouth o' auld nick-nackets :
Rusty airn caps and jinglin' jackets,
Wad haud the Lothians three in tackets,
         A towmont gude ;
And parritch-pats and auld saut-backets
         Before the Flood.

Of Eve's first fire he has a cinder ;
Auld Tubulcain's fire-shool and fender ;
That which distinguishèd the gender
         O' Balaam's ass ;   40
A broom-stick o' the witch of Endor,
         Weel shod wi' brass.

Forbye, he'll shape you aff fu' gleg
The cut of Adam's philibeg ;
The knife that nicket Abel's craig—
         He'll prove you fully
It was a faulding jocteleg,
         Or lang-kail gullie.

But wad ye see him in his glee,
For meikle glee and fun has he,
Then set him down, and twa or three   50
         Guid fellows wi' him ;
And port, O port ! shine thou a wee,
         And then ye'll see him !

Now, by the Pow'rs o' verse and prose !
Thou art a dainty chield, O Grose !
Whae'er o' thee shall ill suppose,
      They sair misca' thee ;
I'd take the rascal by the nose,
      Wad say 'Shame fa' thee !'   60

ON PASTORAL POETRY.

HAIL, Poesie ! thou Nymph reserv'd !
In chase o' thee what crowds hae swerv'd
Frae common sense, or sunk enerv'd
      'Mang heaps o' clavers ;
And oh ! o'er aft thy joes hae starv'd,
      'Mid a' thy favours !

Say, Lassie, why, thy train amang,
While loud the trump's heroic clang,
And sock or buskin skelp alang
      To death or marriage,   10
Scarce ane has tried the shepherd-sang
      But wi' miscarriage ?

In Homer's craft Jock Milton thrives ;
Eschylus' pen Will Shakespeare drives ;
Wee Pope, the knurlin', till him rives
      Horatian fame ;
In thy sweet sang, Barbauld, survives
      Even Sappho's flame.

But thee, Theocritus, wha matches ?
They're no herds' ballats, Maro's catches ;   20
Squire Pope but busks his skinklin' patches
      O' heathen tatters :
I pass by hunders, nameless wretches,
      That ape their betters.

In this braw age o' wit and lear,
Will nane the Shepherd's whistle mair
Blaw sweetly in its native air
   And rural grace;
And wi' the far-fam'd Grecian share
   A rival place?   30

Yes! there is ane—a Scottish callan!
There's ane; come forrit, honest Allan!
Thou need na jouk behint the hallan,
   A chiel sae clever;
The teeth o' Time may gnaw Tamtallan,
   But thou's for ever!

Thou paints auld Nature to the nines,
In thy sweet Caledonian lines;
Nae gowden stream thro' myrtles twines,
   Where Philomel,   40
While nightly breezes sweep the vines,
   Her griefs will tell!

In gowany glens thy burnie strays,
Where bonnie lasses bleach their claes;
Or trots by hazelly shaws and braes,
   Wi' hawthorns gray,
Where blackbirds join the shepherd's lays
   At close o' day.

Thy rural loves are nature's sel';
Nae bombast spates o' nonsense swell;
Nae snap conceits; but that sweet spell   50
   O' witchin' love—
That charm that can the strongest quell,
   The sternest move.

THE HUMBLE PETITION OF BRUAR WATER
TO THE NOBLE DUKE OF ATHOLE.

My Lord, I know your noble ear
    Woe ne'er assails in vain;
Embolden'd thus, I beg you'll hear
    Your humble slave complain,
How saucy Phoebus' scorching beams,
    In flaming summer-pride,
Dry-withering, waste my foamy streams,
    And drink my crystal tide.

The lightly-jumping glowrin' trouts,
    That thro' my waters play,   10
If, in their random wanton spouts,
    They near the margin stray;
If, hapless chance! they linger lang,
    I'm scorching up so shallow,
They're left the whitening stanes amang,
    In gasping death to wallow.

Last day I grat wi' spite and teen,
    As poet Burns came by,
That to a bard I should be seen
    Wi' half my channel dry: 20
A panegyric rhyme, I ween,
    Even as I was, he shor'd me;
But had I in my glory been,
    He, kneeling, wad ador'd me.

Here, foaming down the shelvy rocks,
    In twisting strength I rin;
There high my boiling torrent smokes,
    Wild-roaring o'er a linn:
Enjoying large each spring and well
    As Nature gave them me,   30
I am, altho' I say't mysel,
    Worth gaun a mile to see.

Would then my noble master please
    To grant my highest wishes,
He'll shade my banks wi' tow'ring trees,
    And bonnie spreading bushes.
Delighted doubly then, my Lord,
    You'll wander on my banks,
And listen mony a grateful bird
    Return you tuneful thanks.   40

The sober laverock, warbling wild,
    Shall to the skies aspire ;
The gowdspink, Music's gayest child,
    Shall sweetly join the choir:
The blackbird strong, the lintwhite clear,
    The mavis mild and mellow ;
The robin pensive Autumn cheer,
    In all her locks of yellow.

This, too, a covert shall ensure,
    To shield them from the storm ;   50
And coward maukin sleep secure,
    Low in her grassy form:
Here shall the shepherd make his seat,
    To weave his crown of flow'rs ;
Or find a sheltering safe retreat
    From prone-descending show'rs.

And here, by sweet endearing stealth,
    Shall meet the loving pair,
Despising worlds with all their wealth
    As empty idle care: 60
The flow'rs shall vie in all their charms
    The hour of heav'n to grace,
And birks extend their fragrant arms,
    To screen the dear embrace.

Here haply too, at vernal dawn,
    Some musing bard may stray,
And eye the smoking dewy lawn,
    And misty mountain gray;

Or, by the reaper's nightly beam,
  Mild-chequering thro' the trees,   70
Rave to my darkly dashing stream,
  Hoarse-swelling on the breeze.

Let lofty firs, and ashes cool,
  My lowly banks o'erspread,
And view, deep-bending in the pool,
  Their shadows' wat'ry bed!
Let fragrant birks in woodbines drest
  My craggy cliffs adorn ;
And, for the little songster's nest,
  The close embow'ring thorn.   80

So may Old Scotia's darling hope,
  Your little angel band,
Spring, like their fathers, up to prop
  Their honour'd native land!
So may thro' Albion's farthest ken,
  To social-flowing glasses
The grace be—'Athole's honest men,
  And Athole's bonnie lasses!'

—— •• ——

TO A HAGGIS.

FAIR fa' your honest sonsie face,
Great chieftain o' the puddin'-race!
Aboon them a' ye tak your place,
        Painch, tripe, or thairm :
Weel are ye wordy o' a grace
        As lang's my arm.

The groaning trencher there ye fill,
Your hurdies like a distant hill ;
Your pin wad help to mend a mill
        In time o' need ;   10
While thro' your pores the dews distil
        Like amber bead.

His knife see rustic Labour dight,
An' cut you up wi' ready sleight,
Trenching your gushing entrails bright
      Like ony ditch ;
And then, O what a glorious sight,
        Warm-reekin', rich !

Then, horn for horn they stretch an' strive,
Deil tak the hindmost ! on they drive,   20
Till a' their weel-swall'd kytes belyve
      Are bent like drums ;
Then auld guidman, maist like to rive,
      Bethankit hums.

Is there that o'er his French ragout,
Or olio that wad staw a sow,
Or fricassee wad mak her spew
      Wi' perfect sconner,
Looks down wi' sneering scornfu' view
      On sic a dinner ?   30

Poor devil ! see him owre his trash,
As feckless as a wither'd rash,
His spindle shank a guid whip-lash,
      His nieve a nit :
Thro' bloody flood or field to dash,
      O how unfit !

But mark the Rustic, haggis-fed—
The trembling earth resounds his tread !
Clap in his walie nieve a blade,
      He'll mak it whissle ;
An' legs, an' arms, an' heads will sned,   40
      Like taps o' thrissle.

Ye Pow'rs, wha mak mankind your care,
And dish them out their bill o' fare,
Auld Scotland wants nae skinking ware
      That jaups in luggies ;
But, if ye wish her gratefu' prayer,
      Gie her a Haggis !

ADDRESS TO THE TOOTHACHE.

My curse upon your venom'd stang,
That shoots my tortur'd gums alang,
And thro' my lugs gies mony a twang,
   Wi' gnawing vengeance;
Tearing my nerves wi' bitter pang,
   Like racking engines!

When fevers burn, or ague freezes,
Rheumatics gnaw, or colic squeezes;
Our neighbour's sympathy may ease us,
   Wi' pitying moan;
But thee—thou hell o' a' diseases!
   Aye mocks our groan.

Adown my beard the slavers trickle,
I throw the wee stools o'er the mickle,
As round the fire the giglets keckle
   To see me loup;
While, raving mad, I wish a heckle
   Were in their doup.

O' a' the numerous human dools,
Ill hairsts, daft bargains, cutty-stools,
Or worthy friends rak'd i' the mools—
   Sad sight to see!
The tricks o' knaves, or fash o' fools,
   Thou bear'st the gree.

Where'er that place be priests ca' hell,
Whence a' the tones o' mis'ry yell,
And rankèd plagues their numbers tell,
   In dreadfu' raw,
Thou. Toothache, surely bear'st the bell
   Amang them a'!

10

20

30

O thou grim mischief-making chiel,
That gars the notes of discord squeal,
Till daft mankind aft dance a reel
         In gore a shoe-thick;—
Gie a' the faes o' Scotland's weal
         A towmont's Toothache!

ON CREECH THE BOOKSELLER.

AULD chuckie Reekie's sair distrest,
Down droops her ance weel burnish'd crest,
Nae joy her bonnie buskit nest
         Can yield ava,
Her darling bird that she lo'es best—
         Willie's awa!

O Willie was a witty wight,
And had o' things an unco sleight;
Auld Reekie aye he keepit tight,
         An' trig an' braw: 10
But now they'll busk her like a fright—
         Willie's awa!

The stiffest o' them a' he bow'd;
The bauldest o' them a' he cow'd;
They durst nae mair than he allow'd,
         That was a law:
We've lost a birkie weel worth gowd,
         Willie's awa!

Now gawkies, tawpies, gowks, and fools,
Frae colleges and boarding-schools,
May sprout like simmer puddock-stools   20
         In glen or shaw;
He wha could brush them down to mools—
         Willie's awa!

The brethren o' the Commerce-Cham'er
May mourn their loss wi' doolfu' clamour;
He was a dictionar and grammar
            Amang them a';
I fear they'll now mak mony a stammer—
            Willie's awa!   30

Nae mair we see his levee door
Philosophers and poets pour,
And toothy critics by the score,
            In bloody raw;
The adjutant o' a' the core,
            Willie's awa!

Now worthy Gregory's Latin face,
Tytler's and Greenfield's modest grace;
Mackenzie, Stewart, sic a brace
            As Rome ne'er saw;   40
They a' maun meet some ither place—
            Willie's awa!

Poor Burns e'en Scotch drink canna quicken,
He cheeps like some bewilder'd chicken
Scar'd frae its minnie and the cleckin'
            By hoodie-craw;
Grief's gien his heart an unco kickin'—
            Willie's awa!

Now ev'ry sour-mou'd grinnin' blellum,
And Calvin's folk, are fit to fell him;
Ilk self-conceited critic skellum
            His quill may draw;
He wha could brawlie ward their bellum,
            Willie's awa!   50

Up wimpling stately Tweed I've sped,
And Eden scenes on crystal Jed,
And Ettrick banks, now roaring red,
            While tempests blaw;
But every joy and pleasure's fled—
            Willie's awa!   60

May I be Slander's common speech;
A text for Infamy to preach;
And, lastly, streekit out to bleach
         In winter snaw;
When I forget thee, Willie Creech,
         Tho' far awa!

May never wicked Fortune touzle him!
May never wicked men bamboozle him!
Until a pow as auld 's Methusalem
         He canty claw!   70
Then to the blessed New Jerusalem
         Fleet wing awa!

TO A LOUSE,

ON SEEING ONE ON A LADY'S BONNET AT CHURCH.

HA! wh'are ye gaun, ye crowlin' ferlie!
Your impudence protects you sairly:
I canna say but ye strunt rarely,
         Owre gauze and lace;
Tho' faith! I fear ye dine but sparely
         On sic a place.

Ye ugly, creepin', blastit wonner,
Detested, shunn'd by saunt an' sinner!
How dare ye set your fit upon her,
         Sae fine a lady?   10
Gae somewhere else, and seek your dinner
         On some poor body.

Swith, in some beggar's haffet squattle;
There ye may creep, and sprawl, and sprattle
Wi' ither kindred jumping cattle,
         In shoals and nations;
Where horn nor bane ne'er dare unsettle
         Your thick plantations.

Now haud ye there, ye're out o' sight,
Below the fatt'rels, snug an' tight;   20
Na, faith ye yet! ye'll no be right
        Till ye've got on it,
The very tapmost tow'ring height
        O' Miss's bonnet.

My sooth! right bauld ye set your nose out,
As plump and gray as onie grozet;
O for some rank mercurial rozet,
        Or fell red smeddum!
I'd gie you sic a hearty doze o't,
        Wad dress your droddum!   30

I wad na been surpris'd to spy
You on an auld wife's flannon toy;
Or aiblins some bit duddie boy,
        On's wyliecoat;
But Miss's fine Lunardi! fie,
        How daur ye do't?

O Jenny, dinna toss your head,
An' set your beauties a' abread!
Ye little ken what cursèd speed
        The blastie's makin'!   40
Thae winks and finger-ends, I dread,
        Are notice takin'!

O wad some Pow'r the giftie gie us
To see oursels as others see us!
It wad frae mony a blunder free us,
        And foolish notion:
What airs in dress an' gait wad lea'e us,
        And ev'n devotion!

THE WHISTLE.

I sing of a Whistle, a Whistle of worth,
I sing of a Whistle, the pride of the North,
Was brought to the court of our good Scottish king,
And long with this Whistle all Scotland shall ring.

Old Loda, still rueing the arm of Fingal,
The god of the bottle sends down from his hall—
'This Whistle's your challenge, to Scotland get o'er,
And drink them to hell, Sir, or ne'er see me more!'

Old poets have sung, and old chronicles tell,
What champions ventur'd, what champions fell;   10
The son of great Loda was conqueror still,
And blew on the Whistle their requiem shrill.

Till Robert, the lord of the Cairn and the Scaur,
Unmatch'd at the bottle, unconquer'd in war,
He drank his poor god-ship as deep as the sea;
No tide of the Baltic e'er drunker than he.

Thus Robert, victorious, the trophy has gain'd,
Which now in his house has for ages remain'd;
Till three noble chieftains, and all of his blood,
The jovial contest again have renew'd;   20

Three joyous good fellows, with hearts clear of flaw—
Craigdarroch, so famous for wit, worth, and law,
And trusty Glenriddel, so skill'd in old coins,
And gallant Sir Robert, deep-read in old wines.

Craigdarroch began, with a tongue smooth as oil,
Desiring Glenriddel to yield up the spoil;
Or else he would muster the heads of the clan,
And once more, in claret, try which was the man.

'By the gods of the ancients!' Glenriddel replies,
'Before I surrender so glorious a prize,   30
I'll conjure the ghost of the great Rorie More,
And bumper his horn with him twenty times o'er.'

Sir Robert, a soldier, no speech would pretend,
But he ne'er turn'd his back on his foe—or his friend;
Said ' Toss down the Whistle, the prize of the field,'
And knee-deep in claret, he'd die ere he'd yield.

To the board of Glenriddel our heroes repair,
So noted for drowning of sorrow and care;
But for wine and for welcome not more known to fame,
Than the sense, wit, and taste of a sweet lovely dame. 40

A bard was selected to witness the fray,
And tell future ages the feats of the day;
A bard who detested all sadness and spleen,
And wish'd that Parnassus a vineyard had been.

The dinner being over, the claret they ply,
And ev'ry new cork is a new spring of joy;
In the bands of old friendship and kindred so set,
And the bands grew the tighter the more they were wet.

Gay Pleasure ran riot as bumpers ran o'er;
Bright Phoebus ne'er witness'd so joyous a core, 50
And vow'd that to leave them he was quite forlorn,
Till Cynthia hinted he'd see them next morn.

Six bottles a-piece had well wore out the night,
When gallant Sir Robert, to finish the fight,
Turn'd o'er in one bumper a bottle of red,
And swore 'twas the way that their ancestor did.

Then worthy Glenriddel, so cautious and sage,
No longer the warfare ungodly would wage;
A high-ruling elder to wallow in wine!
He left the foul business to folks less divine. 60

The gallant Sir Robert fought hard to the end;
But who can with Fate and quart bumpers contend?
Though fate said, a hero should perish in light;
So up rose bright Phoebus—and down fell the knight.

Next up rose our bard, like a prophet in drink :
'Craigdarroch, thou'lt soar when creation shall sink !
But if thou would flourish immortal in rhyme,
Come—one bottle more—and have at the sublime !

'Thy line, that have struggled for freedom with Bruce,
Shall heroes and patriots ever produce :   70
So.thine be the laurel, and mine be the bay !
The field thou hast won, by yon bright god of day !'

THE KIRK'S ALARM.

Orthodox, Orthodox, wha believe in John Knox,
    Let me sound an alarm to your conscience :
There's a heretic blast has been blawn i' the wast,
    'That what is not sense must be nonsense.'

Dr. Mac, Dr. Mac, you should stretch on a rack,
    To strike evil-doers wi' terror ;
To join faith and sense upon ony pretence,
    Is heretic, damnable error.

Town of Ayr, town of Ayr, it was mad, I declare,
    To meddle wi' mischief a-brewing ;   10
Provost John is still deaf to the church's relief,
    And orator Bob is its ruin.

D'rymple mild, D'rymple mild, tho' your heart's like a child,
    And your life like the new driven snaw,
Yet that winna save ye, auld Satan must have ye,
    For preaching that three's ane and twa.

Rumble John, Rumble John, mount the steps wi' a groan,
    Cry the book is wi' heresy cramm'd ;
Then lug out your ladle, deal brimstane like adle,
    And roar ev'ry note of the damn'd.   20

Simper James, Simper James, leave the fair Killie dames
  There's a holier chase in your view;
I'll lay on your head, that the pack ye'll soon lead,
  For puppies like you there's but few.

Singet Sawney, Singet Sawney, are ye herding the penny,
  Unconscious what evils await?
Wi' a jump, yell, and howl, alarm every soul,
  For the foul thief is just at your gate.

Daddy Auld, Daddy Auld, there's a tod in the fauld,
  A tod meikle waur than the clerk;   30
Tho' ye can do little skaith, ye'll be in at the death,
  And gif ye canna bite, ye may bark.

Davie Bluster, Davie Bluster, if for a saint ye do muster,
  The corps is no nice of recruits:
Yet to worth let's be just, royal blood ye might boast,
  If the ass was the king of the brutes.

Jamie Goose, Jamie Goose, ye hae made but toom roose,
  In hunting the wicked Lieutenant;
But the Doctor's your mark, for the Lord's haly ark,
  He has cooper'd and ca'd a wrang pin in't.   40

Poet Willie, Poet Willie, gie the Doctor a volley,
  Wi' your 'liberty's chain' and your wit;
O'er Pegasus' side ye ne'er laid a stride,
  Ye but smelt, man, the place where he shit.

Andro Gouk, Andro Gouk, ye may slander the book,
  And the book no the waur, let me tell ye!
Ye are rich, and look big, but lay by hat and wig,
  And ye'll hae a calf's head o' sma' value.

Barr Steenie, Barr Steenie, what mean ye? what mean ye?
  If ye'll meddle nae mair wi' the matter,   50
Ye may hae some pretence to havins and sense,
  Wi' people wha ken ye nae better.

Irvine Side, Irvine Side, wi' your turkeycock pride,
  Of manhood but sma' is your share ;
Ye've the figure, 'tis true, even your faes will allow,
  And your friends they dare grant vou nae mair.

Muirland Jock, Muirland Jock, when the Lord makes a rock
  To crush common sense for her sins,
If ill manners were wit, there 's no mortal so fit
  To confound the poor Doctor at ance.   60

Holy Will, Holy Will, there was wit i' your skull,
  When ye pilfer'd the alms o' the poor ;
The timmer is scant when ye're ta'en for a saint,
  Wha should swing in a rape for an hour.

Calvin's sons, Calvin's sons, seize your sp'ritual guns,
  Ammunition you never can need ;
Your hearts are the stuff will be powther enough,
  And your skulls are storehouses o' lead.

Poet Burns, Poet Burns, wi' your priest-skelping turns,
  Why desert ye your auld native shire?   70
Your muse is a gipsy, e'en tho' she were tipsy
  She cou'd ca' us nae waur than we are.

------◆------

LINES WRITTEN IN FRIARS-CARSE HERMITAGE,

ON NITH-SIDE.

THOU whom chance may hither lead,
Be thou clad in russet weed,
Be thou deckt in silken stole,
Grave these counsels on thy soul.
  Life is but a day at most,
Sprung from night, in darkness lost ;
Hope not sunshine ev'ry hour,
Fear not clouds will always lour.

As Youth and Love, with sprightly dance,
Beneath thy morning star advance,   10
Pleasure with her syren air
May delude the thoughtless pair ;
Let Prudence bless Enjoyment's cup,
Then raptur'd sip, and sip it up.
  As thy day grows warm and high,
Life's meridian flaming nigh,
Dost thou spurn the humble vale ?
Life's proud summits wouldst thou scale ?
Check thy climbing step, elate,
Evils lurk in felon wait :   20
Dangers, eagle-pinioned, bold,
Soar around each cliffy hold,
While cheerful Peace, with linnet song,
Chants the lowly dells among.
  As the shades of ev'ning close,
Beck'ning thee to long repose ;
As life itself becomes disease,
Seek the chimney-nook of ease.
There ruminate with sober thought,
On all thou'st seen, and heard, and wrought ;   30
And teach the sportive younkers round,
Saws of experience, sage and sound.
Say man's true genuine estimate,
The grand criterion of his fate,
Is not—Art thou high or low ?
Did thy fortune ebb or flow ?
Did many talents gild thy span ?
Or frugal Nature grudge thee one ?
Tell them, and press it on their mind,
As thou thyself must shortly find,   40
The smile or frown of awful Heav'n
To Virtue or to Vice is giv'n.
Say to be just, and kind, and wise,—
There solid self-enjoyment lies ;
That foolish, selfish, faithless ways
Lead to be wretched, vile, and base.
  Thus resign'd and quiet, creep
To the bed of lasting sleep ;
Sleep, whence thou shalt ne'er awake,
Night, where dawn shall never break   50

Till future life, future no more,
To light and joy and good restore,
To light and joy unknown before.
  Stranger, go! Heaven be thy guide!
Quod the Beadsman of Nith-side.

GLENRIDDEL HERMITAGE, *June 28th,* 1788.

FROM THE MS.

THOU whom chance may hither lead,
Be thou clad in russet weed,
Be thou deckt in silken stole,
Grave these maxims on thy soul.
  Life is but a day at most,   60
Sprung from night, in darkness lost;
Hope not sunshine every hour,
Fear not clouds will always lour.
  Happiness is but a name,
Make content and ease thy aim;
Ambition is a meteor gleam,
Fame, an idle restless dream:
Peace, the tenderest flower of spring;
Pleasures, insects on the wing;
Those that sip the dew alone—   70
Make the butterflies thy own;
Those that would the bloom devour—
Crush the locusts, save the flower.
  For the future be prepar'd,
Guard, wherever thou canst guard;
But thy utmost duly done,
Welcome what thou canst not shun.
Follies past give thou to air,
Make their consequence thy care:
Keep the name of Man in mind,   80
And dishonour not thy kind.
Reverence, with lowly heart,
HIM whose wondrous work thou art:
Keep His goodness still in view,
Thy trust, and thy example too.
  Stranger, go! Heaven be thy guide!
Quod the Beadsman of Nith-side.

THE LAMENT,

OCCASIONED BY THE UNFORTUNATE ISSUE OF A FRIEND'S AMOUR.

O THOU pale Orb, that silent shines,
  While care-untroubled mortals sleep!
Thou seest a wretch that inly pines,
  And wanders here to wail and weep!
With woe I nightly vigils keep,
  Beneath thy wan, unwarming beam;
And mourn, in lamentation deep,
  How life and love are all a dream.

I joyless view thy rays adorn
  The faintly-markèd, distant hill: 10
I joyless view thy trembling horn,
  Reflected in the gurgling rill:
My fondly-fluttering heart, be still!
  Thou busy pow'r, Remembrance, cease!
Ah! must the agonizing thrill
  For ever bar returning peace!

No idly-feign'd poetic pains,
  My sad love-lorn lamentings claim;
No shepherd's pipe—Arcadian strains;
  No fabled tortures, quaint and tame: 20
The plighted faith, the mutual flame,
  The oft attested Pow'rs above,
The promis'd father's tender name—
  These were the pledges of my love!

Encircled in her clasping arms,
  How have the raptur'd moments flown!
How have I wish'd for fortune's charms,
  For her dear sake, and her's alone!
And must I think it! is she gone,
  My secret heart's exulting boast?   30
And does she heedless hear my groan?
  And is she ever, ever lost?

Oh! can she bear so base a heart,
  So lost to honour, lost to truth,
As from the fondest lover part,
  The plighted husband of her youth?
Alas! life's path may be unsmooth!
  Her way may lie thro' rough distress!
Then who her pangs and pains will soothe,
  Her sorrows share, and make them less?   40

Ye wingèd hours that o'er us past,
  Enraptur'd more, the more enjoy'd,
Your dear remembrance in my breast
  My fondly-treasur'd thoughts employ'd.
That breast, how dreary now, and void,
  For her too scanty once of room!
Ev'n ev'ry ray of hope destroy'd,
  And not a wish to gild the gloom!

The morn that warns th' approaching day
  Awakes me up to toil and woe: 50
I see the hours in long array,
  That I must suffer, lingering slow.
Full many a pang, and many a throe,
  Keen recollection's direful train,
Must wring my soul, ere Phoebus, low,
  Shall kiss the distant western main.

And when my nightly couch I try,
  Sore-harass'd out with care and grief,
My toil-beat nerves, and tear-worn eye,
  Keep watchings with the nightly thief: 60
Or if I slumber, Fancy, chief,
  Reigns, haggard-wild, in sore affright:
Ev'n day, all-bitter, brings relief
  From such a horror-breathing night.

O thou bright Queen, who o'er th' expanse
  Now highest reign'st, with boundless sway!
Oft has thy silent-marking glance
  Observ'd us, fondly-wand'ring, stray!

The 'time, unheeded, sped away,
  While love's luxurious pulse beat high,   70
Beneath thy silver-gleaming ray,
  To mark the mutual-kindling eye.

O scenes in strong remembrance set!
  Scenes never, never to return!
Scenes, if in stupor I forget,
  Again I feel, again I burn!
From ev'ry joy and pleasure torn,
  Life's weary vale I'll wander thro';
And hopeless, comfortless, I'll mourn
  A faithless woman's broken vow.   80

DESPONDENCY.

OPPRESS'D with grief, oppress'd with care,
A burden more than I can bear,
  I set me down and sigh;
O life! thou art a galling load,
Along a rough, a weary road,
  To wretches such as I!
Dim-backward as I cast my view,
  What sick'ning scenes appear!
What sorrows yet may pierce me thro',
  Too justly I may fear!   10
    Still caring, despairing,
      Must be my bitter doom;
    My woes here shall close ne'er,
      But with the closing tomb!

Happy, ye sons of busy life,
Who, equal to the bustling strife,
  No other view regard!
Ev'n when the wishèd end's denied,
Yet, while the busy means are plied,
  They bring their own reward: 20

Whilst I, a hope-abandon'd wight,
  Unfitted with an aim,
Meet ev'ry sad returning night,
  And joyless morn the same ;
    You, bustling, and justling,
      Forget each grief and pain ;
    I, listless, yet restless,
      Find every prospect vain.

How blest the Solitary's lot,
Who, all-forgetting, all-forgot,
  Within his humble cell,
The cavern wild with tangling roots,
Sits o'er his newly-gather'd fruits,
  Beside his crystal well ?
Or, haply, to his ev'ning thought,
  By unfrequented stream,
The ways of men are distant brought,
  A faint collected dream :
    While praising, and raising
      His thoughts to Heav'n on high,
    As wand'ring, meand'ring,
      He views the solemn sky.

Than I, no lonely hermit plac'd
Where never human footstep trac'd,
  Less fit to play the part ;
The lucky moment to improve,
And just to stop and just to move,
  With self-respecting art :
But ah ! those pleasures, loves, and joys,
  Which I too keenly taste,
The Solitary can despise,
  Can want, and yet be blest !
    He needs not, he heeds not,
      Or human love or hate,
    Whilst I here must cry here
      At perfidy ingrate !

Oh ! enviable, early days,
When dancing thoughtless pleasure's maze,
  To care, to guilt unknown !

How ill exchang'd for riper times, 60
To see the follies, or the crimes,
　　Of others, or my own!
Ye tiny elves that guiltless sport,
　　Like linnets in the bush,
Ye little know the ills ye court,
　　When manhood is your wish!
　　　　The losses, the crosses,
　　　　　　That active man engage!
　　　　The fears all, the tears all,
　　　　　　Of dim-declining age. 70

———◆◆———

WILLIE CHALMERS.

Wi' braw new branks in mickle pride,
　　And eke a braw new brechan,
My Pegasus I'm got astride,
　　And up Parnassus pechin';
Whiles owre a bush wi' downward crush,
　　The doited beastie stammers;
Then up he gets, and off he sets
　　For sake o' Willie Chalmers.

I doubt na, lass, that weel kenn'd name
　　May cost a pair o' blushes; 10
I am nae stranger to your fame
　　Nor his warm urgèd wishes.
Your bonnie face sae mild and sweet,
　　His honest heart enamours,
And faith ye'll no be lost a whit,
　　Tho' waired on Willie Chalmers.

Auld Truth hersel might swear ye're fair,
　　Aud Honour safely back her,
And Modesty assume your air,
　　And ne'er a ane mistak' her: 20
And sic twa love-inspiring een
　　Might fire even holy palmers;
Nae wonder then they've fatal been
　　To honest Willie Chalmers.

I doubt na fortune may you shore
   Some mim-mou'd pouther'd priestie,
Fu' lifted up wi' Hebrew lore,
   And band upon his breastie :
But oh ! what signifies to you,
   His lexicons and grammars ;   30
The feeling heart 's the royal blue,
   And that 's wi' Willie Chalmers.

Some gapin' glowrin' country laird
   May warsle for your favour ;
May claw his lug, and straik his beard,
   And host up some palaver.
My bonnie maid, before ye wed
   Sic clumsy-witted hammers,
Seek Heaven for help, and barefit skelp
   Awa' wi' Willie Chalmers.   40

Forgive the Bard ! my fond regard
   For ane that shares my bosom
Inspires my muse to gie 'm his dues,
   For de'il a hair I roose him.
May powers aboon unite you soon,
   · And fructify your amours,
And every year come in mair dear
   To you and Willie Chalmers.

———◆◆———

A BARD'S EPITAPH.

Is there a whim-inspirèd fool,
Owre fast for thought, owre hot for rule,
Owre blate to seek, owre proud to snool,
         Let him draw near ;
And owre this grassy heap sing dool,
         And drap a tear.

Is there a bard of rustic song,
Who, noteless, steals the crowds among,
That weekly this area throng,
    O, pass not by!   10
But, with a frater-feeling strong,
    Here heave a sigh.

Is there a man whose judgment clear,
Can others teach the course to steer,
Yet runs, himself, life's mad career,
    Wild as the wave;
Here pause—and, thro' the starting tear,
    Survey this grave.

The poor inhabitant below
Was quick to learn and wise to know,   20
And keenly felt the friendly glow,
    And softer flame;
But thoughtless follies laid him low,
    And stain'd his name!

Reader, attend! whether thy soul
Soars fancy's flights beyond the pole,
Or darkling grubs this earthly hole,
    In low pursuit;
Know prudent cautious self-control
    Is wisdom's root.   30

EPISTLE TO JOHN RANKINE.

O ROUGH, rude, ready-witted Rankine,
The wale o' cocks for fun and drinkin'!
There's mony godly folks are thinkin'
    Your dreams an' tricks
Will send you, Korah-like a-sinkin',
    Straught to auld Nick's.

Ye hae sae mony cracks an' cants,
And in your wicked, drucken rants,
Ye mak a devil o' the saunts,
    An' fill them fou ;   10
And then their failings, flaws, an' wants,
    Are a' seen thro'.

Hypocrisy, in mercy spare it !
That holy robe, O dinna tear it !
Spare 't for their sakes wha aften wear it,
    The lads in black ;
But your curst wit, when it comes near it,
    Rives 't aff their back.

Think, wicked sinner, wha ye're skaithing,
It 's just the blue-gown badge an' claithing 20
O' saunts ; tak that, ye lea'e them naithing
    To ken them by,
Frae ony unregenerate heathen
    Like you or I.

I've sent you here some rhyming ware,
A' that I bargain'd for, an' mair ;
Sae, when ye hae an hour to spare,
    I will expect
Yon sang ; ye'll sen't, wi' cannie care,
    And no neglect.   30

Tho', faith, sma' heart hae I to sing !
My Muse dow scarcely spread her wing !
I've play'd mysel a bonnie spring,
    An' danc'd my fill !
I'd better gane an' sair'd the king
    At Bunker's Hill.

'Twas ae night lately, in my fun,
I gaed a roving wi' the gun,
An' brought a paitrick to the grun',
    A bonnie hen ;
And, as the twilight was begun,   40
    Thought nane would ken.

The poor wee thing was little hurt;
I straikit it a wee for sport,
Ne'er thinkin they wad fash me for't;
   But, Deil-may-care!
Somebody tells the poacher-court
   The hale affair.

Some auld us'd hands had ta'en a note,
That sic a hen had got a shot;   50
I was suspected for the plot;
   I scorn'd to lie;
So gat the whissle o' my groat,
   An' pay't the fee.

But, by my gun, o' guns the wale,
An' by my pouther an' my hail,
An' by my hen, an' by her tail,
   I vow an' swear!
The game shall pay, o'er moor an' dale,
   For this, niest year.   60

As soon's the clockin'-time is by,
An' the wee pouts begun to cry,
Lord, I'se hae sportin by an' by,
   For my gowd guinea;
Tho' I should herd the buckskin kye
   For't, in Virginia.

Trowth, they had muckle for to blame!
'Twas neither broken wing nor limb,
But twa-three draps about the wame
   Scarce thro' the feathers;   70
An' baith a yellow George to claim,
   An' thole their blethers!

It pits me aye as mad's a hare;
So I can rhyme nor write nae mair;
But pennyworths again is fair,
   When time's expedient:
Meanwhile I am, respected Sir,
   Your most obedient.

EPISTLE TO DAVIE, A BROTHER POET.

W<small>HILE</small> winds frae aff Ben-Lomond blaw,
And bar the doors wi' driving snaw,
 And hing us owre the ingle,
I set me down, to pass the time,
And spin a verse or twa o' rhyme,
 In hamely westlin jingle.
While frosty winds blaw in the drift,
 Ben to the chimla lug,
I grudge a wee the great-folk's gift,
 That live sae bien an' snug ;   10
  I tent less, and want less
   Their roomy fire-side ;
  But hanker and canker
   To see their cursèd pride.

It 's hardly in a body's pow'r,
To keep, at times, frae being sour,
 To see how things are shar'd ;
How best o' chiels are whyles in want,
While coofs on countless thousands rant,
 And ken na how to wair 't :   20
But, Davie, lad, ne'er fash your head,
 Tho' we hae little gear,
We're fit to win our daily bread,
 As lang 's we're hale and fier :
  ' Mair spier na, nor fear na,'
   Auld age ne'er mind a feg ;
  The last o't, the warst o't,
   Is only but to beg.

To lie in kilns and barns at e'en,
When banes are craz'd, and bluid is thin, 30
 Is, doubtless, great distress !

Yet then content could mak us blest;
Ev'n then, sometimes, we'd snatch a taste
   Of truest happiness.
The honest heart that 's free frae a'
   Intended fraud or guile,
However fortune kick the ba',
   Has aye some cause to smile:
     And mind still, you'll find still,
      A comfort this nae sma';   40
     Nae mair then, we'll care then,
      Nae farther can we fa'.

What tho', like commoners of air,
We wander out, we know not where,
   But either house or hal'?
Yet nature's charms, the hills and woods,
The sweeping vales, and foaming floods,
   Are free alike to all.
In days when daisies deck the ground,
   And blackbirds whistle clear,   50
With honest joy our hearts will bound,
   To see the coming year:
     On braes when we please, then,.
      We'll sit and sowth a tune;
     Syne rhyme till 't, we'll time till 't,
      And sing 't when we hae done.

It 's no in titles nor in rank;
It 's no in wealth like Lon'on bank,
   To purchase peace and rest;
It 's no in making muckle, mair: 60
It 's no in books, it 's no in lear,
   To make us truly blest:
If happiness hae not her seat
   And centre in the breast,
We may be wise, or rich, or great,
   But never can be blest:
     Nae treasures, nor pleasures,
      Could make us happy lang;
     The heart aye 's the part aye
      That makes us right or wrang.   70

Think ye, that sic as you and I,
Wha drudge and drive thro' wet an' dry,
  Wi' never-ceasing toil ;
Think ye, are we less blest than they,
Wha scarcely tent us in their way,
  As hardly worth their while ?
Alas ! how oft in haughty mood,
  God's creatures they oppress !
Or else, neglecting a' that 's guid,
  They riot in excess !   80
    Baith careless, and fearless,
      Of either heav'n or hell !
    Esteeming, and deeming
      It 's a' an idle tale !

Then let us cheerfu' acquiesce ;
Nor make our scanty pleasures less,
  By pining at our state ;
And, even should misfortunes come,
I, here wha sit, hae met wi' some,
  An 's thankfu' for them yet.   90
They gie the wit of age to youth ;
  They let us ken oursel ;
They mak us see the naked truth,
  The real guid and ill.
    Tho' losses, and crosses,
      Be lessons right severe,
    There 's wit there, ye'll get there,
      Ye'll find nae other where.

But tent me, Davie, ace o' hearts !
(To say aught less wad wrang the cartes.   100
  And flatt'ry I detest)
This life has joys for you and I ;
And joys that riches ne'er could buy ;
  And joys the very best.
There 's a' the pleasures o' the heart,
  The lover an' the frien' ;
Ye hae your Meg, your dearest part,
  And I my darling Jean !

It warms me, it charms me,
　　To mention but her name :　　　　110
It heats me, it beets me,
　　And sets me a' on flame !

O all ye pow'rs who rule above !
O Thou, whose very self art love !
　　Thou know'st my words sincere !
The life-blood streaming thro' my heart,
Or my more dear immortal part,
　　Is not more fondly dear !
When heart-corroding care and grief
　　Deprive my soul of rest,　　　　120
Her dear idea brings relief
　　And solace to my breast.
　　　　Thou Being, All-seeing,
　　　　　O hear my fervent pray'r ;
　　　　Still take her, and make her
　　　　　Thy most peculiar care !

All hail, ye tender feelings dear !
The smile of love, the friendly tear,
　　The sympathetic glow !
Long since this world's thorny ways　　130
Had number'd out my weary days,
　　Had it not been for you !
Fate still has blest me with a friend,
　　In every care and ill ;
And oft a more endearing band,
　　A tie more tender still.
　　　　It lightens, it brightens
　　　　　The tenebrific scene,
　　　　To meet with, and greet with
　　　　　My Davie or my Jean.　　　　140

O, how that name inspires my style !
The words come skelpin', rank and file,
　　Amaist before I ken !
The ready measure rins as fine,
As Phoebus and the famous Nine
　　Were glowrin' owre my pen.

My spavied Pegasus will limp,
  Till ance he's fairly het;
And then he'll hilch, and stilt, and jimp,
  An' rin an unco fit: 150
    But lest then the beast then
      Should rue this hasty ride,
  I'll light now, and dight now
      His sweaty wizen'd hide.

SECOND EPISTLE TO DAVIE.

Auld neibor,

I'm three times doubly o'er your debtor,
For your auld-farrant, frien'ly letter;
Tho' I maun say't, I doubt ye flatter,
    Ye speak sae fair;
For my puir. silly, rhymin' clatter
    Some less maun sair.

Hale be your heart, hale be your fiddle;
Lang may your elbuck jink and diddle,
To cheer you through the weary widdle
    O' war'ly cares,   10
Till bairns' bairns kindly cuddle
    Your auld gray hairs.

But Davie, lad, I'm red ye're glaikit;
I'm tauld the Muse ye hae negleckit;
An' gif it's sae, ye sud be lickit
    Until ye fyke;
Sic hauns as you sud ne'er be faikit,
    Be hain't wha like.

For me, I'm on Parnassus' brink,
Rivin' the words to gar them clink;   20
Whyles dazed wi' love, whyles dazed wi' drink,
    Wi' jads or masons;
An' whyles, but aye owre late, I think
    Braw sober lessons.

Of a' the thoughtless sons o' man,
Commend me to the Bardie clan :
Except it be some idle plan
        O' rhymin' clink,
The devil-haet, that I sud ban,
          They ever think.   30

Nae thought, nae view, nae scheme o' livin',
Nae cares to gie us joy or grievin' ;
But just the pouchie put the nieve in,
        An' while ought 's there,
Then hiltie skiltie, we gae scrievin',
          An' fash nae mair.

Leeze me on rhyme ! it 's aye a treasure,
My chief, amaist my only pleasure ;
At hame, a-fiel', at wark, or leisure,
        The Muse, poor hizzie !   40
Tho' rough an' raploch be her measure,
          She 's seldom lazy.

Haud to the Muse, my dainty Davie :
The warl' may play you mony a shavie ;
But for the Muse, she'll never leave ye,
        Tho' e'er sae puir,
Na, even tho' limpin' wi' the spavie
          Frae door to door.

EPISTLE TO JOHN LAPRAIK, AN OLD
SCOTTISH BARD.

WHILE briers an' woodbines budding green,
An' paitricks scraichin' loud at e'en,
An' morning poussie whiddin' seen,
        Inspire my Muse,
This freedom, in an unknown frien',
          I pray excuse.

On Fasten-een we had a rockin',
To ca' the crack and weave our stockin';
And there was muckle fun and jokin',
   Ye need na doubt;
At length we had a hearty yokin'
   At sang about.

There was ae sang, amang the rest,
Aboon them a' it pleas'd me best,
That some kind husband had addrest
   To some sweet wife:
It thirl'd the heart-strings thro' the breast,
   A' to the life.

I've scarce heard ought describ'd sae weel,
What gen'rous, manly bosoms feel;
Thought I 'Can this be Pope, or Steele,
   Or Beattie's wark!'
They tauld me 'twas an odd kind chiel
   About Muirkirk.

It pat me fidgin' fain to hear't,
And sae about him there I spier'd;
Then a' that kenn'd him round declar'd
   He had ingine,
That nane excell'd it, few cam near't,
   It was sae fine.

That, set him to a pint of ale,
An' either douce or merry tale,
Or rhymes an' sangs he'd made himsel,
   Or witty catches,
'Tween Inverness and Teviotdale,
   He had few matches.

Then up I gat, an' swoor an aith,
Tho' I should pawn my pleugh and graith,
Or die a cadger pownie's death,
   At some dyke-back,
A pint an' gill I'd gie them baith
   To hear your crack.

But, first an' foremost, I should tell,
Amaist as soon as I could spell,
I to the crambo-jingle fell;
        Tho' rude an' rough,
Yet crooning to a body's sel,
        Does weel eneugh.

I am nae poet, in a sense,
But just a rhymer, like, by chance,   50
An' hae to learning nae pretence,
        Yet what the matter?
Whene'er my Muse does on me glance,
        I jingle at her.

Your critic-folk may cock their nose,
And say 'How can you e'er propose,
You wha ken hardly verse frae prose,
        To mak a sang?'
But, by your leaves, my learnèd foes,
        Ye're maybe wrang.   60

What's a' your jargon o' your schools,
Your Latin names for horns an' stools;
If honest nature made you fools,
        What sairs your grammars?
Ye'd better ta'en up spades and shools,
        Or knappin'-hammers.

A set o' dull conceited hashes
Confuse their brains in college classes!
They gang in stirks, and come out asses,
        Plain truth to speak;   70
An' syne they think to climb Parnassus
        By dint o' Greek!

Gie me ae spark o' Nature's fire,
That's a' the learning I desire;
Then tho' I drudge thro' dub an' mire
        At pleugh or cart,
My Muse, though hamely in attire,
        May touch the heart.

O for a spunk o' Allan's glee,
Or Fergusson's, the bauld an' slee,
Or bright Lapraik's, my friend to be,　　　　80
　　　　If I can hit it!
That would be lear eneugh for me,
　　　　If I could get it.

Now, sir, if ye hae friends enow,
Tho' real friends, I b'lieve, are few,
Yet, if your catalogue be fou,
　　　　I'se no insist,
But gif ye want ae friend that's true,
　　　　I'm on your list.　　　　90

I winna blaw about mysel,
As ill I like my fauts to tell;
But friends, an' folks that wish me well,
　　　　They sometimes roose me;
Tho' I maun own, as mony still
　　　　As far abuse me.

There's ae wee faut they whiles lay to me,
I like the lasses—Gude forgie me!
For mony a plack they wheedle frae me,
　　　　At dance or fair;　　　　100
Maybe some ither thing they gie me
　　　　They weel can spare.

But Mauchline race, or Mauchline fair,
I should be proud to meet you there;
We'se gie ae night's discharge to care,
　　　　If we forgather,
An' hae a swap o' rhymin'-ware
　　　　Wi' ane anither.

The four-gill chap, we'se gar him clatter,
An' kirsen him wi' reekin water;　　　　110
Syne we'll sit down an' tak our whitter,.
　　　　To cheer our heart;
An' faith, we'se be acquainted better
　　　　Before we part.

Awa, ye selfish warly race,
Wha think that havins, sense, an' grace,
Ev'n love an' friendship, should give place
      To catch-the-plack!
I dinna like to see your face,
      Nor hear your crack.   120

But ye whom social pleasure charms,
Whose hearts the tide of kindness warms,
Who hold your being on the terms,
      'Each aid the others,'
Come to my bowl, come to my arms,
      My friends, my brothers!

But to conclude my lang epistle,
As my auld pen's worn to the gristle;
Twa lines frae you wad gar me fissle,
      Who am, most fervent,   130
While I can either sing, or whistle,
      Your friend and servant.

TO THE SAME.

WHILE new-ca'd kye rowte at the stake,
An' pownies reek in pleugh or braik,
This hour on e'enin's edge I take,
      To own I'm debtor,
To honest-hearted auld Lapraik,
      For his kind letter.

Forjeskit sair, with weary legs,
Rattlin' the corn out-owre the rigs,
Or dealing thro' amang the naigs
      Their ten-hours' bite,   10
My awkwart Muse sair pleads and begs
      I would na write.

The tapetless, ramfeezl'd hizzie,
She's saft at best, and something lazy,
Quo' she 'Ye ken we've been sae busy,
    This month an' mair,
That trouth my head is grown quite dizzie,
    An' something sair.'

Her dowff excuses pat me mad;
'Conscience,' says I, 'ye thowless jad!   20
I'll write, an' that a hearty blaud,
    This very night;
So dinna ye affront your trade,
    But rhyme it right.

'Shall bauld Lapraik, the king o' hearts,
Tho' mankind were a pack o' cartes,
Roose you sae weel for your deserts,
    In terms sae friendly,
Yet ye'll neglect to shaw your parts,
    An' thank him kindly?'   30

Sae I gat paper in a blink,
An' down gaed stumpie in the ink:
Quoth I 'Before I sleep a wink,
    I vow I'll close it;
An if ye winna mak it clink,
    By Jove, I'll prose it!'

Sae I've begun to scrawl, but whether
In rhyme, or prose, or baith thegither,
Or some hotch-potch that's rightly neither,
    Let time mak proof;   40
But I shall scribble down some blether
    Just clean aff-loof.

My worthy friend, ne'er grudge an' carp,
Tho' fortune use you hard an' sharp;
Come, kittle up your moorland harp
    Wi' gleesome touch!
Ne'er mind how fortune waft an' warp;
    She's but a bitch.

She's gien me mony a jirt an' fleg,
Sin' I could striddle owre a rig ;   50
But, by the Lord, tho' I should beg
      Wi' lyart pow,
I'll laugh, an' sing, an' shake my leg,
      As lang's I dow!

Now comes the sax-an'-twentieth simmer
I've seen the bud upo' the timmer,
Still persecuted by the limmer,
      Frae year to year:
But yet, despite the kittle kimmer,
      I, Rob, am here.   60

Do ye envy the city gent,
Behind a kist to lie an' sklent,
Or purse-proud, big wi' cent per cent
      An' muckle wame,
In some bit brugh to represent
      A bailie's name?

Or is't the paughty feudal thane,
Wi' ruffl'd sark an' glancing cane,
Wha thinks himsel nae sheep-shank bane,
      But lordly stalks,   70
While caps and bonnets aff are taen,
      As by he walks?

'O Thou wha gies us each guid gift!
Gie me o' wit an' sense a lift,
Then turn me, if Thou please, adrift,
      Thro' Scotland wide ;
Wi' cits nor lairds I wadna shift,
      In a' their pride!'

Were this the charter of our state,
'On pain o' hell be rich an' great,'   80
Damnation then would be our fate,
      Beyond remead ;
But, thanks to Heaven! that's no the gate
      We learn our creed.

For thus the royal mandate ran,
When first the human race began,
'The social, friendly, honest man,
   Whate'er he be,
'Tis he fulfils great Nature's plan,
   And none but he!'   90

O mandate glorious and divine!
The followers of the ragged Nine,
Poor, thoughtless devils! yet may shine,
   In glorious light,
While sordid sons of Mammon's line
   Are dark as night.

Tho' here they scrape, an' squeeze, an' growl,
Their worthless nievefu' of a soul
May in some future carcase howl,
   The forest's fright;   100
Or in some day-detesting owl
   May shun the light.

Then may Lapraik and Burns arise,
To reach their native kindred skies,
And sing their pleasures, hopes, an' joys,
   In some mild sphere,
Still closer knit in friendship's ties
   Each passing year!

————————

TO WILLIAM SIMPSON.

I GAT your letter, winsome Willie;
Wi' gratefu' heart I thank you brawlie;
Tho' I maun say't, I wad be silly,
   An' unco vain,
Should I believe, my coaxin' billie,
   Your flatterin' strain.

But I'se believe ye kindly meant it :
I sud be laith to think ye hinted
Ironic satire, sidelins sklented
   On my poor Musie ;   10
Tho' in sic phraisin' terms ye've penn'd it,
   I scarce excuse ye.

My senses wad be in a creel,
Should I but dare a hope to speel,
Wi' Allan, or wi' Gilbertfield,
   The braes o' fame ;
Or Fergusson, the writer-chiel,
   A deathless name.

(O Fergusson ! thy glorious parts
Ill suited law's dry, musty arts !   20
My curse upon your whunstane hearts,
   Ye E'nbrugh gentry !
The tythe o' what ye waste at cartes
   Wad stow'd his pantry !)

Yet when a tale comes i' my head,
Or lasses gie my heart a screed,
As whiles they're like to be my dead,
   (O sad disease !)
I kittle up my rustic reed ;
   It gies me ease.   30

Auld Coila, now, may fidge fu' fain,
She's gotten poets o' her ain,
Chiels wha their chanters winna hain,
   But tune their lays,
Till echoes a' resound again
   Her weel-sung praise.

Nae poet thought her worth his while,
To set her name in measur'd style ;
She lay like some unkenn'd-of isle,
   Beside New Holland,   40
Or where wild-meeting oceans boil
   Besouth Magellan.

Ramsay an' famous Fergusson
Gied Forth an' Tay a lift aboon;
Yarrow an' Tweed, to mony a tune,
  Owre Scotland rings,
While Irwin, Lugar, Ayr, an' Doon,
  Naebody sings.

Th' Ilissus, Tiber, Thames, an' Seine,
Glide sweet in mony a tunefu' line;   50
But, Willie, set your fit to mine,
  An' cock your crest,
We'll gar our streams an' burnies shine
  Up wi' the best.

We'll sing auld Coila's plains an' fells,
Her moors red-brown wi' heather bells,
Her banks an' braes, her dens an' dells,
  Where glorious Wallace
Aft bure the gree, as story tells,
  Frae Southron billies.   60

At Wallace' name, what Scottish blood
But boils up in a spring-tide flood!
Oft have our fearless fathers strode
  By Wallace' side,
Still pressing onward, red-wat-shod,
  Or glorious died.

O, sweet are Coila's haughs an' woods,
When lintwhites chant amang the buds,
And jinkin' hares, in amorous whids,
  Their loves enjoy,   70
While thro' the braes the cushat croods
  Wi' wailfu' cry!

Ev'n winter bleak has charms to me
When winds rave thro' the naked tree;
Or frost on hills of Ochiltree
  Are hoary gray;
Or blinding drifts wild-furious flee,
  Dark'ning the day!

O Nature! a' thy shews an' forms
To feeling, pensive hearts hae charms!   80
Whether the summer kindly warms,
   Wi' life an' light,
Or winter howls, in. gusty storms,
   The lang, dark night!

The Muse, nae poet ever fand her,
Till by himsel he learn'd to wander
Adown some trottin' burn's meander,
   An' no think lang;
O sweet, to stray an' pensive ponder
   A heart-felt sang!   90

The warly race may drudge an' drive,
Hog-shouther, jundie, stretch, an' strive;
Let me fair Nature's face descrive,
   And I, wi' pleasure,
Shall let the busy, grumbling hive
   Bum owre their treasure.

Fareweel, 'my rhyme-composing brither!'
We've been owre lang unkenn'd to ither:
Now let us lay our heads thegither,
   In love fraternal;   100
May Envy wallop in a tether,
   Black fiend infernal!

While Highlandmen hate tolls an' taxes;
While moorlan' herds like guid fat braxies
While Terra Firma, on her axis,
   Diurnal turns,
Count on a friend, in faith an' practice,
   In Robert Burns.

POSTCRIPT.

My memory's no worth a preen;
I had amaist forgotten clean,   110
Ye bade me write you what they mean
   By this New-Light,
'Bout which our herds sae aft have been
   Maist like to fight.

In days when mankind were but callans
At grammar, logic, an' sic talents,
They took nae pains their speech to balance,
      Or rules to gie,
But spak their thoughts in plain, braid Lallans,
      Like you or me.   120

In thae auld times, they thought the moon,
Just like a sark, or pair o' shoon,
Wore by degrees, till her last roon,
      Gaed past their viewin',
An' shortly after she was done,
      They gat a new one.

This past for certain, undisputed;
It ne'er cam i' their heads to doubt it,
Till chiels gat up an' wad confute it,
      An' ca'd it wrang;   130
An' muckle din there was about it,
      Baith loud an' lang.

Some herds, weel learn'd upo' the beuk,
Wad threap auld folk the thing misteuk;
For 'twas the auld moon turn'd a neuk,
      An' out o' sight,
An' backlins-comin, to the leuk,
      She grew mair bright.

This was deny'd, it was affirm'd;
The herds an' hissels were alarm'd: 140
The rev'rend gray-beards rav'd an' storm'd,
      That beardless laddies
Should think they better were inform'd
      Than their auld daddies.

Frae less to mair it gaed to sticks;
Frae words an' aiths to clours an' nicks;
An' mony a fallow gat his licks,
      Wi' hearty crunt;
An' some, to learn them for their tricks,
      Were hang'd an' brunt.   150

This game was play'd in mony lands,
An' auld-light caddies bure sic hands,
That, faith, the youngsters took the sands
　　　Wi' nimble shanks;
The lairds forbad, by strict commands,
　　　Sic bluidy pranks.

But new-light herds gat sic a cowe,
Folk thought them ruin'd stick-an-stowe,
Till now amaist on ev'ry knowe
　　　Ye'll find ane plac'd;　　　160
An' some, their new-light fair avow,
　　　Just quite barefac'd.

Nae doubt the auld-light flocks are bleatin';
Their zealous herds are vex'd an' sweatin';
Mysel, I've even seen them greetin'
　　　Wi' girnin spite,
To hear the moon sae sadly lied on
　　　By word an' write.

But shortly they will cowe the louns!
Some auld-light herds in neibor-touns　　　170
Are mind't, in things they ca' balloons,
　　　To tak a flight,
An' stay ae month amang the moons,
　　　An' see them right.

Guid observation they will gie them;
An' when the auld moon 's gaun to lea'e them;
The hindmost shaird, they'll fetch it wi' them,
　　　Just i' their pouch,
An' when the new-light billies see them,
　　　I think they'll crouch!　　　180

Sae, ye observe that a' this clatter
Is naething but a 'moonshine matter';
But tho' dull-prose folk Latin splatter
　　　In logic tulzie,
I hope we bardies ken some better
　　　Than mind sic brulzie.

LETTER TO JOHN GOUDIE, KILMARNOCK,

ON THE PUBLICATION OF HIS ESSAYS.

O GOUDIE ! terror of the Whigs,
Dread o' blackcoats and rev'rend wigs,
Sour Bigotry, on her last legs,
      Girnin' looks back,
Wishin' the ten Egyptian plagues
      Wad seize you quick.

Poor gapin', glowrin' Superstition,
Wae 's me ! she 's in a sad condition ;
Fy, bring Black-Jock, her state physician,
      To see her water ;   10
Alas ! there 's ground for great suspicion
      She'll ne'er get better.

Auld Orthodoxy lang did grapple,
But now she 's got an unco' ripple ;
Haste, gie her name up i' the chapel,
      Nigh unto death ;
See how she fetches at the thrapple,
      An' gasps for breath.

Enthusiasm 's past redemption,
Gane in a galloping consumption ;   20
Not a' the quacks, with a' their gumption,
      Will ever mend her ;
Her feeble pulse gies strong presumption,
      Death soon will end her.

'Tis you and Taylor are the chief,
Wha are to blame for this mischief ;
But gin the Lord's ain folk get leave,
      A toom tar-barrel
An' twa red peats wad send relief,
      An' end the quarrel.   30

For me, my skill's but very sma',
An' skill in prose I've nane ava,
But, quietlins-wise, between us twa,
      Weel may ye speed !
An', tho' they sud you sair misca',
       Ne'er fash your head.

E'en swinge the dogs, an' thresh them siccar ;
The mair they squeal, aye chap the thicker ;
An' still, 'mang hands, a hearty bicker
      O' something stout ;—   40
It gars an author's pulse beat quicker,
       An' helps his wit !

There's naething like the honest nappy !
Where will ye e'er see men sae happy,
Or women sousy, saft, an' sappy,
      'Tween morn an' morn,
As them wha like to taste the drappie
      In glass or horn ?

I've seen me dazed upon a time,
I scarce cou'd wink or see a styme ;   50
Just ae half-mutchkin does me prime
      (Ought less is little) ;
Then back I rattle on the rhyme
      As gleg's a whittle !

———◆———

THIRD EPISTLE TO J. LAPRAIK.

Guid speed an' furder to you, Johnny,
Guid health, hale han's, and weather bonnie ;
Now when ye're nickin' down fu' cannie
      The staff o' bread,
May ye ne'er want a stoup o' bran'y
      To clear your head.

May Boreas never thresh your rigs,
Nor kick your rickles aff their legs,
Sendin' the stuff o'er muirs an' hags
   Like drivin' wrack ;   10
But may the tapmast grain that wags
   Come to the sack.

I'm bizzie too, an' skelpin' at it,
But bitter, daudin showers hae wat it ;
Sae my auld stumpie pen I gat it
   Wi' muckle wark,
An' took my jocteleg an' whatt it,
   Like ony clerk.

It's now twa month that I'm your debtor,
For your braw, nameless, dateless letter, 20
Abusin' me for harsh ill-nature
   On holy men,
While Deil a hair yoursel ye're better,
   But mair profane.

But let the kirk-folk ring their bells,
Let's sing about our noble sels ;
We'll cry nae jads frae heathen hills
   To help, or roose us,
But browster wives an' whisky stills,
   They are the Muses.   30

Your friendship, sir, I winna quat it,
An' if ye make objections at it,
Then han' in nieve some day we'll knot it,
   An' witness take,
An' when wi' usquebae we've wat it
   It winna break.

But if the beast and branks be spar'd
Till kye be gaun without the herd,
An' a' the vittel in the yard,
   An' theekit right,   40
I mean your ingle-side to guard
   Ae winter night.

Then muse-inspirin' aqua-vitae
Shall make us baith sae blithe an' witty,
Till ye forget ye're auld an' gatty,
      An' be as canty
As ye were nine years less than thretty,—
      Sweet ane an' twenty!

But stooks are cowpit wi' the blast,
An' now the sinn keeks in the west,   50
Then I maun rin amang the rest
      An' quit my chanter;
Sae I subscribe mysel in haste,
      Yours, Rab the Ranter.

————◦◦————

TO THE REV. JOHN M'MATH.

ENCLOSING A COPY OF HOLY WILLIE'S PRAYER, WHICH HE
HAD REQUESTED.

WHILE at the stook the shearers cow'r
To shun the bitter blaudin' show'r,
Or in gulravage rinnin' scour;
      To pass the time,
To you I dedicate the hour
      In idle rhyme.

My Musie, tir'd wi' mony a sonnet
On gown, an' ban', an' douce black bonnet,
Is grown right eerie now she's done it,
      Lest they shou'd blame her,   10
An' rouse their holy thunder on it,
      And anathem her.

I own 'twas rash, an' rather hardy,
That I, a simple country bardie,
Shou'd meddle wi' a pack so sturdy,
      Wha, if they ken me,
Can easy, wi' a single wordie,
      Lowse hell upon me.

But I gae mad at their grimaces,
Their sighin', cantin', grace-proud faces,　　　20
Their three-mile prayers, and half-mile graces,
　　　　　Their raxin' conscience,
Whase greed, revenge, an' pride disgraces
　　　　　Waur nor their nonsense.

There's Gawn, misca't waur than a beast,
Wha has mair honour in his breast
Than mony scores as guid's the priest
　　　　　Wha sae abus'd him:
An' may a bard no crack his jest
　　　　　What way they've used him?　30

See him the poor man's friend in need,
The gentleman in word an' deed,
An' shall his fame an' honour bleed
　　　　　By worthless skellums,
An' not a Muse erect her head
　　　　　To cowe the blellums?

O Pope, had I thy satire's darts
To gie the rascals their deserts,
I'd rip their rotten, hollow hearts,
　　　　　An' tell aloud　　　40
Their jugglin' hocus-pocus arts
　　　　　To cheat the crowd.

God knows I'm no the thing I shou'd be,
Nor am I even the thing I could be,
But, twenty times, I rather would be
　　　　　An atheist clean,
Than under gospel colours hid be,
　　　　　Just for a screen.

An honest man may like a glass,
An honest man may like a lass,　　　50
But mean revenge, an' malice fause,
　　　　　He'll still disdain,
An' then cry zeal for gospel laws,
　　　　　Like some we ken.

They tak religion in their mouth;
They talk o' mercy, grace, an' truth,
For what? to gie their malice skouth
        On some puir wight,
An' hunt him down, o'er right an' ruth,
        To ruin straight.   60

All hail, Religion, maid divine!
Pardon a muse sae mean as mine,
Who in her rough imperfect line
        Thus daurs to name thee;
To stigmatize false friends of thine
        Can ne'er defame thee.

Tho' blotcht an' foul wi' mony a stain,
An' far unworthy of thy train,
Wi' trembling voice I tune my strain
        To join wi' those,   70
Who boldly daur thy cause maintain
        In spite o' foes:

In spite o' crowds, in spite o' mobs,
In spite of undermining jobs,
In spite o' dark banditti stabs
        At worth an' merit,
By scoundrels, even wi' holy robes,
        But hellish spirit.

O Ayr, my dear, my native ground!
Within thy presbyterial bound,   80
A candid lib'ral band is found
        Of public teachers,
As men, as Christians too, renown'd,
        An' manly preachers.

Sir, in that circle you are nam'd,
Sir, in that circle you are fam'd;
An' some, by whom your doctrine's blam'd,
        (Which gies you honour)—
Even, sir, by them your heart's esteem'd,
        An' winning manner.   90

Pardon this freedom I have ta'en,
An' if impertinent I've been,
Impute it not, good sir, in ane
　　　　　　　Whase heart ne'er wrang'd ye,
But to his utmost would befriend
　　　　　　Ought that belang'd ye.

———◦◦———

TO JAMES SMITH.

Dear Smith, the sleeest pawkie thief
That e'er attempted stealth or rief,
Ye surely hae some warlock-breef
　　　　　　Owre human hearts;
For ne'er a bosom yet was prief
　　　　　　Against your arts.

For me,. I swear by sun an' moon,
And ev'ry star that blinks aboon,
Ye've cost me twenty pair o' shoon
　　　　　　Just gaun to see you;　　　　　10
And ev'ry ither pair that's done,
　　　　　　Mair taen I'm wi' you.

That auld capricious carlin', Nature.
To mak amends for scrimpit stature,
She's turn'd you aff, a human creature
　　　　　　On her first plan,
And in her freaks, on ev'ry feature,
　　　　　　She's wrote 'The Man.'

Just now I've taen the fit o' rhyme,
My barmie noddle's working prime,　　　20
My fancie yerkit up sublime
　　　　　　Wi' hasty summon:
Hae ye a leisure-moment's time
　　　　　　To hear what's comin'?

Some rhyme a neebor's name to lash ;
Some rhyme (vain thought !) for needfu' cash ;
Some rhyme to court the country clash,
       An' raise a din ;
For me, an aim I never fash ;
       I rhyme for fun.   30

The star that rules my luckless lot,
Has fated me the russet coat,
An' damn'd my fortune to the groat ;
       But, in requit,
Has blest me with a random shot
       O' country wit.

This while my notion 's taen a sklent,
To try my fate in guid, black prent ;
But still the mair I'm that way bent,
       Something cries ' Hoolie !   40
I red you, honest man, tak tent !
       Ye'll shaw your folly.

'There 's ither poets, much your betters,
Far seen in Greek, deep men o' letters,
Hae thought they had ensured their debtors
       A' future ages ;
Now moths deform in shapeless tatters
       Their unknown pages.'

Then fareweel hopes o' laurel-boughs,
To garland my poetic brows !   50
Henceforth I'll rove where busy ploughs
       Are whistling thrang,
An' teach the lanely heights an' howes
       My rustic sang.

I'll wander on, wi' tentless heed
How never-halting moments speed,
Till fate shall snap the brittle thread ;
       Then, all unknown,
I'll lay me with th' inglorious dead,
       Forgot and gone !   60

But why o' death begin a tale?
Just now we're living sound an' hale;
Then top and maintop crowd the sail,
         Heave Care o'er side!
And large, before Enjoyment's gale,
         Let's tak the tide.

This life, sae far's I understand,
Is a' enchanted fairy-land,
Where pleasure is the magic wand,
         That, wielded right,   70
Maks hours like minutes, hand in hand,
         Dance by fu' light.

The magic wand then let us wield:
For, ance that five-an'-forty's speel'd,
See, crazy, weary, joyless Eild,
         Wi' wrinkled face,
Comes hoastin', hirplin' owre the field,.
         Wi' creepin' pace.

When ance life's day draws near the gloamin',
Then fareweel vacant careless roamin';   80
An' fareweel cheerfu' tankards foamin',
         An' social noise;
An' fareweel dear deluding woman,
         The joy of joys!

O life, how pleasant is thy morning,
Young Fancy's rays the hills adorning!
Cold-pausing Caution's lesson scorning,
         We frisk away,
Like schoolboys, at th' expected warning,
         To joy and play.   90

We wander there, we wander here,
We eye the rose upon the brier,
Unmindful that the thorn is near,
         Among the leaves:
And tho' the puny wound appear,
         Short while it grieves.

Some, lucky, find a flow'ry spot,
For which they never toil'd nor swat;
They drink the sweet and eat the fat,
   But care or pain;   100
And, haply, eye the barren hut
   With high disdain.

With steady aim, some Fortune chase;
Keen hope does ev'ry sinew brace;
Thro' fair, thro' foul, they urge the race,
   And seize the prey;
Then cannie, in some cozie place,
   They close the day.

And others, like your humble servan',
Poor wights! nae rules nor roads observin', 110
To right or left, eternal swervin',
   They zig-zag on;
Till curst with age, obscure an' starvin',
   They often groan.

Alas! what bitter toil an' straining—
But truce wi' peevish, poor complaining!
Is Fortune's fickle Luna waning?
   E'en let her gang!
Beneath what light she has remaining,
   Let's sing our sang.   120

My pen I here fling to the door,
And kneel 'Ye Pow'rs!' and warm implore,
'Tho' I should wander Terra o'er,
   In all her climes,
Grant me but this, I ask no more,
   Aye rowth o' rhymes.

'Gie dreeping roasts to country lairds,
Till icicles hing frae their beards;
Gie fine braw claes to fine life-guards,
   And maids of honour;   130
And yill an' whisky gie to cairds,
   Until they sconner.

'A title, Dempster merits it;
A garter gie to Willie Pitt;
Gie wealth to some be-ledger'd cit,
   In cent per cent;
But gie me real, sterling wit,
    And I'm content.

'While ye are pleased to keep me hale,
I'll sit down o'er my scanty meal,   140
Be't water-brose, or muslin-kail,
    Wi' cheerfu' face,
As lang's the Muses dinna fail
    To say the grace.'

An anxious e'e I never throws
Behint my lug, or by my nose;
I jouk beneath misfortune's blows
    As weel's I may;
Sworn foe to sorrow, care, and prose,
    I rhyme away.   150

O ye douce folk, that live by rule,
Grave, tideless-blooded, calm, and cool,
Compar'd wi' you—O fool! fool! fool!
    How much unlike!
Your hearts are just a standing pool,
    Your lives a dyke!

Nae hare-brain'd sentimental traces,
In your unletter'd, nameless faces!
In arioso trills and graces
    Ye never stray,
But gravissimo, solemn basses,   160
    Ye hum away.

Ye are sae grave, nae doubt ye're wise;
Nae ferly tho' ye do despise
The hairum-scairum, ram-stam boys,
    The rattlin' squad:
I see you upward cast your eyes—
    Ye ken the road.

Whilst I—but I shall haud me there—
Wi' you I'll scarce gang ony where—   170
Then, Jamie, I shall say nae mair,
      But quat my sang,
Content with You to mak a pair,
      Where'er I gang.

TO GAVIN HAMILTON, ESQ., MAUCHLINE,

RECOMMENDING A BOY.

I HOLD it, Sir, my bounden duty,
To warn you how that Master Tootie,
      Alias Laird M'Gaun,
Was here to lure the lad away
'Bout whom ye spak the tither day,
      An' wad hae done 't aff han' :
But lest he learn the callan tricks,
    As faith I muckle doubt him,
Like scrapin' out auld Crummie's nicks,
    An' tellin' lies about them ;   10
    As lieve then I'd have then
      Your clerkship he should sair,
    If sae be ye may be
      Not fitted otherwhere.

Altho' I say 't, he's gleg enough,
An' 'bout a house that's rude an' rough,
      The boy might learn to swear ;
But then wi' you, he'll be sae taught,
An' get sic fair example straught,
      I hae na ony fear.   20
Ye'll catechize him every quirk,
    An' shore him weel wi' hell ;
An' gar him follow to the kirk——
    Aye when ye gang yoursel.
    If ye then, maun be then
      Frae hame this comin' Friday,
    Then please, sir, to lea'e, sir,
      The orders wi' your lady.

My word of honour I ha'e gi'en,
In Paisley John's, that night at e'en,   30
    To meet the Warld's worm :
To try to get the twa to gree,
An' name the airles an' the fee,
    In legal mode an' form :
I ken he weel a snick can draw,
    When simple bodies let him ;
An' if a Devil be at a',
    In faith he's sure to get him.
To phrase you an' praise you
    Ye ken your Laureat scorns :   40
The pray'r still, you share still,
    Of grateful Minstrel Burns.

———◆———

EPISTLE TO MR. M'ADAM,

OF CRAIGEN-GILLAN, IN ANSWER TO AN OBLIGING LETTER HE SENT IN THE COMMENCEMENT OF MY POETIC CAREER.

SIR, o'er a gill I gat your card,
    I trow it made me proud ;
'See wha taks notice o' the Bard !'
    I lap and cried fu' loud.

'Now deil-ma-care about their jaw,
    The senseless, gawkie million ;
I'll cock my nose aboon them a',
    I'm roos'd by Craigen-Gillan !'

'Twas noble, sir ; 'twas like yoursel,
    To grant your high protection :   10
A great man's smile, ye ken fu' weel,
    Is aye a blest infection.

Tho', by his banes wha in a tub
    Match'd Macedonian Sandy !
On my ain legs, thro' dirt and dub,
    I independent stand aye.

And when those legs to gude, warm kail,
  Wi' welcome canna bear me :
A lee dyke-side, a sybow-tail,
  And barley-scone shall cheer me.   20

Heaven spare you lang to kiss the breath
  O' mony flow'ry simmers !
And bless your bonnie lasses baith,—
  I'm tald they're loosome kimmers !

And God bless young Dunaskin's laird,
  The blossom of our gentry !
And may he wear an auld man's beard,
  A credit to his country.

--------•--------

EPISTLE TO MAJOR LOGAN.

Hail, thairm-inspirin', rattlin' Willie !
Though fortune's road be rough an' hilly
To every fiddling, rhyming billie,
     We never heed,
But take it like the unback'd filly,
     Proud o' her speed.

When idly govin' whyles we saunter,
Yirr, fancy barks, awa' we canter
Uphill, down brae, till some mishanter,
     Some black bog-hole,   10
Arrests us, then the scathe an' banter
     We're forced to thole.

Hale be your heart ! hale be your fiddle !
Lang may your elbuck jink and diddle,
To cheer you through the weary widdle
     O' this wild warl',
Until you on a crummock driddle
     A gray-hair'd carl.

Come wealth, come poortith, late or soon,
Heaven send your heart-strings aye in tune,　20
And screw your temper-pins aboon,
　　A fifth or mair,
The melancholious lazy croon,
　　O' cankrie care.

May still your life from day to day
Nae 'lente largo' in the play,
But 'allegretto forte' gay
　　Harmonious flow,
A sweeping, kindling, bauld strathspey—
　　Encore! Bravo!　30

A blessing on the cheery gang
Wha dearly like a jig or sang,
An' never think o' right an' wrang
　　By square an' rule,
But as the clegs o' feeling stang
　　Are wise or fool.

My hand-waled curse keep hard in chase
The harpy, hoodock, purse-proud race,
Wha count on poortith as disgrace—
　　Their tuneless hearts!　40
May fire-side discords jar a base
　　To a' their parts!

But come, your hand, my careless brither,
I' th' ither warl' if there's anither,
An' that there is I've little swither
　　About the matter;
We cheek for chow shall jog thegither,
　　I'se ne'er bid better.

We've faults and failings—granted clearly,
We're frail backsliding mortals merely,　50
Eve's bonnie squad priests wyte them sheerly
　　For our grand fa';
But still, but still, I like them dearly—
　　God bless them a'!

Ochone for poor Castalian drinkers,
When they fa' foul o' earthly jinkers,
The witching cursed delicious blinkers
      Hae put me hyte,
And gart me weet my waukrife winkers,
        Wi' girnin' spite.   60

But by yon moon!—and that's high swearin'—
An' every star within my hearin'!
An' by her een wha was a dear ane!
      I'll ne'er forget;
I hope to gie the jads a clearin'
      In fair play yet.

My loss I mourn, but not repent it,
I'll seek my pursie where I tint it;
Ance to the Indies I were wonted,
      Some cantraip hour,   70
By some sweet elf I'll yet be dinted,
      Then *vive l'amour!*

Faites mes baissemains respectueuse
To sentimental sister Susie,
An' honest Lucky; no to roose you,
      Ye may be proud
That sic a couple Fate allows ye
      To grace your blood.

Nea mair at present can I measure,
An' trowth my rhymin' ware's nae treasure; 80
But when in Ayr, some half hour's leisure,
      Be't light, be't dark,
Sir Bard will do himself the pleasure
      To call at Park.

Mossgiel, October 30, 1786.

A POETICAL EPISTLE TO A TAILOR.

WHAT ails ye now, ye lousie bitch,
To thresh my back at sic a pitch?
Losh, man! hae mercy wi' your natch,
  Your bodkin's bauld,
I didna suffer half sae much
  Frae Daddie Auld.

What tho' at times when I grow crouse,
I gi'e their wames a random pouse,
Is that enough for you to souse
  Your servant sae? 10
Gae mind your seam, ye prick-the-louse
  An' jag-the-flae!

King David o' poetic brief,
Wrought 'mang the lasses such mischief
As fill'd his after life wi' grief
  An' bloody rants,
An' yet he's rank'd amang the chief
  O' lang-syne saunts.

And maybe, Tam, for a' my cants,
My wicked rhymes, an' drucken rants, 20
I'll gie auld cloven Clooty's haunts
  An unco slip yet,
An' snugly sit amang the saunts,
  At Davie's hip yet.

But fegs! the Session says I maun
Gae fa' upo' anither plan,
Than garrin' lasses cowp the cran
  Clean heels owre body,
And sairly thole their mither's ban
  Afore the howdy. 30

This leads me on to tell for sport
How I did wi' the Session sort—
Auld Clinkum at the Inner port
  Cried three times, 'Robin!
Come hither, lad, an' answer for't,—
  Ye're blam'd for jobbin'.'

Wi' pinch I put a Sunday's face on,
An' snoov'd awa' before the Session;
I made an open fair confession,
  I scorn'd to lie;
An' syne Mess John, beyond expression,
  Fell foul o' me.

A furnicator-loun he call'd me,
An' said my fau't frae bliss expell'd me;
I own'd the tale was true he tell'd me,
  'But what the matter?'
Quo' I 'I fear unless ye geld me,
  I'll ne'er be better.'

'Geld you!' quo' he, 'and whatfor no?
If that your right hand, leg or toe,
Should ever prove your sp'ritual foe,
  You shou'd remember
To cut it aff, an' whatfor no
  Your dearest member?'

'Na, na,' quo' I, 'I'm no for that,
Gelding's nae better than 'tis ca't,
I'd rather suffer for my faut
  A hearty flewit,
As sair owre hip as ye can draw't,
  Tho' I should rue it.

'Or gin ye like to end the bother,
To please us a', I've just ae ither,
When next wi' yon lass I forgather,
  Whate'er betide it,
I'll frankly gi'e her 't a' thegither,
  An' let her guide it.'

40

50

60

But, Sir, this pleas'd them warst ava,
An' therefore, Tam, when that I saw,
I said 'Gude night,' and cam awa,
   And left the Session;   70
I saw they were resolvèd a'
   On my oppression.

ANSWER TO VERSES ADDRESSED TO THE POET

BY THE GUIDWIFE OF WAUCHOPE-HOUSE.

GUIDWIFE,
I mind it weel, in early date,
When I was beardless, young and blat
 An' first could thresh the barn,
Or haud a yokin' at the pleugh,
An' tho' forfoughten sair eneugh,
 Yet unco proud to learn,—
When first amang the yellow corn
 A man I reckon'd was,
And wi' the lave ilk merry morn
 Could rank my rig and lass,   10
  Still shearing, and clearing
   The tither stooked raw,
  Wi' claivers, an' haivers,
   Wearing the day awa,—

Ev'n then a wish! (I mind its power)
A wish that to my latest hour
 Shall strongly heave my breast;
That I for poor auld Scotland's sake,
Some usefu' plan or beuk could make,
 Or sing a sang at least.   20

The rough bur-thistle, spreading wide
 Amang the bearded bear,
I turn'd the weeder-clips aside,
 An' spar'd the symbol dear:

No nation, no station,
  My envy e'er could raise ;
A Scot still, but blot still,
  I knew nae higher praise.

But still the elements o' sang
In formless jumble, right an' wrang,   30
  Wild floated in my brain ;
Till on that hairst I said before,
My partner in the merry core,
  She rous'd the forming strain :
I see her yet, the sonsie quean,
  That lighted up my jingle,
Her witching smile, her pauky een,
  That gart my heart-strings tingle ;
    I fir'd, inspir'd,
      At ev'ry kindling keek,   40
    But bashing, and dashing,
      I fear'd aye to speak.

Health to the sex ! ilk guid chiel says,
Wi' merry dance in winter days,
  An' we to share in common :
The gust o' joy, the balm of woe,
The saul o' life, the heav'n below,
  Is rapture-giving woman.
Ye surly sumphs, who hate the name,
  Be mindfu' o' your mither :   50
She, honest woman, may think shame
  That ye're connected with her !
    Ye're wae men, ye're nae men,
      That slight the lovely dears ;
    To shame ye, disclaim ye,
      Ilk honest birkie swears.

For you, no bred to barn or byre,
Wha sweetly tune the Scottish lyre,
  Thanks to you for your line :
The marled plaid ye kindly spare,   60
By me should gratefully be ware ;
  'Twad please me to the nine.

I'd be mair vauntie o' my hap,
  Douce hingin' owre my curple,
Than ony ermine ever lap,
  Or proud imperial purple.
    Farewell then, lang hale then,
      An' plenty be your fa';
    May losses and crosses
      Ne'er at your hallan ca'.   70

EPISTLE TO HUGH PARKER.

IN this strange land, this uncouth clime,
A land unknown to prose or rhyme;
Where words ne'er crost the Muse's heckles,
Nor limpit in poetic shackles;
A land that prose did never view it,
Except when drunk he stacher't through it;
Here, ambush'd by the chimla cheek,
Hid in an atmosphere of reek,
I hear a wheel thrum i' the neuk,
I hear it—for in vain I leuk.   10
The red peat gleams, a fiery kernel,
Enhuskèd by a fog infernal;
Here, for my wonted rhyming raptures,
I sit and count my sins by chapters;
For life and spunk like ither Christians,—
I'm dwindled down to mere existence;
Wi' nae converse but Gallowa' bodies,
Wi' nae kend face but Jenny Geddes.
Jenny, my Pegasean pride!
Dowie she saunters down Nithside,   20
And ay a westlin leuk she throws,
While tears hap o'er her auld brown nose!
Was it for this, wi' canny care,
Thou bure the Bard through many a shire?
At howes or hillocks never stumbled,
And late or early never grumbled?

O, had I power like inclination,
I'd heeze thee up a constellation,
To canter with the Sagitarre,
Or loup the ecliptic like a bar;   30
Or turn the pole like any arrow;
Or, when auld Phoebus bids good-morrow,
Down the zodiac urge the race,
And cast dirt on his godship's face;
For I could lay my bread and kail
He'd ne'er cast saut upo' thy tail.
Wi' a' this care and a' this grief,
And sma', sma' prospect of relief,
And nought but peat reek i' my head,
How can I write what ye can read?   40
Tarbolton, twenty-fourth o' June,
Ye'll find me in a better tune;
But till we meet and weet our whistle,
Tak this excuse for nae epistle.

EPISTLE TO ROBERT GRAHAM, ESQ.,
OF FINTRY.

WHEN Nature her great master-piece design'd,
And fram'd her last, best work, the human mind,
Her eye intent on all the mazy plan,
She form'd of various parts the various man.
  Then first she calls the useful many forth;
Plain plodding industry, and sober worth:
Thence peasants, farmers, native sons of earth,
And merchandise' whole genus take their birth:
Each prudent cit a warm existence finds,
And all mechanics' many-apron'd kinds.   10
Some other rarer sorts are wanted yet,
The lead and buoy are needful to the net:
The caput mortuum of gross desires
Makes a material for mere knights and squires;

The martial phosphorus is taught to flow,
She kneads the lumpish philosophic dough,
Then marks the unyielding mass with grave designs,
Law, physic, politics, and deep divines:
Last, she sublimes th' Aurora of the poles,
The flashing elements of female souls.   20

The order'd system fair before her stood,
Nature, well-pleas'd, pronounc'd it very good;
But ere she gave creating labour o'er,
Half-jest, she try'd one curious labour more;
Some spumy, fiery, ignis fatuus matter,
Such as the slightest breath of air might scatter;
With arch alacrity and concious glee
(Nature may have her whim as well as we,
Her Hogarth-art perhaps she meant to show it)
She forms the thing, and christens it a Poet,—   30
Creature, tho' oft the prey of care and sorrow,
When blest to-day, unmindful of to-morrow;
A being form'd t' amuse his graver friends,
Admir'd and prais'd—and there the homage ends;
A mortal quite unfit for Fortune's strife,
Yet oft the sport of all the ills of life;
Prone to enjoy each pleasure riches give,
Yet haply wanting wherewithal to live;
Longing to wipe each tear, to heal each groan,
Yet frequent all unheeded in his own.   40

But honest Nature is not quite a Turk,
She laugh'd at first, then felt for her poor work.
Pitying the propless climber of mankind,
She cast about a standard tree to find;
And, to support his helpless woodbine state,
Attach'd him to the generous truly great—
A title, and the only one I claim,
To lay strong hold for help on bounteous Graham.

Pity the tuneful muses' hapless train,
Weak, timid landsmen on life's stormy main!   50
Their hearts no selfish stern absorbent stuff,
That never gives—tho' humbly takes enough;
The little fate allows, they share as soon,
Unlike sage proverb'd wisdom's hard wrung boon.
The world were blest did bliss on them depend:
Ah, that 'the friendly e'er should want a friend!'

Let prudence number o'er each sturdy son,
Who life and wisdom at one race begun,
Who feel by reason, and who give by rule,
(Instinct's a brute, and sentiment a fool!)   60
Who make poor 'will do' wait upon 'I should'—
We own they're prudent, but who feels they're good?
Ye wise ones, hence! ye hurt the social eye!
God's image rudely etch'd on base alloy!
But come ye who the godlike pleasure know,
Heaven's attribute distinguish'd—to bestow!
Whose arms of love would grasp the human race:
Come thou who giv'st with all a courtier's grace;
Friend of my life, true patron of my rhymes!
Prop of my dearest hopes for future times.   70
Why shrinks my soul, half-blushing, half-afraid,
Backward, abash'd to ask thy friendly aid?
I know my need, I know thy giving hand,
I crave thy friendship at thy kind command;
But there are such who court the tuneful nine—
Heavens! should the branded character be mine!
Whose verse in manhood's pride sublimely flows,
Yet vilest reptiles in their begging prose.
Mark how their lofty independent spirit
Soars on the spurning wing of injur'd merit!   80
Seek not the proofs in private life to find;
Pity the best of words should be but wind!
So to heaven's gates the lark's shrill song ascends,
But grovelling on the earth the carol ends.
In all the clam'rous cry of starving want,
They dun benevolence with shameless front;
Oblige them, patronize their tinsel lays,
They persecute you all your future days!
Ere my poor soul such deep damnation stain,
My horny fist assume the plough again;   90
The piebald jacket let me patch once more;
On eighteen-pence a week I've liv'd before.
Tho', thanks to Heaven, I dare even that last shift,
I trust, meantime, my boon is in thy gift;
That, plac'd by thee upon the wish'd-for height,
Where, man and nature fairer in her sight,
My muse may imp her wing for some sublimer flight.

TO DR. BLACKLOCK.

Wow, but your letter made me vauntie!
And are ye hale, and weel, and cantie?
I kenn'd it still your wee bit jauntie
  Wad bring ye to:
Lord send you aye as weel's I want ye,
  And then ye'll do.

The ill-thief blaw the Heron south!
And never drink be near his drouth!
He tauld mysel by word o' mouth,
  He'd tak my letter;   10
I lippen'd to the chiel in trouth,
  And bade nae better.

But aiblins honest Master Heron
Had at the time some dainty fair one,
To ware his theologic care on,
  And holy study;
And tir'd o' sauls to waste his lear on,
  E'en tried the body.

But what d'ye think, my trusty fier,
I'm turn'd a gauger—Peace be here!   20
Parnassian queans, I fear, I fear,
  Ye'll now disdain me!
And then my fifty pounds a year
  Will little gain me.

Ye glaiket, gleesome, dainty damies,
Wha by Castalia's wimplin' streamies,
Lowp, sing, and lave your pretty limbies,
  Ye ken, ye ken,
That strang necessity supreme is
  'Mang sons o' men.   30

I hae a wife and twa wee laddies,
They maun hae brose and brats o' duddies;
Ye ken yoursels my heart right proud is—
       I need na vaunt,
But I'll sned besoms—thraw saugh woodies,
       Before they want.

Lord help me thro' this warld o' care!
I'm weary sick o't late and air!
Not but I hae a richer share
       Than mony ithers;   40
But why should ae man better fare,
       And a' men brithers?

Come, Firm Resolve, take thou the van,
Thou stalk o' carl-hemp in man!
And let us mind, faint heart ne'er wan
       A lady fair;
Wha does the utmost that he can,
       Will whyles do mair.

But to conclude my silly rhyme
(I'm scant o' verse, and scant o' time)—   50
To make a happy fire-side clime
       To weans and wife,
That's the true pathos and sublime
       Of human life.

My compliments to sister Beckie;
And eke the same to honest Lucky,
I wat she is a daintie chuckie,
       As e'er tread clay!
And gratefully, my guid auld cockie,
       I'm yours for aye.   60

LETTER TO JAMES TENNANT, GLENCONNER.

AULD comrade dear and brither sinner,
How 's a' the folk about Glenconner?
How do you this blae eastlin wind,
That 's like to blaw a body blind?
For me, my faculties are frozen,
My dearest member nearly dozen'd.
I've sent you here by Johnie Simson,
Twa sage philosophers to glimpse on;
Smith, wi' his sympathetic feeling,
An' Reid, to common sense appealing.   10
Philosophers have fought an' wrangled,
An' meikle Greek an' Latin mangled,
Till wi' their logic-jargon tir'd,
An' in the depth of Science mir'd,
To common sense they now appeal,
What wives an' wabsters see an' feel.
But, hark ye, friend, I charge you strictly,
Peruse them, an' return them quickly;
For now I'm grown sae cursèd douce,
I pray an' ponder but the house;   20
My shins, my lane, I there sit roastin',
Perusing Bunyan, Brown, an' Boston;
Till by an' by, if I haud on,
I'll grunt a real Gospel-groan:
Already I begin to try it,
To cast my een up like a pyet,
When by the gun she tumbles o'er,
Flutt'ring an' gaspin' in her gore:
Sae shortly you shall see me bright,
A burning an' a shining light.   30
  My heart-warm love to guid auld Glen,
The ace an' wale of honest men:
When bending down wi' auld grey hairs,
Beneath the load of years and cares,
May He who made him still support him,
An' views beyond the grave comfort him.
His worthy fam'ly far and near,
God bless them a' wi' grace and gear!

My auld school-fellow, Preacher Willie,
The manly tar, my mason billie,   40
An' Auchenbay, I wish him joy ;
If he's a parent, lass or boy,
May he be dad, and Meg the mither
Just five-and-forty years thegither !
An' no forgetting wabster Charlie,
I'm tauld he offers very fairly.
An' Lord, remember singing Sannock,
Wi' hale-breeks, saxpence, an' a bannock.
An' next, my auld acquaintance, Nancy,
Since she is fitted to her fancy,   50
An' her kind stars hae airted till her
A good chiel wi' a pickle siller.
My kindest, best respects I sen' it,
To cousin Kate an' sister Janet ;
Tell them frae me, wi' chiels be cautious,
For, faith, they'll aiblins fin' them fashious :
To grant a heart is fairly civil,
But to grant a maidenhead's the devil.
An' lastly, Jamie, for yoursel,
May guardian angels tak a spell,   60
An' steer you seven miles south o' hell :
But first, before you see heav'n's glory,
May ye get mony a merry story,
Mony a laugh, and mony a drink,
An' aye enough o' needfu' clink.
    Now fare ye weel, an' joy be wi' you !
For my sake, this I beg it o' you,
Assist poor Simson a' ye can,
Ye'll fin' hin just an honest man ;
Sae I conclude and quat my chanter,   70
Yours, saint or sinner,
                  ROB THE RANTER.

EPISTLE TO ROBERT GRAHAM, ESQ.,
OF FINTRY:

ON THE CLOSE OF THE DISPUTED ELECTION BETWEEN SIR JAMES JOHNSTONE AND CAPTAIN MILLER, FOR THE DUMFRIES DISTRICT OF BOROUGHS.

FINTRY, my stay in worldly strife,
Friend o' my Muse, friend o' my life,
　　Are ye as idle 's I am?
Come then, wi' uncouth, kintra fleg,
O'er Pegasus I'll fling my leg,
　　And ye shall see me try him.

But where shall I go rin a ride,
That I may splatter nane beside?
　　I wad na be uncivil:
In manhood's various paths and ways　　　　10
There 's aye some doytin' body strays,
　　And *I* ride like the devil.

Thus I break off wi' a' my birr,
An' down yon dark deep alley spur,
　　Where Theologics daunder:
Alas! curst wi' eternal fogs,
And damned in everlasting bogs,
　　As sure 's the creed I'll blunder.

I'll stain a band, or jaup a gown,
Or rin my reckless guilty crown　　　　　20
　　Against the haly door.
Sair do I rue my luckless fate
When, as the muse an' deil wad hae 't,
　　I rade that road before.

Suppose I take a spurt, and mix
Amang the wilds o' Politics,
　　Electors and elected;
Where dogs at Court (sad sons of bitches!)
Septennially a madness touches,
　　Till all the land 's infected.　　　　　30

All hail! Drumlanrig's haughty Grace,
Discarded remnant of a race
      Once godlike great in story;
Thy forbears' virtues all contrasted,
The very name of Douglas blasted,
      Thine that inverted glory!

Hate, envy, oft the Douglas bore;
But thou hast superadded more,
      And sunk them in contempt;
Follies and crimes have stained the name,   40
But, Queensberry, thine the virgin claim—
      From all that's good exempt!

I'll sing the zeal Drumlanrig bears
Who left the all-important cares
      Of princes and their darlings;
And, bent on winning borough towns,
Came shaking hands wi' wabster loons,
      And kissing barefit carlins.

Combustion thro' our boroughs rode
Whistling his roaring pack abroad   50
      Of mad unmuzzled lions;
As Queensberry buff and blue unfurl'd,
And Westerha' and Hopeton hurl'd
      To every Whig defiance.

But cautious Queensberry left the war,
Th' unmannor'd dust might soil his star;
      Besides, he hated bleeding;
But left behind him heroes bright,
Heroes in Cæsarean fight,
      Or Ciceronian pleading.   60

O! for a throat like huge Mons-Meg,
To muster o'er each ardent Whig
      Beneath Drumlanrig's banner!
Heroes and heroines commix,
All in the field of politics,
      To win immortal honour.

M'Murdo and his lovely spouse,
(Th' enamour'd laurels kiss her brows!)
      Led on the loves and graces:
She won each gaping burgess' heart,   70
While he, all-conquering, play'd his part
      Among their wives and lasses.

Craigdarroch led a light-arm'd corps,
Tropes, metaphors and figures pour,
      Like Hecla streaming thunder:
Glenriddel, skill'd in rusty coins,
Blew up each Tory's dark designs,
      And bared the treason under.

In either wing two champions fought,
Redoubted Staig, who set at nought   80
      The wildest savage Tory:
And Welsh, who ne'er yet flinch'd his ground,
High-waved his magnum-bonum round
      With Cyclopean fury.

Miller brought up th' artillery ranks,
The many-pounders of the Banks,
      Resistless desolation!
While Maxwelton, that baron bold,
'Mid Lawson's port entrench'd his hold,
      And threaten'd worse damnation.   90

To these what Tory hosts oppos'd,
With these what Tory warriors clos'd,
      Surpasses my descriving:
Squadrons extended long and large,
With furious speed rush to the charge,
      Like raving devils driving.

What verse can sing, what prose narrate,
The butcher deeds of bloody fate
      Amid this mighty tulzie!
Grim Horror girn'd—pale Terror roar'd,   100
As Murther at his thrapple shor'd,
      And Hell mix'd in the brulzie.

As Highland crags by thunder cleft,
When lightnings fire the stormy lift,
   Hurl down with crashing rattle;
As flames among a hundred woods;
As headlong foam a hundred floods;
   Such is the rage of battle!

The stubborn Tories dare to die;
As soon the rooted oaks would fly 110
   Before th' approaching fellers:
The Whigs come on like Ocean's roar,
When all his wintry billows pour
   Against the Buchan Bullers.

Lo, from the shades of Death's deep night,
Departed Whigs enjoy the fight,
   And think on former daring:
The muffled murtherer of Charles
The Magna Charta flag unfurls,
   All deadly gules its bearing. 120

Nor wanting ghosts of Tory fame,
Bold Scrimgeour follows gallant Graham,
   Auld Covenanters shiver.
(Forgive, forgive, much-wrong'd Montrose!
Now death and hell engulf thy foes,
   Thou liv'st on high for ever!)

Still o'er the field the combat burns,
The Tories, Whigs, give way by turns;
   But Fate the word has spoken,
For woman's wit and strength o' man 130
Alas! can do but what they can!
   The Tory ranks are broken.

O that my een were flowing burns!
My voice a lioness that mourns
   Her darling cubs' undoing;
That I might greet, that I might cry,
While Tories fall, while Tories fly,
   And furious Whigs pursuing!

What Whig but melts for good Sir James?
Dear to his country by the names   140
      Friend, patron, benefactor!
Not Pulteney's wealth can Pulteney save!
And Hopeton falls, the generous brave!
      And Stewart, bold as Hector!

Thou, Pitt, shalt rue this overthrow;
And Thurlow growl a curse of woe;
      And Melville melt in wailing!
How Fox and Sheridan rejoice!
And Burke shall sing, 'O Prince, arise,
      Thy power is all-prevailing!'   150

For your poor friend, the Bard, afar
He only hears and sees the war,
      A cool spectator purely!
So, when the storm the forest rends,
The robin in the hedge descends,
      And sober chirps securely.

Now for my friends' and brethren's sakes,
And for my dear-loved Land o' Cakes,
      I pray with holy fire—
Lord send a rough-shod troop o' hell   160
Owre a' wad Scotland buy or sell,
      To grind them in the mire!

———•◦•———

EPISTLE TO ROBERT GRAHAM, ESQ.,

OF FINTRY.

Late crippl'd of an arm, and now a leg,
About to beg a pass for leave to beg;
Dull, listless, teas'd, dejected, and depress'd
(Nature is adverse to a cripple's rest):
Will generous Graham list to his Poet's wail?
(It soothes poor Misery, heark'ning to her tale,)

And hear him curse the light he first survey'd,
And doubly curse the luckless rhyming trade?
 Thou, Nature, partial Nature, I arraign;
Of thy caprice maternal I complain.   10
The lion and the bull thy care have found,
One shakes the forests, and one spurns the ground:
Thou giv'st the ass his hide, the snail his shell,
Th' envenom'd wasp, victorious, guards his cell.
Thy minions, kings defend, control, devour,
In all th' omnipotence of rule and power.
Foxes and statesmen, subtile wiles ensure;
The cit and polecat stink, and are secure.
Toads with their poison, doctors with their drug,
The priest and hedgehog in their robes, are snug.   20
Ev'n silly woman has her warlike arts,
Her tongue and eyes, her dreaded spear and darts.
 But Oh! thou bitter step-mother and hard,
To thy poor, fenceless, naked child—the Bard!
A thing unteachable in world's skill,
And half an idiot too, more helpless still.
No heels to bear him from the op'ning dun;
No claws to dig, his hated sight to shun; ·
No horns, but those by luckless Hymen worn,
And those, alas! not Amalthea's horn: 30
No nerves olfact'ry, Mammon's trusty cur,
Clad in rich Dulness' comfortable fur,
In naked feeling, and in aching pride,
He bears th' unbroken blast from ev'ry side:
Vampyre booksellers drain him to the heart,
And scorpion critics cureless venom dart.
 Critics—appall'd I venture on the name,
Those cut-throat bandits in the paths of fame,
Bloody dissectors, worse than ten Monroes;
He hacks to teach, they mangle to expose.   40
 His heart by causeless, wanton malice wrung,
By blockheads' daring into madness stung;
His well-won bays, than life itself more dear,
By miscreants torn, who ne'er one sprig must wear ·
Foil'd, bleeding, tortur'd in th' unequal strife,
The hapless Poet flounders on thro' life.
Till fled each hope that once his bosom fired,
And fled each Muse that glorious once inspired,

Low sunk in squalid, unprotected age,
Dead even resentment for his injur'd page,   50
He heeds or feels no more the ruthless critic's rage!
  So, by some hedge, the generous steed deceas'd,
For half-starv'd snarling curs a dainty feast;
By toil and famine wore to skin and bone,
Lies, senseless of each tugging bitch's son.
  O Dulness! portion of the truly blest!
Calm shelter'd haven of eternal rest!
Thy sons ne'er madden at the fierce extremes
Of Fortune's polar frost, or torrid beams.
If mantling high she fills the golden cup,   60
With sober selfish ease they sip it up;
Conscious the bounteous meed they well deserve,
They only wonder 'some folks' do not starve.
The grave sage hern thus easy picks his frog,
And thinks the mallard a sad worthless dog,
When disappointment snaps the clue of hope,
And thro' disastrous night they darkling grope,
With deaf endurance sluggishly they bear,
And just conclude that 'fools are fortune's care.'
So heavy, passive to the tempest's shocks,   70
Strong on the sign-post stands the stupid ox.
  Not so the idle Muses' mad-cap train,
Not such the workings of their moon-struck brain;
In equanimity they never dwell,
By turns in soaring heav'n, or vaulted hell.
  I dread thee, Fate, relentless and severe,
With all a poet's, husband's, father's fear!
Already one strong-hold of hope is lost,
Glencairn, the truly noble, lies in dust;
(Fled, like the sun eclips'd as noon appears,   80
And left us darkling in a world of tears:)
Oh! hear my ardent, grateful, selfish pray'r!
Fintry, my other stay, long bless and spare!
Thro' a long life his hopes and wishes crown,
And bright in cloudless skies his sun go down!
May bliss domestic smoothe his private path;
Give energy to life; and soothe his latest breath,
With many a filial tear circling the bed of death!

TO TERRAUGHTY, ON HIS BIRTHDAY.

HEALTH to the Maxwells' veteran Chief!
Health, aye unsour'd by care or grief:
Inspired, I turned Fate's sibyl leaf
   This natal morn,
I see thy life is stuff o' prief,
    Scarce quite half worn.

This day thou metes threescore eleven,
And I can tell that bounteous Heaven
(The second-sight, ye ken, is given
   To ilka poet)   10
On thee a tack o' seven times seven
    Will yet bestow it.

If envious buckies view wi' sorrow
Thy lengthen'd days on this blest morrow,
May desolation's lang-teeth'd harrow,
   Nine miles an hour,
Rake them, like Sodom and Gomorrah,
    In brunstane stoure.

But for thy friends,—and they are mony,
Baith honest men and lassies bonnie,—   20
May couthie fortune, kind and cannie,
   In social glee,
Wi' mornings blithe and o'enings funny
    Bless them and thee!

Fareweel, auld birkie! Lord be near ye,
And then the Deil he daurna steer ye:
Your friends aye love, your faes aye fear ye;
   For me, shame fa' me,
If neist my heart I dinna wear ye
    While BURNS they ca' me.   30

EPISTLE FROM ESOPUS TO MARIA.

FROM those drear solitudes and frowsy cells,
Where infamy with sad repentance dwells;
Where turnkeys make the jealous portal fast,
And deal from iron hands the spare repast;
Where truant 'prentices, yet young in sin,
Blush at the curious stranger peeping in;
Where strumpets, relics of the drunken roar,
Resolve to drink, nay, half to whore, no more;
Where tiny thieves not destin'd yet to swing,
Beat hemp for others, riper for the string: 10
From these dire scenes my wretched lines I date,
To tell Maria her Esopus' fate.
'Alas! I feel I am no actor here!'
'Tis real hangmen real scourges bear!
Prepare, Maria, for a horrid tale
Will turn thy very rouge to deadly pale;
Will make thy hair, tho' erst from gipsy poll'd,
By barber woven, and by barber sold,
Though twisted smooth with Harry's nicest care,
Like hoary bristles to erect and stare.   20
The hero of the mimic scene, no more
I start in Hamlet, in Othello roar;
Or, haughty Chieftain, 'mid the din of arms,
In Highland bonnet woo Malvina's charms;
While sans-culottes stoop up the mountain high,
And steal from me Maria's prying eye.
Bless'd Highland bonnet! once my proudest dress,
Now prouder still, Maria's temples press.
I see her wave thy towering plumes afar,
And call each coxcomb to the wordy war.   30
I see her face the first of Ireland's sons,
And even out-Irish his Hibernian bronze;
The crafty colonel leaves the tartan'd lines,
For other wars, where he a hero shines:
The hopeful youth, in Scottish senate bred,
Who owns a Bushby's heart without the head,

Comes 'mid a string of coxcombs to display
That *veni, vidi, vici,* is his way;
The shrinking bard adown an alley skulks,
And dreads a meeting worse than Woolwich hulks; 40
Though there his heresies in church and state
Might well award him Muir and Palmer's fate:
Still she undaunted reels and rattles on,
And dares the public like a noontide sun.
What scandal call'd Maria's jaunty stagger
The ricket reeling of a crooked swagger?
Whose spleen? e'en worse than Burns's venom when
He dips in gall unmix'd his eager pen,
And pours his vengeance in the burning line!
Who christen'd thus Maria's lyre divino   50
The idiot strum of vanity bemused,
And even th' abuse of poesy abused?
Who call'd her verse a parish workhouse, made
For motley, foundling fancies, stolen or stray'd?
A workhouse! ah, that sound awakes my woes,
And pillows on the thorn my rack'd repose!
In durance vile here must I wake and weep,
And all my frowsy couch in sorrow steep;
That straw where many a rogue has lain of yore,
And vermin'd gipsies litter'd heretofore.   60

Why, Lonsdale, thus thy wrath on vagrants pour?
Must earth no rascal, save thyself, endure?
Must thou alone in guilt immortal swell,
And make a vast monopoly of hell?
Thou know'st the virtues cannot hate thee worse;
The vices also, must they club their curse?
Or must no tiny sin to others fall,
Because thy guilt's supreme enough for all?

Maria, send me too thy griefs and cares;
In all of thee sure thy Esopus shares.   70
As thou at all mankind the flag unfurls,
Who on my fair one satire's vengeance hurls?
Who calls thee pert, affected, vain coquette,
A wit in folly, and a fool in wit?
Who says that fool alone is not thy due,
And quotes thy treacheries to prove it true?

Our force united on thy foes we'll turn,
And dare the war with all of woman born:
For who can write and speak as thou and I?
My periods that decyphering defy,   80
And thy still matchless tongue that conquers all reply.

————+————

EPISTLE TO COLONEL DE PEYSTER.

My honour'd Colonel, deep I feel
Your interest in the Poet's weal;
Ah! now sma' heart hae I to speel
    The steep Parnassus,
Surrounded thus by bolus pill,
    And potion glasses.

O what a canty warld were it,
Would pain, and care, and sickness spare it;
And fortune favour worth and merit,
    As they deserve: 10
And aye a rowth, roast beef and claret:
    Syne wha wad starve?

Dame Life, tho' fiction out may trick her,
And in paste gems and fripp'ry deck her,
Oh! flick'ring, feeble, and unsicker
    I've found her still,
Aye wav'ring like the willow wicker,
    'Tween good and ill.

Then that curst carmagnole, auld Satan,
Watches, like baudrons by a rattan,   20
Our sinfu' saul to get a claut on
    Wi' felon ire;
Syne, whip! his tail ye'll ne'er cast saut on,
    He's off like fire.

Ah Nick! ah Nick! it isna fair,
First showing us the tempting ware,
Bright wines and bonnie lasses rare,
   To put us daft;
Syne weave, unseen, thy spider snare
    O' hell's damn'd waft.   30

Poor man, the flee, aft bizzes by,
And aft as chance he comes thee nigh,
Thy auld damn'd elbow yeuks wi' joy,
   And hellish pleasure;
Already in thy fancy's eye,
   Thy sicker treasure.

Soon heels-o'er-gowdie! in he gangs,
And like a sheep-head on a tangs,
Thy girning laugh enjoys his pangs
   And murd'ring wrestle,   40
As, dangling in the wind, he hangs
   A gibbet's tassel.

But lest you think I am uncivil,
To plague you with this draunting drivel,
Abjuring a' intentions evil,
   I quat my pen:
The Lord preserve us frae the Devil!
   Amen! amen!

———◆◆———

WINTER.

The wintry wast extends his blast,
 And hail and rain does blaw;
Or the stormy north sends driving forth
 The blinding sleet and snaw:
While, tumbling brown, the burn comes down,
 And roars frae bank to brae:
And bird and beast in covert rest,
 And pass the heartless day.

'The sweeping blast, the sky o'ercast,'
  The joyless winter-day,   10
Let others fear, to me more dear
  Than all the pride of May:
The tempest's howl, it soothes my soul,
  My griefs it seems to join;
The leafless trees my fancy please,
  Their fate resembles mine!

Thou Pow'r Supreme, whose mighty scheme
  These woes of mine fulfil,
Here, firm, I rest,—they must be best,
  Because they are Thy will!   20
Then all I want (Oh! do thou grant
  This one request of mine!)
Since to enjoy thou dost deny,
  Assist me to resign.

———•———

A PRAYER IN THE PROSPECT OF DEATH.

O Thou unknown Almighty Cause
  Of all my hope and fear!
In whose dread presence, ere an hour,
  Perhaps I must appear!

If I have wander'd in those paths
  Of life I ought to shun;
As something, loudly in my breast,
  Remonstrates I have done;

Thou know'st that Thou hast formèd me
  With passions wild and strong;   10
And list'ning to their witching voice
  Has often led me wrong.

Where human weakness has come short,
  Or frailty stept aside,
Do thou, All-Good! for such Thou art,
  In shades of darkness hide.

Where with intention I have err'd,
  No other plea I have,
But Thou art good ; and Goodness still
  Delighteth to forgive.   20

STANZAS ON THE SAME OCCASION.

Why am I loath to leave this earthly scene?
  Have I so found it full of pleasing charms?
Some drops of joy with draughts of ill between ;
  Some gleams of sunshine 'mid renewing storms!
Is it departing pangs my soul alarms?
  Or Death's unlovely, dreary, dark abode?
For guilt, for guilt, my terrors are in arms ;
  I tremble to approach an angry God,
And justly smart beneath his sin-avenging rod.

Fain would I say, 'Forgive my foul offence !'   10
  Fain promise never more to disobey ;
But, should my Author health again dispense,
  Again I might desert fair virtue's way ;
Again in folly's path might go astray ;
  Again exalt the brute, and sink the man ;
Then how should I for Heavenly mercy pray,
  Who act so counter Heavenly mercy's plan?
Who sin so oft have mourn'd, yet to temptation ran?

O Thou, great Governor of all below !
  If I may dare a lifted eye to Thee,   20
Thy nod can make the tempest cease to blow,
  And still the tumult of the raging sea :
With that controlling pow'r assist ev'n me
  Those headlong furious passions to confine,
For all unfit I feel my powers to be,
  To rule their torrent in th' allowèd line ;
O, aid me with Thy help, Omnipotence Divine !

THE FIRST PSALM.

The man, in life wherever plac'd,
  Hath happiness in store,
Who walks not in the wicked's way,
  Nor learns their guilty lore:

Nor from the seat of scornful pride
  Casts forth his eyes abroad,
But with humility and awe
  Still walks before his God.

That man shall flourish like the trees
  Which by the streamlets grow;   10
The fruitful top is spread on high,
  And firm the root below.

But he whose blossom buds in guilt
  Shall to the ground be cast,
And like the rootless stubble tost
  Before the sweeping blast.

For-why that God the good adore
  Hath giv'n them peace and rest,
But hath decreed that wicked men
  Shall ne'er be truly blest.   20

———·———

A PRAYER, UNDER THE PRESSURE OF
VIOLENT ANGUISH.

O Thou great Being! what Thou art
  Surpasses me to know:
Yet sure I am, that known to Thee
  Are all Thy works below.

Thy creature here before Thee stands,
  All wretched and distrest;
Yet sure those ills that wring my soul
  Obey Thy high behest.

Sure Thou, Almighty, canst not act
  From cruelty or wrath!   10
O free my weary eyes from tears,
  Or close them fast in death!

But if I must afflicted be,
  To suit some wise design;
Then man my soul with firm resolves
  To bear and not repine!

———•———

THE FIRST SIX VERSES OF THE NINETIETH
PSALM.

O THOU, the first, the greatest friend
  Of all the human race!
Whose strong right hand has ever been
  Their stay and dwelling-place!

Before the mountains heav'd their heads
  Beneath Thy forming hand,
Before this ponderous globe itself
  Arose at Thy command;

That pow'r which rais'd and still upholds
  This universal frame,   10
From countless unbeginning time
  Was ever still the same.

Those mighty periods of years
  Which seem to us so vast,
Appear no more before Thy sight
  Than yesterday that's past.

Thou giv'st the word; Thy creature, man,
  Is to existence brought;
Again Thou say'st, 'Ye sons of men,
  Return ye into nought!'   20

Thou layest them, with all their cares,
    In everlasting sleep;
As with a flood thou tak'st them off
    With overwhelming sweep.

They flourish like the morning flow'r,
    In beauty's pride array'd;
But long ere night cut down it lies
    All wither'd and decay'd.

THE POET'S WELCOME TO HIS LOVE-BEGOTTEN DAUGHTER.

Thou 's welcome, wean! mishanter fa' me,
If ought of thee, or of thy mammy,
Shall ever daunton me, or awe me,
            My sweet wee lady,
Or if I blush when thou shalt ca' me
            Tit-ta or daddy.

Wee image of my bonnie Betty,
I fatherly will kiss and daut thee,
As dear an' near my heart I set thee
            Wi' as guid will,   10
As a' the priests had seen me get thee
            That 's out o' hell.

What tho' they ca' me fornicator,
An' tease my name in kintra clatter:
The mair they talk I'm kent the better,
            E'en let them clash;
An auld wife's tongue 's a feckless matter
            To gie ane fash.

Welcome, my bonnie, sweet wee dochter—
Tho' ye come here a wee unsought for,   20
An' tho' your comin' I hae fought for
            Baith kirk an' queir;
Yet, by my faith, ye're no unwrought for!
            That I shall swear!

Sweet fruit o' mony a merry dint,
My funny toil is now a' tint,
Sin' thou came to the warl asklent,
      Which fools may scoff at;
In my last plack thy part's be in't—
      The better half o't.   30

An' if thou be what I wad hae thee,
An' tak the counsel I shall gie thee,
A lovin' father I'll be to thee,
      If thou be spar'd;
Thro' a' thy childish years I'll ee thee,
      An' think't weel war'd.

Tho' I should be the waur bested,
Thou's be as braw an' bienly clad,
An' thy young years as nicely bred
      Wi' education,   40
As ony brat o' wedlock's bed
      In a' thy station.

Gude grant that thou may aye inherit
Thy mither's person, grace, an' merit,
An' thy poor worthless daddy's spirit,
      Without his failins;
'Twill please me mair to see and hear o't,
      Than stockit mailins.

———+·+———

ELEGY ON THE DEATH OF ROBERT RUISSEAUX.

Now Robin lies in his last lair,
He'll gabble rhyme, nor sing nae mair,
Cauld poverty, wi' hungry stare,
      Nae mair shall fear him;
Nor anxious fear, nor cankert care,
      E'er mair come near him.

To tell the truth, they seldom fasht him,
Except the moment that they crusht him;
For sune as chance or fate had husht 'em,
  Tho' e'er sae short,   10
Then wi' a rhyme or sang he lasht 'em,
  And thought it sport.

Tho' he was bred to kintra wark,
And counted was baith wight and stark,
Yet that was never Robin's mark
  To mak a man;
But tell him he was learn'd and clark,
  Ye roos'd him than!

—◆—

A DEDICATION TO GAVIN HAMILTON, ESQ.

EXPECT na, Sir, in this narration,
A fleechin', fleth'rin' Dedication,
To roose you up, an' ca' you guid,
An' sprung o' great an' noble bluid,
Because ye're sirnam'd like his Grace,
Perhaps related to the race;
Then when I'm tir'd—and sae are ye,
Wi' mony a fulsome, sinfu' lie,
Set up a face how I stop short
For fear your modesty be hurt.   10

 This may do—maun do, Sir, wi' them wha
Maun please the great folk for a wamefou;
For me! sae laigh I needna bow,
For, Lord be thankit, I can plough;
And when I downa yoke a naig,
Then, Lord be thankit, I can beg;
Sae I shall say, an' that's nae flatt'rin',
It's just sic Poet an' sic Patron.

 The Poet, some guid angel help him,
Or else, I fear, some ill ane skelp him! 20

He may do weel for a' he's done yet,
But only—he's no just begun yet.

The Patron (Sir, ye maun forgie me,
I winna lie, come what will o' me)—
On ev'ry hand it will allow'd be,
He's just—nae better than he should be.

I readily and freely grant,
He downa see a poor man want;
What's no his ain he winna tak it,
What ance he says he winna break it;   30
Ought he can lend he'll not refus't,
Till aft his guidness is abus'd;
And rascals whyles that do him wrang,
Ev'n that, he does na mind it lang:
As master, landlord, husband, father,
He does na fail his part in either.

But then, nae thanks to him for a' that;
Nae godly symptom ye can ca' that;
It's naething but a milder feature
Of our poor, sinfu', corrupt nature: 40
Ye'll get the best o' moral works,
'Mang black Gentoos and pagan Turks,
Or hunters wild on Ponotaxi,
Wha never heard of orthodoxy.
That he's the poor man's friend in need,
The gentleman in word and deed,
It's no thro' terror of damnation;
It's just a carnal inclination.

Morality, thou deadly bane,
Thy tens o' thousands thou hast slain!   50
Vain is his hope, whase stay and trust is
In moral mercy, truth, and justice!

No—stretch a point to catch a plack;
Abuse a brother to his back;
Steal thro' the winnock frae a whore,
But point the rake that taks the door:
Be to the poor like ony whunstane,
And haud their noses to the grunstane.

Ply ev'ry art o' legal thieving;
No matter—stick to sound believing.   60

Learn three-mile pray'rs, an' half-mile graces,
Wi' weel-spread looves, an' lang, wry faces;
Grunt up a solemn, lengthen'd groan,
And damn a' parties but your own;
I'll warrant then ye're nae deceiver,
A steady, sturdy, staunch believer.

O ye wha leave the springs of Calvin,
For gumlie dubs of your ain delvin!
Ye sons of heresy and error,
Ye'll some day squeal in quaking terror!   70
When vengeance draws the sword in wrath,
And in the fire throws the sheath;
When Ruin, with his sweeping besom,
Just frets till Heav'n commission gies him:
While o'er the harp pale mis'ry moans, ⎫
And strikes the ever-deep'ning tones, ⎬
Still louder shrieks, and heavier groans! ⎭

Your pardon, Sir, for this digression,
I maist forgat my Dedication;
But when divinity comes 'cross me,   80
My readers still are sure to lose me.

So, Sir, ye see 'twas nae daft vapour.
But I maturely thought it proper,
When a' my works I did review,
To dedicate them, Sir, to You:
Because (ye need na tak it ill)
I thought them something like yoursel'.

Then patronize them wi' your favour,
And your petitioner shall ever—
I had amaist said ever pray: 90
But that's a word I need na say:
For prayin' I hae little skill o't;
I'm baith dead-sweer, an wretched ill o't;
But I'se repeat each poor man's pray'r,
That kens or hears about you, Sir.

'May ne'er misfortune's gowling bark
Howl thro' the dwelling o' the Clerk!
May ne'er his gen'rous, honest heart,
For that same gen'rous spirit smart!
May Kennedy's far-honour'd name   100
Lang beet his hymeneal flame,
Till Hamiltons, at least a dizen,
Are frae their nuptial labours risen!
Five bonnie lasses round their table,
And seven braw fellows, stout an' able,
To serve their King and Country weel,
By word, or pen, or pointed steel!
May health and peace, in mutual rays,
Shine on the evening o' his days;
Till his wee, curlie John's ier-oe,   110
When ebbing life nae mair shall flow,
The last, sad, mournful rites bestow!'

I will not wind a lang conclusion
Wi' complimentary effusion:
But whilst your wishes and endeavours
Are blest with Fortune's smiles and favours,
I am, dear Sir, with zeal most fervent,
Your much indebted, humble servant.

But if (which Pow'rs above prevent)
That iron-hearted carl, Want,   120
Attended in his grim advances,
By sad mistakes, and black mischances,
While hopes, and joys, and pleasures fly him,
Make you as poor a dog as I am,
Your humble servant then no more;
For who would humbly serve the poor?
But, by a poor man's hopes in Heav'n!
While recollection's pow'r is given,
If, in the vale of human life,
The victim sad of fortune's strife,   130
I, thro' the tender gushing tear,
Should recognize my Master dear,
If friendless, low, we meet together,
Then, Sir, your hand—my Friend and Brother!

THE INVENTORY,

IN ANSWER TO THE USUAL MANDATE SENT BY A SURVEYOR OF THE TAXES, REQUIRING A RETURN OF THE NUMBER OF HORSES, SERVANTS, CARRIAGES, ETC. KEPT.

SIR, as your mandate did request,
I send you here a faithfu' list
O' gudes an' gear, an' a' my graith,
To which I'm clear to gi'e my aith.

Imprimis then, for carriage cattle,
I have four brutes o' gallant mettle,
As ever drew before a pettle;
My han' afore's a gude auld has-been,
An' wight an' wilfu' a' his days been;
My han' ahin's a weel gaun fillie,   10
That aft has borne me hame frae Killie,
An' your auld burrough mony a time,
In days when riding was nae crime—
But ance whan in my wooing pride
I like a blockhead boost to ride,
The wilfu' creature sae I pat to,
(Lord, pardon a' my sins an' that too!)
I play'd my fillie sic a shavie,
She's a' bedevil'd wi' the spavie.
My furr-ahin's a wordy beast,   20
As e'er in tug or tow was trac'd.
The fourth's, a Highland Donald hastie,
A damn'd red-wud Kilburnie blastie.
Foreby a Cowte, o' Cowte's the wale,
As ever ran afore a tail;
If he be spar'd to be a beast,
He'll draw me fifteen pun at least.

Wheel carriages I ha'e but few,
Three carts, an' twa are feckly new;
An auld wheel barrow, mair for token,   30
Ae leg, an' baith the trams, are broken;
I made a poker o' the spin'le,
An' my auld mother burnt the trin'le.

For men, I've three mischievous boys,
Run de'ils for rantin' an' for noise;

A gaudsman ane, a thrasher t'other,
Wee Davock hauds the nowte in fother.
I rule them as I ought discreetly,
An' often labour them completely.
An' aye on Sundays duly nightly,   40
I on the questions tairge them tightly;
Till faith, wee Davock's grown sae gleg,
Tho' scarcely langer than my leg
He'll screed you aff Effectual Calling,
As fast as ony in the dwalling.

I've nane in female servan' station,
(Lord keep me aye frae a' temptation!)
I ha'e nae wife, and that my bliss is,
An' ye have laid nae tax on misses;
An' then if kirk folks dinna clutch me,   50
I ken the devils dare na touch me.
Wi' weans I'm mair than weel contented,
Heav'n sent me ane mae than I wanted.
My sonsie smirking dear-bought Bess,
She stares the daddy in her face,
Enough of ought ye like but grace.
But her, my bonnie sweet wee lady,
I've paid enough for her already,
An' gin ye tax her or her mither,
B' the Lord, ye'se get them a' thegither.   60

And now, remember, Mr. Aiken,
Nae kind of license out I'm takin';
Frae this time forth, I do declare,
I'se ne'er ride horse nor hizzie mair;
Thro' dirt and dub for life I'll paidle,
Ere I sae dear pay for a saddle;
My travel a' on foot I'll shank it,
I've sturdy bearers, Gude be thankit!
The Kirk an' you may tak' you that,
It puts but little in your pat;   70
Sae dinna put me in your buke,
Nor for my ten white shillings luke.

This list wi' my ain han' I wrote it,
The day an' date as under notit:
Then know all ye whom it concerns,
Subscripsi huic—ROBERT BURNS.

Mossgiel, February 22, 1786.

ADDRESS OF BEELZEBUB

TO THE PRESIDENT OF THE HIGHLAND SOCIETY.

LONG life, my Lord, an' health be yours,
Unskaith'd by hunger'd Highland boors ;
Lord grant nae duddie desperate beggar,
Wi' dirk, claymore, or rusty trigger,
May twin auld Scotland o' a life
She likes—as lambkins like a knife.
Faith, you and Applecross were right
To keep the Highland hounds in sight !
I doubt na', they wad bid nae better
Than let them ance out owre the water ;   10
Then up amang thae lakes and seas
They'll mak' what rules and laws they please ;
Some daring Hancock, or a Franklin,
May set their Highland bluid a ranklin' ;
Some Washington again may head them,
Or some Montgomery fearless lead them,
Till God knows what may be effected
When by such heads and hearts directed ;
Poor dunghill sons of dirt and mire
May to Patrician rights aspire !   20
Nae sage North, now, nor sager Sackville,
To watch and premier o'er the pack vile ;
An' where will ye get Howes and Clintons
To bring them to a right repentance,
To cowe the rebel generation,
An' save the honour o' the nation ?
They an' be d—d ! what right hae they
To meat or sleep, or light o' day !
Far less to riches, pow'r, or freedom,
But what your lordship likes to gie them ?   30

But hear, my lord ! Glengarry, hear !
Your hand 's owre light on them, I fear ;
Your factors, grieves, trustees, and bailies,
I canna' say but they do gaylies ;
They lay aside a' tender mercies,
An' tirl the hallions to the birses ;

Yet while they're only poind't and herriet,
They'll keep their stubborn Highland spirit;
But smash them! crash them a' to spails!
An' rot the dyvors i' the jails!　　　　　　　40
The young dogs, swinge them to the labour!
Let wark an' hunger mak' them sober!
The hizzies, if they're aughtlins fawsont,
Let them in Drury Lane be lesson'd!
An' if the wives an' dirty brats
Come thiggin' at your doors an' yetts,
Flaffin' wi' duds an' grey wi' beas',
Frightin' awa your deucks an' geese,
Get out a horsewhip or a jowler,
The langest thong, the fiercest growler,　　　50
An' gar the tatter'd gypsies pack
Wi' a' their bastards on their back!
Go on, my lord! I lang to meet you,
An' in my house at hame to greet you;
Wi' common lords ye shanna mingle,
The benmost neuk beside the ingle,
At my right han' assign'd your seat
'Tween Herod's hip an' Polycrate;
Or (if you on your station tarrow)
Between Almagro and Pizarro,—　　　　　60
A seat, I'm sure, ye're weel deservin't;
An' till ye come—Your humble servant,
　　　　　　　　　　　　BEELZEBUB.

June 1, Anno Mundi 5790.

——◆——

NATURE'S LAW.

LET other heroes boast their scars,
　　The marks of sturt and strife;
And other poets sing of wars,
　　The plagues of human life;
Shame fa' the fun; wi' sword and gun
　　To slap mankind like lumber!
I sing his name and nobler fame,
　　Wha multiplies our number.

Great Nature spoke, with air benign,
  'Go on, ye human race!   10
This lower world I you resign;
  Be fruitful and increase.
The liquid fire of strong desire
  I've pour'd it in each bosom;
Here, on this hand, does mankind stand,
  And there is Beauty's blossom!'

The Hero of these artless strains,
  A lowly Bard was he,
Who sung his rhymes in Coila's plains
  With meikle mirth an' glee;   20
Kind Nature's care had given his share,
  Large, of the flaming current;
And, all devout, he never sought
  To stem the sacred torrent.

He felt the powerful, high behest,
  Thrill, vital, thro' and thro';
And sought a correspondent breast
  To give obedience due;
Propitious Powers screen'd the young flow'rs,
  From mildews of abortion;   30
And lo! the bard, a great reward,
  Has got a double portion!

Auld, cantie Coil may count the day,
  As annual it returns,
The third of Libra's equal sway,
  That gave another Burns,
With future rhymes, in other times,
  To emulate his sire;
To sing auld Coil in nobler style
  With more poetic fire.   40

Ye Powers of peace, and peaceful song,
  Look down with gracious eyes;
And bless auld Coila, large and long,
  With multiplying joys.

Long may she stand to prop the land,
  The flow'r of ancient nations ;
And Burnses spring, her fame to sing,
  To endless generations !

---+--

TO MR. JOHN KENNEDY.

Now Kennedy, if foot or horse
E'er bring you in by Mauchline Corss,
Lord ! man, there 's lasses there wad force
    A hermit's fancy,
And down the gate in faith they're worse
    And mair unchancy.

But, as I'm sayin', please step to Dow's
And taste sic gear as Johnny brews,
Till some bit callan brings me news ,
    That you are there,   10
And if we dinna had a bouze
    I'se ne'er drink mair.

It 's no I like to sit an' swallow,
Then like a swine to puke an' wallow,
But gie me just a true good fallow
    Wi' right ingine,
And spunkie ance to make us mellow,
    And then we'll shine.

Now if ye're ane o' warl's folk,
Wha rate the wearer by the cloak,
An' sklent on poverty their joke,   20
    Wi' bitter sneer,
Wi' you no friendship I will troke,
    Nor cheap nor dear.

But if, as I'm informèd weel,
Ye hate as ill 's the very deil,
The flinty hearts that canna feel—
            Come, Sir, here 's tae you ;
Hae ! there 's my haun' ; I wiss you weel,
            And gude be wi' you.   30

——•◦•——

THE CALF.

TO THE REV. MR. JAMES STEVEN, ON HIS TEXT,

' And ye shall go forth, and grow up as calves of the stall.'—Mal. iv. 2.

RIGHT, Sir ! your text I'll prove it true,
    Tho' Heretics may laugh ;
For instance, there 's yoursel just now,
    God knows, an unco Calf !

And should some Patron be so kind,
    As bless you wi' a kirk,
I doubt na, Sir, but then we'll find,
    Ye're still as great a Stirk.

But, if the Lover's raptur'd hour,
    Shall ever be your lot,   10
Forbid it, ev'ry heavenly Power,
    You e'er should be a Stot !

Tho', when some kind, connubial Dear,
    Your but-and-ben adorns,
The like has been that you may wear
    A noble head of horns.

And, in your lug, most reverend James,
    To hear you roar and rowte,
Few men o' sense will doubt your claims
    To rank amang the Nowte.   20

And when ye're number'd wi' the dead,
  Below a grassy hillock,
Wi' justice they may mark your head—
  'Here lies a famous Bullock!'

—+—

LINES ON AN INTERVIEW WITH LORD DAER.

THIS wot ye all whom it concerns,
I, Rhymer Robin, alias Burns,
      October twenty-third,
A ne'er to be forgotten day,
Sae far I sprachled up the brae,
      I dinner'd wi' a Lord.

I've been at drunken writers' feasts,
Nay, been bitch-fou 'mang godly priests,
      Wi' rev'rence be it spoken!
I've even join'd the honour'd jorum,   10
When mighty Squireships of the quorum
      Their hydra drouth did sloken.

But wi' a Lord—stand out my shin;
A Lord—a Peer—an Earl's son,
      Up higher yet, my bonnet!
And sic a Lord!—lang Scotch ells twa,
Our Peerage he o'erlooks them a',
      As I look o'er my sonnet.

But O for Hogarth's magic pow'r!
To show Sir Bardie's willyart glow'r,   20
      And how he star'd and stammer'd,
When govin', as if led wi' branks,
An' stumpin' on his ploughman shanks,
      He in the parlour hammer'd.

I sidling shelter'd in a nook,
An' at his Lordship steal't a look,
　　Like some portentous omen;
Except good sense and social glee,
An' (what surprised me) modesty,
　　I markèd nought uncommon.　　　　30

I watch'd the symptoms o' the Great,
The gentle pride, the lordly state,
　　The arrogant assuming;
The fient a pride, nae pride had he,
Nor sauce, nor state that I could see,
　　Mair than an honest ploughman.

Then from his lordship I shall learn
Henceforth to meet with unconcern
　　One rank as weel 's another;
Nae honest worthy man need care　　　　40
To meet with noble youthful Daer,
　　For he but meets a brother.

LYING AT A REVEREND FRIEND'S HOUSE
ONE NIGHT

THE AUTHOR LEFT THE FOLLOWING VERSES IN THE ROOM
WHERE HE SLEPT.

O Thou dread Pow'r, who reign'st above,
　　I know Thou wilt me hear
When for this scene of peace and love,
　　I make my pray'r sincere.

The hoary sire—the mortal stroke,
　　Long, long be pleas'd to spare;
To bless his little filial flock,
　　And show what good men are.

She, who her lovely offspring eyes
 With tender hopes and fears,   10
O bless her with a mother's joys,
 But spare a mother's tears!

Their hope, their stay, their darling youth,
 In manhood's dawning blush—
Bless him, thou God of love and truth,
 Up to a parent's wish.

The beauteous, seraph sister-band,
 With earnest tears I pray,
Thou know'st the snares on ev'ry hand,
 Guide Thou their steps alway.   20

When soon or late they reach that coast,
 O'er life's rough ocean driven,
May they rejoice, no wand'rer lost,
 A family in Heaven!

THE FAREWELL.

Farewell, old Scotia's bleak domains,
Far dearer than the torrid plains
 Where rich ananas blow!
Farewell, a mother's blessing dear!
A brother's sigh! a sister's tear!
 My Jean's heart-rending throe!
Farewell, my Bess! tho' thou'rt bereft
 Of my parental care,
A faithful brother I have left,
 My part in him thou'lt share!   10
  Adieu too, to you too,
   My Smith, my bosom frien';
  When kindly you mind me,
   O then befriend my Jean!

When bursting anguish tears my heart,
From thee, my Jeany, must I part?
  Thou weeping answ'rest 'no!'
Alas! misfortune stares my face,
And points to ruin and disgrace;
  I for thy sake must go!
Thee, Hamilton, and Aiken dear,
  A grateful, warm adieu!
I, with a much-indebted tear,
  Shall still remember you!
    All-hail then the gale then,
      Wafts me from thee, dear shore!
    It rustles, and whistles,
      I'll never see thee more!

20

---- •• ----

INSCRIPTION ON THE TOMBSTONE

ERECTED BY BURNS TO THE MEMORY OF FERGUSSON.

No sculptur'd marble here, nor pompous lay,
  'No storied urn nor animated bust;'
This simple stone directs pale Scotia's way
  To pour her sorrows o'er her Poet's dust.

She mourns, sweet tuneful youth, thy hapless fate:
  Tho' all the powers of song thy fancy fir'd,
Yet Luxury and Wealth lay by in State,
  And thankless·starv'd what they so much admir'd.

This humble tribute with a tear he gives,
  A brother Bard, who can no more bestow:
But dear to fame thy Song immortal lives,
  A nobler monument than Art can show.

10

VERSES WRITTEN UNDER THE PORTRAIT OF FERGUSSON THE POET,

IN A COPY OF THAT AUTHOR'S WORKS PRESENTED TO A YOUNG LADY IN EDINBURGH, MARCH 19, 1787.

CURSE on ungrateful man, that can be pleas'd,
And yet can starve the author of the pleasure!
O thou, my elder brother in misfortune,
By far my elder brother in the Muses,
With tears I pity thy unhappy fate!
Why is the Bard unpitied by the world,
Yet has so keen a relish of its pleasures?

ON SCARING SOME WATER FOWL

IN LOCH-TURIT, A WILD SCENE AMONG THE HILLS OF OCHTERTYRE.

WHY, ye tenants of the lake,
For me your wat'ry haunt forsake?
Tell me, fellow-creatures, why
At my presence thus you fly?
Why disturb your social joys,
Parent, filial, kindred ties?—
Common friend to you and me,
Nature's gifts to all are free:
Peaceful keep your dimpling wave,
Busy feed, or wanton lave;   10
Or, beneath the sheltering rock,
Bide the surging billow's shock.

Conscious, blushing for our race,
Soon, too soon, your fears I trace.
Man, your proud, usurping foe,
Would be lord of all below;

Plumes himself in Freedom's pride,
Tyrant stern to all beside.
   The eagle, from the cliffy brow,
Marking you his prey below,   20
In his breast no pity dwells,
Strong Necessity compels.
But Man, to whom alone is giv'n
A ray direct from pitying Heav'n,
Glories in his heart humane—
And creatures for his pleasure slain.
   In these savage, liquid plains,
Only known to wand'ring swains,
Where the mossy riv'let strays,
Far from human haunts and ways;   30
All on Nature you depend,
And life's poor season peaceful spend.
   Or, if man's superior might
Dare invade your native right,
On the lofty ether borne,
Man with all his pow'rs you scorn;
Swiftly seek, on clanging wings,
Other lakes and other springs;
And the foe you cannot brave,
Scorn at least to be his slave.   40

WRITTEN WITH A PENCIL

OVER THE CHIMNEY-PIECE IN THE PARLOUR OF THE INN AT KENMORE, TAYMOUTH.

ADMIRING Nature in her wildest grace,
These northern scenes with weary feet I trace;
O'er many a winding dale and painful steep,
Th' abodes of covey'd grouse and timid sheep,
My savage journey, curious, I pursue,
Till fam'd Bredalbane opens to my view.
The meeting cliffs each deep-sunk glen divides,
The woods, wild scatter'd, clothe their ample sides;

Th' outstretching lake, embosom'd 'mong the hills,
The eye with wonder and amazement fills ;   10
The Tay meand'ring sweet in infant pride,
The palace rising on his verdant side ;
The lawns wood-fringed in Nature's native taste,
The hillocks dropt in Nature's careless haste ;
The arches striding o'er the new-born stream ;
The village, glittering in the noontide beam—

*   *   *   *   *   *

Poetic ardours in my bosom swell,
Lone wand'ring by the hermit's mossy cell :
The sweeping theatre of hanging woods ;
Th' incessant roar of headlong tumbling floods—   20

*   *   *   *   *   *

Here Poesy might wake her heav'n-taught lyre,
And look through Nature with creative fire ;
Here, to the wrongs of Fate half reconcil'd,
Misfortune's lighten'd steps might wander wild ;
And Disappointment, in these lonely bounds,
Find balm to soothe her bitter, rankling wounds :
Here heart-struck Grief might heav'nward stretch her scan,
And injur'd Worth forget and pardon man.

*   *   *   *   *   *

——+——

WRITTEN WITH A PENCIL

STANDING BY THE FALL OF FYERS, NEAR LOCH-NESS.

AMONG the heathy hills and ragged woods
The roaring Fyers pours his mossy floods ;
Till full he dashes on the rocky mounds,
Where, thro' a shapeless breach, his stream resounds.
As high in air the bursting torrents flow,
As deep recoiling surges foam below,
Prone down the rock the whitening sheet descends,
And viewless Echo's ear, astonished, rends.

Dim-seen, thro' rising mists and ceaseless show'rs,
The hoary cavern, wide-surrounding, lours.   10
Still thro' the gap the struggling river toils,
And still, below, the horrid cauldron boils—

*   *   *   *   *   *

---♦♦---

ON THE DEATH OF ROBERT DUNDAS, ESQ.

OF ARNISTON, LATE LORD PRESIDENT OF THE COURT OF SESSION.

Lone on the bleaky hills the straying flocks
Shun the fierce storms among the sheltering rocks;
Down from the rivulets, red with dashing rains,
The gathering floods burst o'er the distant plains;
Beneath the blasts the leafless forests groan;
The hollow caves return a sullen moan.

Ye hills, ye plains, ye forests, and ye caves,
Ye howling winds, and wintry swelling waves!
Unheard, unseen, by human ear or eye,
Sad to your sympathetic glooms I fly;   10
Where to the whistling blast and water's roar,
Pale Scotia's recent wound I may deplore.

O heavy loss, thy country ill could bear!
A loss these evil days can ne'er repair!
Justice, the high vicegerent of her God,
Her doubtful balance eyed, and sway'd her rod;
Hearing the tidings of the fatal blow,
She sunk, abandon'd to the wildest woe.

Wrongs, injuries, from many a darksome den,
Now gay in hope explore the paths of men: 20
See from his cavern grim Oppression rise,
And throw on Poverty his cruel eyes;
Keen on the helpless victim see him fly,
And stifle, dark, the feebly bursting cry:

Mark ruffian Violence, distain'd with crimes,
Rousing elate in these degenerate times ;
View unsuspecting Innocence a prey,
As guileful Fraud points out the erring way :
While subtile Litigation's pliant tongue
The life-blood equal sucks of Right and Wrong : 30
Hark, injured Want recounts th' unlisten'd tale,
And much-wrong'd Mis'ry pours th' unpitied wail !

Ye dark waste hills, and brown unsightly plains,
To you I sing my grief-inspirèd strains :
Ye tempests, rage ! ye turbid torrents, roll !
Ye suit the joyless tenor of my soul.
Life's social haunts and pleasures I resign ;
Be nameless wilds and lonely wanderings mine,
To mourn the woes my country must endure,
That wound degenerate ages cannot cure. 40

ON THE DEATH OF SIR JAMES HUNTER BLAIR.

THE lamp of day, with ill-presaging glare,
  Dim, cloudy, sunk beneath the western wave ;
Th' inconstant blast howl'd thro' the dark'ning air,
  And hollow whistled in the rocky cave.

Lone as I wander'd by each cliff and dell,
  Once the lov'd haunts of Scotia's royal train ;
Or mus'd where limpid streams, once hallow'd, well ;
  Or mould'ring ruins mark the sacred fane.

Th' increasing blast roar'd round the beetling rocks,
  The clouds swift-wing'd flew o'er the starry sky, 10
The groaning trees untimely shed their locks,
  And shooting meteors caught the startled eye.

The paly moón rose in the livid east,
  And 'mong the cliffs disclos'd a stately Form,
In weeds of woe, that frantic beat her breast,
  And mix'd her wailings with the raving storm.

Wild to my heart the filial pulses glow,
   'Twas Caledonia's trophied shield I view'd:
Her form majestic droop'd in pensive woe,
   The lightning of her eye in tears imbued.   20

Revers'd that spear, redoubtable in war,
   Reclin'd that banner, erst in fields unfurl'd,
That like a deathful meteor gleam'd afar,
   And brav'd the mighty monarchs of the world.

'My patriot son fills an untimely grave!'
   With accents wild and lifted arms she cried;
'Low lies the hand that oft was stretch'd to save,
   Low lies the heart that swell'd with honest pride!

'A weeping country joins a widow's tear,
   The helpless poor mix with the orphan's cry;   30
The drooping arts surround their patron's bier,
   And grateful science heaves the heartfelt sigh.

'I saw my sons resume their ancient fire;
   I saw fair Freedom's blossoms richly blow;
But, ah! how hope is born but to expire!
   Relentless fate has laid their guardian low.

'My patriot falls: but shall he lie unsung,
   While empty greatness saves a worthless name?
No; every Muse shall join her tuneful tongue,
   And future ages hear his growing fame.   40

'And I will join a mother's tender cares,
   Thro' future times to make his virtues last,
That distant years may boast of other Blairs,'—
   She said, and vanish'd with the sweeping blast.

PROLOGUE,

SPOKEN BY MR. WOODS, ON HIS BENEFIT-NIGHT, MONDAY,
APRIL 16. 1787.

When by a generous public's kind acclaim,
That dearest meed is granted—honest fame;
When here your favour is the actor's lot,
Nor even the man in private life forgot;
What breast so dead to heav'nly virtue's glow,
But heaves impassion'd with the grateful throe?
  Poor is the task to please a barb'rous throng,
It needs no Siddons' power in Southern's song:
But here an ancient nation, fam'd afar
For genius, learning high, as great in war—   10
Hail, Caledonia! name for ever dear!
Before whose sons I'm honour'd to appear!
Where every science, every nobler art,
That can inform the mind, or mend the heart,
Is known; as grateful nations oft have found,
Far as the rude barbarian marks the bound.
Philosophy, no idle, pedant dream,
Here holds her search, by heaven-taught Reason's beam;
Here History paints with elegance and force,
The tide of Empire's fluctuating course;   20
Here Douglas forms wild Shakespeare into plan,
And Harley rouses all the god in man.
When well-form'd taste and sparkling wit unite,
With manly love, or female beauty bright
(Beauty, where faultless symmetry and grace
Can only charm us in the second place)—
Witness my heart, how oft with panting fear,
As on this night, I've met these judges here!
But still the hope Experience taught to live,
Equal to judge—you're candid to forgive.   30
No hundred-headed Riot here we meet,
With decency and law beneath his feet,
Nor Insolence assumes fair Freedom's name;
Like Caledonians, you applaud or blame.

O Thou, dread Power! whose empire-giving hand
Has oft been stretch'd to shield the honour'd land,
Strong may she glow with all her ancient fire;
May every son be worthy of his sire;
Firm may she rise with generous disdain
At Tyranny's, or direr Pleasure's chain;   40
Still self-dependent in her native shore,
Bold may she brave grim Danger's loudest roar,
Till Fate the curtain drop on worlds to be no more.

PROLOGUE

SPOKEN AT THE THEATRE, DUMFRIES, ON NEW YEAR'S DAY
EVENING [1790].

No song nor dance I bring from yon great city
That queens it o'er our taste—the more's the pity;
Tho', by-the-by, abroad why will you roam?
Good sense and taste are natives here at home:
But not for panegyric I appear,
I come to wish you all a good New-Year!
Old Father Time deputes me here before ye,
Not for to preach, but tell his simple story:
The sage grave Ancient cough'd, and bade me say,
'You're one year older this important day.'   10
If wiser too—he hinted some suggestion,
But 'twould be rude, you know, to ask the question;
And with a would-be roguish leer and wink,
Said, 'Sutherland, in one word, bid them *think*!'
Ye sprightly youths quite flush with hope and spirit,
Who think to storm the world by dint of merit,
To you the dotard has a deal to say,
In his sly, dry, sententious, proverb way!
He bids you mind, amid your thoughtless rattle,
That the first blow is ever half the battle;   20
That tho' some by the skirt may try to snatch him;
Yet by the forelock is the hold to catch him;
That whether doing, suffering, or forbearing,
You may do miracles by persevering.

Last, tho' not least in love, ye youthful fair,
Angelic forms, high Heaven's peculiar care!
To you old Bald-pate smoothes his wrinkled brow,
And humbly begs you'll mind the important—*Now!*
To crown your happiness he asks your leave,
And offers bliss to give and to receive.   30

For our sincere, tho' haply weak endeavours,
With grateful pride we own your many favours;
And howsoe'er our tongues may ill reveal it,
Believe our glowing bosoms truly feel it.

PROLOGUE

FOR MR. SUTHERLAND'S BENEFIT-NIGHT, DUMFRIES.

WHAT needs this din about the town o' Lon'on,
How this new play an' that new sang is comin'?
Why is outlandish stuff sae meikle courted?
Does nonsense mend like brandy, when imported?
Is there nae poet, burning keen for fame,
Will try to gie us sangs and plays at hame?
For comedy abroad he need na toil,
A fool and knave are plants of every soil;
Nor need he hunt as far as Rome and Greece
To gather matter for a serious piece;   10
There's themes enow in Caledonian story,
Would show the tragic muse in a' her glory.
Is there no daring Bard will rise, and tell
How glorious Wallace stood, how hapless fell?
Where are the Muses fled that could produce
A drama worthy o' the name o' Bruce;
How here, even here, he first unsheath'd the sword
'Gainst mighty England and her guilty lord;
And after mony a bloody, deathless doing,
Wrench'd his dear country from the jaws of ruin?   20
O for a Shakespeare or an Otway scene,
To draw the lovely, hapless Scottish Queen!
Vain all th' omnipotence of female charms
'Gainst headlong, ruthless, mad Rebellion's arms.

She fell, but fell with spirit truly Roman,
To glut the vengeance of a rival woman;
A woman, tho' the phrase may seem uncivil,
As able and as wicked as the devil!
One Douglas lives in Home's immortal page,
But Douglases were heroes every age: 30
And tho' your fathers, prodigal of life,
A Douglas follow'd to the martial strife,
Perhaps, if bowls row right, and Right succeeds,
Ye yet may follow where a Douglas leads!

As ye hae generous done, if a' the land
Would tak the Muses' servants by the hand;
Not only hear, but patronize, befriend them,
And where ye justly can commend, commend them;
And aiblins when they winna stand the test,
Wink hard, and say the folks hae done their best!   40
Would a' the land do this, then I'll be cation
Ye'll soon hae poets o' the Scottish nation
Will gar Fame blaw until her trumpet crack,
And warsle time, an' lay him on his back!

For us and for our stage should ony spier,
'Whase aught thae chiels maks a' this bustle here?
My best leg foremost, I'll set up my brow.
We hae the honour to belong to you!
We're your ain bairns, e'en guide us as ye like,
But like good mithers, shore before ye strike—   50
And gratefu' still I hope ye'll ever find us,
For a' the patronage and meikle kindness
We've got frae a' professions, sets and ranks:
God help us! we're but poor—ye'se get but thanks.

————◆————

THE RIGHTS OF WOMAN.

PROLOGUE SPOKEN BY MISS FONTENELLE ON HER BENEFIT-
NIGHT. [NOV. 26, 1792.]

WHILE Europe's eye is fix'd on mighty things,
The fate of Empires, and the fall of Kings;
While quacks of State must each produce his plan,
And even children lisp the Rights of Man;

Amid the mighty fuss just let me mention,
The Rights of Woman merit some attention.
  First, in the Sexes' intermix'd connexion,
One sacred Right of Woman is, Protection.
The tender flower that lifts its head, elate,
Helpless, must fall before the blasts of Fate,   10
Sunk on the earth, defac'd its lovely form,
Unless your shelter ward th' impending storm.
  Our second Right—but needless here is caution,
To keep that Right inviolate 's the fashion,
Each man of sense has it so full before him,
He'd die before he'd wrong it—'tis Decorum.
There was, indeed, in far less polished days,
A time, when rough rude man had naughty ways;
Would swagger, swear, get drunk, kick up a riot,
Nay, even thus invade a Lady's quiet!   20
Now, thank our stars! those Gothic times are fled;
Now, well-bred men—and you are all well-bred!
Most justly think (and we are much the gainers)
Such conduct neither spirit, wit, nor manners.
  For Right the third, our last, our best, our dearest,
That Right to fluttering female hearts the nearest,
Which even the Rights of Kings in low prostration
Most humbly own—'tis dear, dear admiration!
In that blest sphere alone we live and move;
There taste that life of life—immortal love.   30
Sighs, tears, smiles, glances, fits, flirtations, airs,
'Gainst such an host what flinty savage dares?
When awful Beauty joins with all her charms,
Who is so rash as rise in rebel arms?
  Then truce with kings, and truce with constitutions,
With bloody armaments and revolutions!
Let Majesty your first attention summon,
Ah! ça ira! THE MAJESTY OF WOMAN!

ADDRESS, SPOKEN BY MISS FONTENELLE,

ON HER BENEFIT-NIGHT, DECEMBER 4, 1793, AT THE THEATRE, DUMFRIES.

STILL anxious to secure your partial favour,
And not less anxious, sure, this night, than ever,
A Prologue, Epilogue, or some such matter,
'Twould vamp my bill, said I, if nothing better;
So sought a Poet, roosted near the skies,
Told him I came to feast my curious eyes;
Said nothing like his works was ever printed;
And last, my Prologue-business slily hinted.
'Ma'am, let me tell you,' quoth my man of rhymes,
'I know your bent—these are no laughing times: 10
Can you—but, Miss, I own I have my fears—
Dissolve in pause, and sentimental tears?
With laden sighs, and solemn-rounded sentence,
Rouse from his sluggish slumbers fell Repentance,
Paint Vengeance as he takes his horrid stand,
Waving on high the desolating brand,
Calling the storms to bear him o'er a guilty land?'
     I could no more—askance the creature eyeing,
D'ye think, said I, this face was made for crying?
I'll laugh, that's poz—nay, more, the world shall know it;
And so, your servant! gloomy Master Poet!   21
     Firm as my creed, Sirs, 'tis my fix'd belief,
That Misery's another word for Grief;
I also think—so may I be a bride!
That so much laughter, so much life enjoy'd.
     Thou man of crazy care and ceaseless sigh,
Still under bleak Misfortune's blasting eye;
Doom'd to that sorest task of man alive—
To make three guineas do the work of five:
Laugh in Misfortune's face—the beldam witch!   30
Say you'll be merry, tho' you can't be rich.
     Thou other man of care, the wretch in love,
Who long with jiltish arts and airs hast strove;
Who, as the boughs all temptingly project,
Measur'st in desperate thought—a rope—thy neck—

Or, where the beetling cliff o'erhangs the deep,
Peerest to meditate the healing leap:
Would'st thou be cur'd, thou silly, moping elf?
Laugh at her follies—laugh e'en at thyself:
Learn to despise those frowns now so terrific,   40
And love a kinder: that's your grand specific.
  To sum up all, be merry, I advise;
And as we're merry, may we still be wise.

ON SEEING MISS FONTENELLE

IN A FAVOURITE CHARACTER.

SWEET naïveté of feature,
  Simple, wild, enchanting elf,
Not to thee, but thanks to Nature,
  Thou art acting but thyself.

Wert thou awkward, stiff, affected,
  Spurning nature, torturing art;
Loves and graces all rejected,
  Then indeed thou'dst act a part.

ODE, SACRED TO THE MEMORY OF
MRS. OSWALD.

DWELLER in yon dungeon dark,
Hangman of creation! mark
Who in widow-weeds appears,
Laden with unhonour'd years,
Noosing with care a bursting purse,
Baited with many a deadly curse!

STROPHE.

View the wither'd beldam's face—
Can thy keen inspection trace
Aught of humanity's sweet melting grace?

Note that eye, 'tis rheum o'erflows,   10
Pity's flood there never rose.
See those hands, ne'er stretch'd to save
Hands that took—but never gave.
Keeper of Mammon's iron chest,
Lo, there she goes, unpitied and unblest;
She goes, but not to realms of everlasting rest!

ANTISTROPHE.

Plunderer of armies, lift thine eyes
(Awhile forbear, ye torturing fiends!)—
Seest thou whose step unwilling hither bends?
No fallen angel, hurl'd from upper skies;   20
'Tis thy trusty quondam mate,
Doom'd to share thy fiery fate,
She, tardy, hell-ward plies.

EPODE.

And are they of no more avail,
Ten thousand glitt'ring pounds a year?
In other worlds can Mammon fail,
Omnipotent as he is here?
O, bitter mock'ry of the pompous bier,
While down the wretched vital part is driv'n!
The cave-lodg'd beggar, with a conscience clear,   30
Expires in rags, unknown, and goes to Heav'n.

—◦◦—

ELEGY ON THE YEAR 1788.

For Lords or Kings I dinna mourn,
E'en let them die—for that they're born:
But oh! prodigious to reflec'!
A Towmont, Sirs, is gane to wreck!
O Eighty-eight, in thy sma' space
What dire events hae taken place!
Of what enjoyments thou hast reft us!
In what a pickle thou hast left us!

The Spanish empire's tint a head,
And my auld teethless Bawtie's dead!   10
The tulzie's sair 'tween Pitt an' Fox,
An' our gudewife's wee birdy cocks;
The tane is game, a bludie devil,
But to the hen-birds unco civil;
The tither's something dour o' treadin,
But better stuff ne'er claw'd a midden.

Ye ministers, come mount the poupit,
An' cry till ye be hearse an' roupet,
For Eighty-eight he wish'd you weel,
And gied you a' baith gear an' meal;   20
E'en mony a plack, and mony a peck,
Ye ken yoursels, for little feck.

Ye bonnie lasses, dight your een,
For some o' you hae tint a frien';
In Eighty-eight, ye ken, was ta'en
What ye'll ne'er hae to gie again.

Observe the very nowt an' sheep,
How dowf and daviely they creep;
Nay, even the yirth itsel does cry,
For E'mbrugh wells are grutten dry.   30

O Eighty-nine, thou's but a bairn,
An' no owre auld, I hope, to learn!
Thou beardless boy, I pray tak care,
Thou now hast got thy daddie's chair,
Nae hand-cuff'd, mizzl'd, hap-shackl'd Regent,
But, like himsel, a full free agent.
Be sure ye follow out the plan
Nae waur than he did, honest man:
As muckle better as you can.

January 1, 1789.

ON SEEING A WOUNDED HARE LIMP BY ME,

WHICH A FELLOW HAD JUST SHOT AT.

INHUMAN man! curse on thy barb'rous art,
  And blasted be thy murder-aiming eye;
  May never pity soothe thee with a sigh,
Nor ever pleasure glad thy cruel heart!

Go, live, poor wanderer of the wood and field,
  The bitter little that of life remains;
  No more the thickening brakes and verdant plains
To thee shall home, or food, or pastime yield.

Seek, mangled wretch, some place of wonted rest,
  No more of rest, but now thy dying bed!   10
  The sheltering rushes whistling o'er thy head,
The cold earth with thy bloody bosom prest.

Perhaps a mother's anguish adds its woe;
  The playful pair crowd fondly by thy side:
  Ah, helpless nurslings! who will now provide
That life a mother only can bestow?

Oft as by winding Nith, I, musing, wait
  The sober eve, or hail the cheerful dawn.
  I'll miss thee sporting o'er the dewy lawn,
And curse the ruffian's aim, and mourn thy hapless fate.

———————◆◆———————

THE SELKIRK GRACE.

SOME hae meat, and canna eat,
  And some wad eat that want it;
But we hae meat and we can eat,
  And sae the Lord be thankit.

II.

Songs and Ballads.

— ·· —

MARY MORISON.

O MARY, at thy window be,
  It is the wish'd, the trysted hour!
Those smiles and glances let me see,
  That make the miser's treasure poor:
How blythely wad I bide the stoure,
  A weary slave frae sun to sun.
Could I the rich reward secure,
  The lovely Mary Morison.

Yestreen, when to the trembling string
  The dance gaed thro' the lighted ha'.   10
To thee my fancy took its wing,
  I sat, but neither heard nor saw:
Tho' this was fair, and that was braw.
  And yon the toast of a' the town.
I sigh'd, and said amang them a',
  'Ye are na Mary Morison.'

O Mary, canst thou wreck his peace,
  Wha for thy sake wad gladly die?
Or canst thou break that heart of his.
  Whase only faut is loving thee?   20
If love for love thou wilt na gie,
  At least be pity to me shown!
A thought ungentle canna be
  The thought o' Mary Morison.

MY LOVE IS LIKE A RED RED ROSE.

My love is like a red red rose
　　That's newly sprung in June:
My love is like the melodie
　　That's sweetly play'd in tune.

So fair art thou, my bonnie lass,
　　So deep in love am I:
And I will love thee still, my dear,
　　Till a' the seas gang dry.

Till a' the seas gang dry, my dear,
　　And the rocks melt wi' the sun:　　　10
And I will love thee still, my dear,
　　While the sands o' life shall run.

And fare thee weel, my only love.
　　And fare thee weel awhile!
And I will come again, my love,
　　Tho' it were ten thousand mile.

———————

AFTON WATER.

Flow gently, sweet Afton, among thy green braes,
Flow gently, I'll sing thee a song in thy praise;
My Mary's asleep by thy murmuring stream,
Flow gently, sweet Afton, disturb not her dream.

Thou stock-dove whose echo resounds thro' the glen,
Ye wild whistling blackbirds in yon thorny den,
Thou green-crested lapwing, thy screaming forbear,
I charge you disturb not my slumbering fair.

How lofty, sweet Afton, thy neighbouring hills,
Far mark'd with the courses of clear winding rills ;   10
There daily I wander as noon rises high,
My flocks and my Mary's sweet cot in my eye.

How pleasant thy banks and green valleys below,
Where wild in the woodlands the primroses blow ;
There oft as mild ev'ning weeps over the lea,
The sweet-scented birk shades my Mary and me.

Thy crystal stream, Afton, how lovely it glides,
And winds by the cot where my Mary resides ;
How wanton thy waters her snowy feet lave,
As gathering sweet flow'rets she stems thy clear wave.   20

Flow gently, sweet Afton, among thy green braes,
Flow gently, sweet river, the theme of my lays ;
My Mary's asleep by thy murmuring stream,
Flow gently, sweet Afton, disturb not her dream.

———••———

GO FETCH TO ME A PINT O' WINE.

Go fetch to me a pint o' wine,
    An' fill it in a silver tassie ;
That I may drink, before I go,
    A service to my bonnie lassie.
The boat rocks at the pier o' Leith,
    Fu' loud the wind blaws frae the ferry,
The ship rides by the Berwick-law,
    And I maun leave my bonnie Mary.

The trumpets sound, the banners fly,
    The glittering spears are rankèd ready ;   10
The shouts o' war are heard afar,
    The battle closes thick and bloody ;
But it's no the roar o' sea or shore
    Wad mak me langer wish to tarry ;
Nor shout o' war that's heard afar,
    It's leaving thee, my bonnie Mary.

HIGHLAND MARY.

YE banks, and braes, and streams around
 The castle o' Montgomery,
Green be your woods, and fair your flowers,
 Your waters never drumlie!
There simmer first unfauld her robes,
 And there the langest tarry;
For there I took the last fareweel
 O' my sweet Highland Mary.

How sweetly bloom'd the gay green birk,
 How rich the hawthorn's blossom,   10
As underneath their fragrant shade
 I clasp'd her to my bosom!
The golden hours on angel wings
 Flew o'er me and my dearie;
For dear to me as light and life
 Was my sweet Highland Mary.

Wi' mony a vow, and lock'd embrace,
 Our parting was fu' tender;
And, pledging aft to meet again,
 We tore oursels asunder;   20
But oh! fell death's untimely frost,
 That nipt my flower sae early!
Now green's the sod, and cauld's the clay,
 That wraps my Highland Mary!

O pale, pale now, those rosy lips,
 I aft have kiss'd sae fondly!
And closed for aye the sparkling glance,
 That dwelt on me sae kindly!
And mould'ring now in silent dust,
 That heart that lo'ed me dearly!   30
But still within my bosom's core
 Shall live my Highland Mary.

TO MARY IN HEAVEN.

THOU lingering star, with lessening ray,
  That lov'st to greet the early morn,
Again thou usherest in the day
  My Mary from my soul was torn.
O Mary! dear departed shade!
  Where is thy place of blissful rest?
Seest thou thy lover lowly laid?
  Hear'st thou the groans that rend his breast?

That sacred hour can I forget?
  Can I forget the hallow'd grove,   10
Where by the winding Ayr we met,
  To live one day of parting love?
Eternity will not efface
  Those records dear of transports past;
Thy image at our last embrace—
  Ah! little thought we 'twas our last!

Ayr gurgling kiss'd his pebbled shore,
  O'erhung with wild woods, thickening green;
The fragrant birch, and hawthorn hoar,
  Twin'd amorous round the raptur'd scene.   20
The flowers sprang wanton to be prest,
  The birds sang love on ev'ry spray,
Till too too soon, the glowing west
  Proclaim'd the speed of wingèd day.

Still o'er these scenes my memory wakes,
  And fondly broods with miser care!
Time but the impression deeper makes,
  As streams their channels deeper wear.
My Mary, dear departed shade!
  Where is thy blissful place of rest?   30
Seest thou thy lover lowly laid?
  Hear'st thou the groans that rend his breast?

MY NANNIE O.

BEHIND yon hills where Lugar flows,
  'Mang moors an' mosses many O,
The wintry sun the day has clos'd,
  And I'll awa' to Nannie O.

The westlin wind blaws loud an' shill,
  The night's baith mirk and rainy O;
But I'll get my plaid, an' out I'll steal,
  An' owre the hill to Nannie O.

My Nannie's charming, sweet, an' young:
  Nae artfu' wiles to win ye O: 10
May ill befa' the flattering tongue
  That wad beguile my Nannie O.

Her face is fair, her heart is true,
  As spotless as she's bonnie O:
The opening gowan, wat wi' dew,
  Nae purer is than Nannie O.

A country lad is my degree,
  An' few there be that ken me O;
But what care I how few they be,
  I'm welcome aye to Nannie O.   20

My riches a's my penny-fee,
  An' I maun guide it cannie O;
But warl's gear ne'er troubles me,
  My thoughts are a' my Nannie O.

Our auld Guidman delights to view
  His sheep an' kye thrive bonnie O;
But I'm as blythe that hauds his pleugh,
  An' has nae care but Nannie O.

Come weel, come woe, I care na by,
  I'll tak what Heav'n will send me O;   30
Nae ither care in life have I,
  But live, an' love my Nannie O.

AE FOND KISS.

AE fond kiss, and then we sever!
Ae fareweel, alas, for ever!
Deep in heart-wrung tears I'll pledge thee,
Warring sighs and groans I'll wage thee.
Who shall say that fortune grieves him
While the star of hope she leaves him?
Me, nae cheerfu' twinkle lights me,
Dark despair around benights me.

I'll ne'er blame my partial fancy,
Naething could resist my Nancy;   10
But to see her was to love her,
Love but her, and love for ever.
Had we never lov'd sae kindly,
Had we never lov'd sae blindly,
Never met—or never parted,
We had ne'er been broken-hearted.

Fare thee weel, thou first and fairest!
Fare thee weel, thou best and dearest!
Thine be ilka joy and treasure,
Peace, enjoyment, love, and pleasure.   20
Ae fond kiss, and then we sever;
Ae fareweel, alas, for ever!
Deep in heart-wrung tears I'll pledge thee,
Warring sighs and groans I'll wage thee.

————◆————

MY NANNIE'S AWA.

Now in her green mantle blythe Nature arrays,
And listens the lambkins that bleat o'er the braes,
While birds warble welcomes in ilka green shaw;
But to me it's delightless—my Nannie's awa.

The snaw-drap and primrose our woodlands adorn,
And violets bathe in the weet o' the morn:
They pain my sad bosom, sae sweetly they blaw,
They mind me o' Nannie—and Nannie's awa

Thou laverock that springs frae the dews o' the lawn
The shepherd to warn o' the grey-breaking dawn,   10
And thou, mellow mavis, that hails the night-fa',
Gie over for pity—my Nannie's awa.

Come autumn sae pensive, in yellow and gray,
And soothe me wi' tidings o' nature's decay;
The dark, dreary winter, and wild-driving snaw,
Alane can delight me—now Nannie's awa.

YE BANKS AND BRAES.

Ye banks and braes o' bonnie Doon,
    How can ye bloom sae fresh and fair?
How can ye chant, ye little birds,
    And I sae weary fu' o' care?
Thou'lt break my heart, thou warbling bird,
    That wantons thro' the flowering thorn:
Thou minds me o' departed joys,
    Departed never to return.

Aft hae I rov'd by bonnie Doon,
    To see the rose and woodbine twine;   10
And ilka bird sang o' its love,
    And fondly sae did I o' mine.
Wi' lightsome heart I pu'd a rose,
    Fu' sweet upon its thorny tree;
And my fause lover stole my rose,
    But ah! he left the thorn wi' me.

(Earlier Version.)

Ye flowery banks o' bonnie Doon,
    How can ye blume sae fair?
How can ye chant, ye little birds,
    And I sae fu' o' care?

Thou'll break my heart, thou bonnie bird,
   That sings upon the bough ;
Thou minds me o' the happy days,
   When my fause luve was true.

Thou'll break my heart, thou bonnie bird,
   That sings beside thy mate ;   10
For sae I sat, and sae I sang,
   And wist na o' my fate.

Aft hae I rov'd by bonnie Doon,
   To see the wood-bine twine,
And ilka bird sang o' its love,
   And sae did I o' mine.

Wi' lightsome heart I pu'd a rose
   Frae off its thorny tree :
But my fause luver staw my rose,
   And left the thorn wi' me.   20

Wi' lightsome heart I pu'd a rose
   Upon a morn in June ;
And sae I flourish'd on the morn,
   And sae was pu'd ere noon.

———◦◦———

OF A' THE AIRTS.

Of a' the airts the wind can blaw,
   I dearly like the west,
For there the bonnie lassie lives,
   The lassie I lo'e best :
There 's wild woods grow, and rivers row,
   And mony a hill between ;
But day and night my fancy's flight
   Is ever wi' my Jean.

I see her in the dewy flowers,
  I see her sweet and fair :
I hear her in the tunefu' birds,
  I hear her charm the air :
There 's not a bonnie flower that springs
  By fountain, shaw, or green ;
There 's not a bonnie bird that sings,
  But minds me o' my Jean.

——◆◆——

THERE WAS A LAD.

THERE was a lad was born in Kyle,
But what'n a day o' what'n a style
I doubt it 's hardly worth the while
  To be sae nice wi' Robin.

    Robin was a rovin' boy,
      Rantin' rovin', rantin' rovin' ;
    Robin was a rovin' boy,
      Rantin' rovin' Robin.

Our monarch's hindmost year but ane
Was five-and-twenty days begun,
'Twas then a blast o' Janwar win'
  Blew hansel in on Robin.

The gossip keekit in his loof,
Quo' scho, Wha lives will see the proof,
This waly boy will be nae coof,
  I think we'll ca' him Robin.

He'll hae misfortunes great and sma',
But aye a heart aboon them a' ;
He'll be a credit till us a'.
  We'll a' be proud o' Robin.

But sure as three times three mak nine,
I see by ilka score and line,
This chap will dearly like our kin',
  So leeze me on thee, Robin.

Guid faith, quo' scho, I doubt you, Sir,
Ye gar the lasses lie aspar,
But twenty fauts ye may hae waur,
   So blessings on thee, Robin!

    Robin was a rovin' boy,
      Rantin' rovin', rantin' rovin';   30
    Robin was a rovin' boy,
      Rantin' rovin' Robin.

GREEN GROW THE RASHES.

GREEN grow the rashes O,
   Green grow the rashes O;
The sweetest hours that e'er I spend,
   Are spent amang the lasses O!

There's nought but care on ev'ry han',
   In ev'ry hour that passes O;
What signifies the life o' man,
   An' 'twere na for the lasses O.

The warly race may riches chase,
   An' riches still may fly them O;   10
An' tho' at last they catch them fust,
   Their hearts can ne'er enjoy them O.

But gie me a canny hour at e'en,
   My arms about my dearie O;
An' warly cares, an' warly men,
   May a' gae tapsalteerie O!

For you sae douce, ye sneer at this,
   Ye're nought but senseless asses O:
The wisest man the warl' saw,
   He dearly lov'd the lasses O.   20

Auld nature swears, the lovely dears
   Her noblest work she classes O;
Her prentice han' she tried on man,
   An' then she made the lasses O.

FOR A' THAT AND A' THAT.

Is there, for honest poverty,
  That hangs his head, and a' that?
The coward-slave, we pass him by,
  We dare be poor for a' that!
    For a' that, and a' that,
      Our toils obscure, and a' that;
    The rank is but the guinea stamp;
      The man's the gowd for a' that.

What tho' on hamely fare we dine,
  Wear hodden-gray, and a' that;   10
Gie fools their silks, and knaves their wine,
  A man's a man for a' that.
    For a' that, and a' that,
      Their tinsel show, and a' that;
    The honest man, tho' e'er sae poor,
      Is King o' men for a' that.

Ye see yon birkie, ca'd a lord,
  Wha struts, and stares, and a' that;
Tho' hundreds worship at his word,
  He's but a coof for a' that: 20
    For a' that, and a' that,
      His riband, star, and a' that,
    The man of independent mind,
      He looks and laughs at a' that.

A prince can mak a belted knight,
  A marquis, duke, and a' that;
But an honest man's aboon his might,
  Guid faith he mauna fa' that!
    For a' that, and a' that,
      Their dignities, and a' that,   30
    The pith o' sense, and pride o' worth,
      Are higher rank than a' that.

Then let us pray that come it may,
　　As come it will for a' that ;
That sense and worth, o'er a' the earth,
　　May bear the gree, and a' that.
　　　　For a' that and a' that,
　　　　　It 's coming yet, for a' that,
　　　　That man to man the warld o'er
　　　　　Shall brothers be for a' that.　　　40

-- ◦◦ --

AULD LANG SYNE.

SHOULD auld acquaintance be forgot,
　　And never brought to min' ?
Should auld acquaintance be forgot,
　　And auld lang syne ?

　　　　For auld lang syne, my dear.
　　　　　For auld lang syne,
　　　　We'll tak a cup o' kindness yet,
　　　　　For auld lang syne.

We twa hae run about the braes,
　　And pu'd the gowans fine ;　　　　　　10
But we've wander'd mony a weary foot
　　Sin' auld lang syne.

We twa hae paidled i' the burn,
　　From morning sun till dine ;
But seas between us braid hae roar'd
　　Sin' auld lang syne.

And there 's a hand, my trusty fiere,
　　And gie 's a hand o' thine ;
And we'll tak a right guid-willie waught,
　　For auld lang syne.　　　　　　　20

And surely ye'll be your pint-stowp,
　　And surely I'll be mine ;
And we'll tak a cup o' kindness yet
　　For auld lang syne.

SCOTS WHA HAE.

ROBERT BRUCE'S ADDRESS TO HIS ARMY, BEFORE
THE BATTLE OF BANNOCKBURN.

Scots, wha hae wi' Wallace bled,
Scots, wham Bruce has aften led,
Welcome to your gory bed,
    Or to victorie.

Now 's the day, and now 's the hour ;
See the front o' battle lour !
See approach proud Edward's power—
    Chains and slaverie !

Wha will be a traitor knave ?
Wha can fill a coward's grave ?   10
Wha sae base as be a slave ?
    Let him turn and flee !

Wha for Scotland's King and law
Freedom's sword will strongly draw,
Freeman stand, or freeman fa' ?
    Let him follow me !

By oppression's woes and pains !
By your sons in servile chains !
We will drain our dearest veins,
    But they shall be free !   20

Lay the proud usurpers low !
Tyrants fall in every foe !
Liberty 's in every blow !
    Let us do or die !

Glossary.

A', *all.*
Aback, *behind, at the back.*
Abeigh, *at bay, aloof.*
Aboon, *above.*
Abread, *abroad.*
Abreed, *in breadth.*
Acquent, *acquainted.*
A'-day, *all day.*
Adle, *putrid water.*
Ae, *one; only.*
Aff, *off.*
Aff-hand, *at once, offhand.*
Aff-loof, *off-hand.*
Afore, *before.*
Aften, *often.*
A-gley, *off the right line; asquint.*
Aiblins, *perhaps.*
Aik, *an oak.*
Aiken, *oaken.*
Ain, *own.*
Air or ear', *early.*
Airl-penny, *earnest-money.*
Airles, *earnest-money.*
Airn, *iron.*
Airns, *irons.*
Airt, *point or quarter of the earth or sky; to direct.*
Airted, *directed.*
Aith, *an oath.*
Aiths, *oaths.*
Aits, *oats.*
Aiver, *horse no longer young.*
Aizle, *a hot cinder.*
Ajee, *to the one side.*
Alake! *alas!*
Alang, *along.*
Amaist, *almost.*
Amang, *among.*
An', *and.*
An 's, *and is.*
Ance, *once.*
Ane, *one.*
Anes, *ones.*
Anither, *another.*
Arles, *earnest-money.*

Ase, *ashes.*
Asklent, *obliquely.*
Asteer, *astir.*
A'thegither, *altogether.*
Athort, *athwart.*
Atween, *between.*
Aught, *eight.*
Aughteen, *eighteen.*
Aughtlins, *anything, in the least.*
Auld, *old.*
Auldfarran, *sagacious, old-fashioned.*
Aumous, *alms.*
Ava, *at all.*
Awa, *away.*
Awe, *to owe.*
Awee, *a little time.*
Awfu', *awful.*
Awnie, *bearded* (said of barley).
Aye, *always.*
Ayont, *beyond.*

Ba', *a ball.*
Babie-clouts, *baby-clothes.*
Backets, *buckets.*
Bade, *endured, desired.*
Baggie (dim. of *bag', the stomach.*
Bainie, *bony, muscular.*
Bairns, *children.*
Bairntime, *all the children of one mother.*
Baith, *both.*
Bakes, *biscuits.*
Ballats, *ballads.*
Ban', *band.*
Banes, *bones.*
Bang, *a stroke.*
Bannet, *a bonnet.*
Bannock, *a cake of oatmeal bread, or a barley scon.*
Bardie, dim of *bard.*
Barefit, *barefooted.*
Barkit, *barked.*
Barin' (of a stone-pit), *laying bare the stones by removing the turf.*
Barley-bree, *ale or whisky.*

Barm, *yeast.*

Barmie, *frothing or fermenting.*

Batch, *a party or quantity.*

Batts, *the botts or colic.*

Bauckie-bird, *the bat.*

Baudrons, *a cat.*

Bauks, *cross-beams.*

Bauk-en', *end of a bank or cross-beam.*

Bauld, *bold.*

Baumy, *balmy.*

Bawk, *a ridge left untilled.*

Baws'nt, *having a white stripe down the face.*

Bawtie, *a familiar name for a dog.*

Be't, *be it.*

Bear, *barley.*

Beets, *adds fuel to fire, incites.*

Befa', *befall.*

Behint, *behind.*

Belang, *belong to.*

Beld, *bald.*

Bellyfu', *bellyfull.*

Belyve, *by-and-by.*

Ben, *the inner or best room of a cottage.*

Benmost bore, *the innermost recess, or hole.*

Bethankit, *the grace after meat.*

Beuk, *a book.* Devil's pictur'd beuks, *cards.*

Bicker, *a wooden bowl,* or *a short race.*

Bid, *to wish, or ask.*

Bide, *to stand, to endure.*

Biel, *a habitation.*

Bield, *shelter.*

Bien (*of a person*) *well-to-do ;* (*of a place*) *comfortable.*

Big, *to build.*

Biggin, *building.*

Bill, *a bull.*

Billie, *a comrade, fellow, young man.*

Bings, *heaps.*

Birk, *the birch.*

Birken-shaw, *a small birch-wood.*

Birkie, *a lively, young, forward fellow.*

Birring, *whirring.*

Birses, *bristles.*

Bit, *crisis ;* also, *little.*

Bizzard gled, *a kite.*

Bizz, *a bustling haste.*

Bizzy, *busy.*

Bizzies, *buzzes.*

Black Bonnet, *the elder.*

Blae, *blue, sharp, keen.*

Blastie, *a term of contempt.*

Blastit, *blasted, withered.*

Blate, *shamefaced, sheepish.*

Blather, *bladder.*

Blaud, *to slap ; a quantity of anything.*

Blaudin', *pelting or beating.*

Blaw, *to blow, to brag.*

Blawn, *blown.*

Bleerit, *bleared.*

Bleeze, *a blaze.*

Bleezin, *blazing.*

Blellum, *an idle talking fellow.*

Blether, *the bladder, nonsense.*

Blethers, *nonsense.*

Bleth'rin, *talking idly.*

Blin', *blind.*

Blink, *a short time, a look.*

Blinks, *looks smilingly.*

Blinkers, *a term of contempt, pretty girls.*

Blinkin, *smirking.*

Blitter, *the mire snipe.*

Blue-gown, *one of those beggars who get annually on the king's birthday a blue cloak or gown with a badge, a beggar, a bedesman.*

Blude, *blood.*

Bluid, *blood.*

Blume, *bloom.*

Bluntie, *a stupid person.*

Blypes, *peelings.*

Bocked, *vomited.*

Boddle, *a small coin, a halfpenny.*

Bogles, *hobgoblins.*

Bonnie, *beautiful.*

Bonnocks, *thick cakes of oatmeal bread.*

Boord, *board.*

Boortrees, *elder bushes.*

Boost, *must needs.*

Bore, *a hole or rent.*

Bouk, *a corpse.*

Bouses, *drinks.*

Bow-hough'd, *crook-thighed.*

Bow-kail, *cabbage.*

Bow't, *crooked.*

Brae, *the slope of a hill.*

Braid, *broad.*

Braid-claith, *broad-cloth.*

Braid Scots, *broad Scotch.*

Braik, *a harrow to break the clods.*

Braing't, *rushed forward.*

Brak, *did break.*

Brak's, *broke his.*

Brankie, *well attired.*

Branks, *a kind of wooden curb for horses.*

Brany, *brandy.*

Brash, *a sudden short illness.*

Brats, *clothes, aprons.*

Brattle, *a shore race.*

Braw, *handsome, gaily dressed.*

Brawly, *perfectly.*

Braxies, *sheep which have died of a disease called 'braxy.'*

Breastie, *dim. of breast.*

Breastit, *did spring up or forward.*

Brechan, *a horse-collar.*

Breckan, *fern.*

Bree, *juice, liquid.*

Breeks, *breeches.*

Brent, *high, smooth, unwrinkled.*

Brief, *a writing.*

Brig, *bridge.*

Brither, *brother.*

Brithers, *brothers.*

Brock, *a badger.*

Brogue, *a trick.*

Broo, *water, broth.*

Brooses, *races at country weddings who shall first reach the bridegroom's house on returning from church.*

Browst, *as much malt liquor as brewed at a time.*

Browster-wives, *ale-house wives.*

Brugh, *burgh.*

Brulzie, *a broil.*

Brunstane, *brimstone.*

Brunt, *burned.*

Brust, *burst.*

Buckie, *dim. of buck.*

Buckskin, *an inhabitant of Virginia.*

Buff, *to beat.*

Bughtin-time, *the time of collecting the ewes in the pens to be milked.*

Buirdly, *strong, well-knit.*

Buke, *book.*

Bum, *to hum.*

Bum-clock, *a beetle.*

Bumming, *humming.*

Bummle, *a blunderer.*

Bunker, *a seat in a window.*

Burdies, *damsels.*

Bure, *bore, did bear.*

Burns, *streams.*

Burnie, *streamlet.*

Burnewin, *i.e. burn the wind, a blacksmith.*

Bur-thistle, *the spear-thistle.*

Busking, *dressing, decorating.*

Buskit, *dressed.*

Busks, *adorns.*

Buss, *a bush.*

Bussle, *a bustle.*

But, *without, or wanting.*

But an' ben, *kitchen and parlour.*

By, *past, apart.*

By attour, *in the neighbourhood, outside.*

Byke, *a bee-hive.*

Byre, *cowshed.*

Ca', *to drive ; a call.*

Ca'd, *named, driven ; calved.*

Ca't, *called.*

Ca' throu', *to push forward.*

Cadger, *a carrier or travelling dealer.*

Cadie, *a fellow.*

Caff, *chaff.*

Cairds, *tinkers.*

Calf-ward, *a small inclosure for calves.*

Callans, *boys.*

Callor, *fresh.*

Callet, *a trull.*

Cam, *came.*

Cankert, *cankered.*

Cankrie, *cankered.*

Canna, *cannot.*

Cannie, *carefully, softly.*

Cantie, *cheerful, lively.*

Cantrip, *a charm, a spell.*

Cape-stane, *cope-stone.*

Carl, *a carle, a man.*

Carlin, *an old woman.*

Cartes, *cards for playing.*

Cartie, *dim. of cart.*

Caudrons, *cauldrons.*

Cauf, *a calf.*

Cauk and keel, *chalk and ruddle.*

Cauld, *cold.*

Caups, *wooden bowl.*

Causey, *causeway.*

Cavie, *a hen-coop.*

Chamer, *chamber*.
Change-house, *a tavern*.
Chap, *a fellow*.
Chapman, *a pedlar*.
Chaup, *a blow*.
Cheek for chow, *cheek for jowl*.
Cheep, *chirp*.
Chiels, *young fellows*.
Chimla, *chimney*.
Chittering, *shivering with cold*.
Chows, *chews*.
Chuckie, dim. of *chuck*.
Christendie, *Christendom*.
Chuffie, *fat-faced*.
Clachan, *a hamlet*.
Claise, *clothes*.
Claith, *cloth*.
Claithing, *clothing*.
Claiver, *to talk idly or foolishly*.
Clamb, *clomb*.
Clankie, *a sharp stroke*.
Clap, *a clapper*.
Clark, *clerky, scholarly*.
Clarkit, *wrote*.
Clarty, *dirty*.
Clash, *gossip ; to talk*.
Clatter, *to talk idly*.
Claught, *clutched*.
Claughtin, *catching at anything greedily*.
Claut, *to snatch at, to lay hold of a quantity scraped together*.
Claver, *clover*.
Clavers, *idle stories*.
Claw, *scratch*.
Cleckin, *a brood*.
Cleed, *to clothe*.
Cleeding, *clothing*.
Cleek, *to seize*.
Cleekit, *linked themselves*.
Clegs, *gad-flies*.
Clink, *to rhyme; money*.
Clinkin, *sitting down neatly*.
Clinkumbell, *the church bell-ringer*.
Clips, *shears*.
Clishmaclaver, *idle talk*.
Clockin-time, *hatching-time*.
Cloot, *the hoof*.
Clootie, *Satan*.
Clours, *bumps or swellings after a blow*.
Clouts, *clothes*.
Clout, *patch*.

Clud, *a cloud*.
Coble, *a fishing-boat*.
Cock, *to erect*.
Cocks, *good fellows*.
Cod, *a pillow*.
Co'er, *to cover*.
Coft, *bought*.
Cog, *a wooden dish*.
Coggie, dim. of *cog*.
Coila, *from Kyle, a district of Ayrshire*.
Collie, *a sheep dog*.
Collieshangie, *an uproar, a quarrel*.
Commans, *commandments*.
Compleenin, *complaining*.
Cood, *the cud*.
Coofs, *fools, ninnies*.
Cookit, *appeared and disappeared, or peeped*.
Coost, *did cast*.
Cootie, *a kind of large spoon, or spade; also, feathered at the ancles*.
Corbies, *crows*.
Corn't, *fed with oats*.
Corss, *the market-cross*.
Couldna, *could not*.
Countra, *country*.
Couthie, *kindly, loving, comfortable*.
Cowp, *to tumble over*.
Cowpit, *tumbled*.
Cow'rin, *cowering*.
Cowr, *to cover*.
Cour, *to cover*.
Cowte, *a colt*.
Crack, *a story or harangue, talk*.
Crackin, *conversing, gossiping*.
Craft, *a croft*.
Craig, *the throat*.
Craigs, *crags*.
Craigy, *craggy*.
Craiks, *landrails*.
Crambo-clink, *rhymes, or doggerel verses crammed together*.
Crambo-jingle, *rhymes*.
Crankous, *fretful*.
Cranreuch, *hoar frost*.
Crap, *crop*.
Craw, *to crow*.
Creel, *a basket*.
Creepie-chair, *the chair or stool of repentance*.
Creeshie, *greasy*.

Crocks, *old sheep.*
Croods, *coos.*
Crooded, *cooed.*
Cronie, *an intimate comrade.*
Croon, *a groaning or murmuring sound.*
Crouchie, *crook-backed.*
Crouse, *brisk and bold.*
Crowdie, *porridge.*
Crowdie-time, *breakfast-time.*
Crummock, *a staff with a crooked head.*
Crump, *crisp or crumbly.*
Crunt, *a blow on the head with a cudgel.*
Cuddle, *to fondle.*
Cuifs, *blockheads, ninnies.*
Cummock, *a staff with a crooked head.*
Curch, *a female head-dress.*
Curchie, *a curtsy.*
Curmurring, *rumbling.*
Curpin, *the crupper.*
Curple, *the crupper.*
Cushats, *wood-pigeons.*
Custock, *the heart of a stalk of cabbage.*
Cutty, *short.*

Daddie, *father.*
Daes't, *stupefied, dazed.*
Daffin, *merriment.*
Daft, *foolish, sportive.*
Dails, *deals of wood.*
Daimen-icker, *an occasional ear of corn.*
Damies, dim. *of dames.*
Dam, *water.*
Dang, *knocked, pushed.*
Danton, *to subdue.*
Darklins, *darkling.*
Daud, *a lump; to knock.*
Daudin', *pelting.*
Dauntingly, *dauntlessly.*
Daur, *to dare.*
Daurna, *dare not.*
Daut, *to fondle, to doat on.*
Daw, *to dawn.*
Dawtit, *fondled, caressed.*
Daurg, *a day's work.*
Daviely, *spiritless.* [Dowiely.]
Davie's, *King David's.*

Dead-sweer, *extremely reluctant.*
Deave, *to deafen.*
Deils, *devils.*
Deil ma care, *devil may care, no matter for all that.*
Deil haet, *devil a thing; devil have it!*
Deleerit, *delirious.*
Delvin, *delving.*
Descrive, *to describe.*
Deservin't, *deserving of it.*
Deuk, *a duck.*
Devel, *a stunning blow.*
Diddle, *to jog, or fiddle.*
Differ, *difference.*
Dight, *cleaned from chaff, to wipe away.*
Din, *dun in colour.*
Ding, *to surpass, to beat.*
Dink, *neat; trim.*
Dinna, *do not.*
Dirl, *a thrilling blow.*
Dizzen, *a dozen.*
Dochter, *daughter.*
Doited, *stupefied.*
Donsie, *stupid, unmanageable.*
Dooked, *ducked.*
Dool, *sorrow.*
Doolfu', *sorrowful.*
Doos, *pigeons.*
Dorty, *saucy, sullen.*
Douce, *grave, sober, modest, gentle.*
Doucely, *soberly.*
Doudled, *dandled.*
Dought, *could, might.*
Dought na, *did not, or did not choose to.*
Doup, *the backside, the bottom.*
Dour, *stubborn.*
Dow, *do, can.*
Dowff, *pithless, dull.*
Dowie, *faded or worn with sorrow, sad.*
Downa bide, *cannot stand.*
Downa do, *impotence.*
Doylt, *stupid.*
Doytin, *walking stupidly.*
Dozen'd, *impotent, torpid or be-numbed.*
Draiglit, *draggled.*
Drants, *sullen fits.*
Drap, *drop, a small quantity.*
Drappie, dim. *of drap.*
Drapping, *dropping.*

Draunting, *drawling, of a slow enunciation.*

Dree, *to endure.*

Dreeping, *dripping.*

Dreigh, *tedious and slow.*

Driddle, *to play on the fiddle without skill.*

Drift, *a drove.* Fell aff the drift, *wandered from his companions.*

Droddum, *the breech.*

Drone, *the bagpipe.*

Droop-rumpl't, *that droops at the crupper.*

Drouk, *to drench.*

Droukit, *wet, drenched.*

Drouth, *thirst.*

Drouthy, *thirsty.*

Druken, *drunken.*

Drumly, *muddy.*

Drummock, *meal and water mixed raw.*

Drunt, *pet, sullen humour.*

Dry, *thirsty.*

Dubs, *puddles.*

Duds, *garments.*

Duddie, *ragged.*

Duddies, *garments.*

Dung, *knocked, exhausted.*

Dunted, *beat, thumped.*

Dunts, *blows, knocks.*

Durk, *a dirk.*

Dusht, *pushed.*

Dwalling, *dwelling.*

Dwalt, *dwelt.*

Dyvors, *bankrupts, disreputable fellows.*

Earns, *eagles.*

Eastlin, *eastern.*

Ee, *eye ; to watch.*

Een, *eyen.*

E'e brie, *the eyebrow.*

E'en *evening.*

E'enins, *evenings.*

Eerie, *having or producing a superstitious feeling of dread ; dismal.*

Eild, *age.*

Eke, *also.*

Elbucks, *elbows.*

Eldritch, *elvish ; strange, wild, hideous.*

Eleckit, *elected.*

Eller, *an elder.*

En', *end.*

Enbrugh, *Edinburgh.*

Em'brugh, *Edinburgh.*

Enow, *enough.*

Erse, *Gaelic.*

Ether-stane, *adder-stone.*

Ettle, *design.*

Expeckit, *expected.*

Eydent, *diligent.*

Fa', *lot ; also, have as one's lot, obtain.*

Faddom't, *fathomed.*

Fae, *foe.*

Faem, *foam.*

Faikit, *bated, forgiven, excused.*

Failins, *failings.*

Fair-fa', *may good befall !*

Fairin, *a present, a reward.*

Fairly, *entirely, completely.*

Fallow, *a fellow.*

Fa'n or fa'en, *have fallen.*

Fan, *found.*

Fand, *found.*

Farls, *cakes of oat-bread.*

Fash, *trouble myself.*

Fash your thumb, *trouble yourself in the least.*

Fashous, *troublesome.*

Fasten-een, *Fasten's-even (before Lent).*

Fatt'rels, *ribbon-ends.*

Faught, *a fight.*

Fauld, *a fold.*

Faulding, *folding.*

Faulding slap, *the gate of the fold.*

Fause, *false.*

Faut, *fault.*

Fautor, *a transgressor.*

Fawsont, *seemly, respectably.*

Fearfu', *fearful.*

Feat, *spruce.*

Fecht, *to fight.*

Feck, *the greater portion.*

Feckly, *mostly.*

Fecket, *an under waistcoat with sleeves.*

Feckless, *powerless, without effect.*

Feg, *a fig.*

Feide, *feud.*

Fell, *the flesh immediately under the skin ; keen, biting ; tasty.*

Fen, *a shift. provision.*

Fend, *to keep off, to live comfortably.*

Ferlie, *wonder.*

Fetch't, *pulled by fits and starts.*

Fey, *fated.*

Fidge, *to fidget.*

Fidgin-fain, *fidgetting with eagerness.*

Fiel, *soft, smooth.*

Fient, *fiend.* The fient a, *the devil a.*

Fier, *healthy, sound ; brother, friend.*

Fiere, *companion.*

Fillie, *a filly.*

Fin', *find.*

Fissle, *bustle or rustle.*

Fit, *foot.*

Fittie-lan, *the near horse of the hindermost pair in the plough.*

Fizz, *to make a hissing noise like fermentation.*

Flaffin, *flapping, fluttering.*

Flae, *a flea.*

Flang, *did fling or caper.*

Flannen, *flannel.*

Fleech'd, *supplicated, flattered.*

Flee, *a fly.*

Fleesh, *a fleece.*

Fleg, *a fright, a random stroke.*

Fleth'rin, *flattering.*

Flewit, *a sharp blow.*

Fley'd, *scared.*

Flichterin', *fluttering.*

Flinders, *shreds.*

Flinging, *dancing wildly.*

Flingin-tree, *a flail.*

Fliskit, *fretted and capered.*

Flittering, *fluttering.*

Flyte, *to scold*

Fodgel, *squat, plump.*

Foor, *fared, went.*

Foord, *a ford.*

Foorsday, *Thursday.*

Forbears, *forefathers.*

Forbye, *besides.*

Forfairn, *worn out, jaded.*

Forfoughten, *fatigued.*

Forgather, *meet, fall in with.*

Forgie, *forgive.*

Forjesket, *jaded with fatigue.*

Forrit, *forward.*

Fother, *fodder.*

Fou, *full, tipsy.*

Foughten, *troubled.*

Fouth, *abundance.*

Fow, *full measure of corn, bushel.*

Frae, *from.*

Freath, *to froth.*

Fremit, *strange, foreign.*

Frien', *friend.*

Fu', *full.*

Fud, *hare's tail.*

Fufft, *puffed, blew.*

Furder, *furtherance, success.*

Furms, *wooden forms or seats.*

Furr-ahin, *the hindmost horse on the right hand of the plough.*

Furrs, *furrows.*

Fushionless, *pithless.*

Fy, *an exclamation of haste.*

Fyke, *trouble, fuss.*

Fyle, *to soil or dirty.*

Gab, *the mouth ; to prate.*

Gae, *go, gave.*

Gaed, *went.*

Gaets, *manners, or ways.*

Gairs, *'purple patches.'*

Gane, *gone.*

Gang, *to go.*

Gangrel, *vagrant.*

Gar, *to make.*

Garten, *garter.*

Gash, *sagacious.*

Gashin, *conversing.*

Gat, *got.*

Gate, *manner, way or road.*

Gatty, *swelled.*

Gaucie, *large, bushy, full, stately.*

Gaud, *the plough shaft.*

Gaudsman, *a ploughboy, the boy who drives the horses in the plough.*

Gaun, *going.*

Gaunted, *yawned.*

Gawcie, *jolly, large, flourishing.*

Gawkies, *foolish persons.*

Gawn, *Gavin.*

Gaylies, *pretty well.*

Gear, *wealth, goods.*

Geck, *to toss the head in scorn.*

Geds, *pike.*

Genty, *slender.*

Geordie, *George.* The yellow letter'd Geordie, *a guinea.*

Get, *child.*

Ghaists, *ghosts.*

Gie, *give.*

Gied, *gave.*

Gien, *given.*

Gi'en, *given.*

Gies, *give us.*

Gif, *if.*

Giftie, *dim. of gift.*

Giglets. *laughing children.*

Gillie, *dim. of gill.*

Gilpey, *a young person.*

Gimmer, *a ewe two years old.*

Gin, *if.*

Girdle, *a circular plate of iron for toasting cakes on the fire.*

Girn, *to grin.*

Girrs, *hoops.*

Gizz, *a wig.*

Glaikit, *thoughtless, giddy.*

Glaizie, *smooth, glossy.*

Glamour, *effect of a charm.*

Glaum'd, *grasped.*

Gled, *a kite.*

Gleed, *a live coal.*

Gleg, *sharp; cleverly, swiftly.*

Gleib, *a gleb or portion.*

Glib-gabbet, *that speaks smoothly and readily.*

Glinted, *glanced.*

Gloamin, *twilight.*

Gloamin-shot, *a twilight interview.*

Glowrin, *staring.*

Glowr'd, *looked earnestly, stared.*

Glunch, *a frown.*

Goavan, *moving and looking vacantly.*

Gotten, *got.*

Gowan, *the daisy.*

Gowd, *gold.*

Gowden, *golden.*

Gowff'd, *golfed.*

Gowk, *a fool.*

Gowling, *howling.*

Graff, *a grave.*

Grained, *groaned.*

Graip, *a pronged instrument.*

Graith, *harness accoutrements.*

Granes, *groans.*

Grannie, *grandmother.*

Grape, *to grope.*

Grapit, *groped.*

Grat, *wept.*

Gree, *a prize; to agree.*

Gree't, *agreed.*

Greet, *to weep.*

Griens, *longs for.*

Grippet, *gripped, caught hold of.*

Grissle, *gristle.*

Grit, *great.*

Grozet, *a gooseberry.*

Grumphie, *the sow.*

Grun', *the ground.*

Grunstane, *a grindstone.*

Gruntle, *the countenance, a grunting noise.*

Grunzie, *the mouth.*

Grushie, *thick, of thriving growth.*

Grusome, *ill favoured.*

Grutten, *wept.*

Gudeen, *good even.*

Gudeman, *goodman.*

Gudes, *goods.*

Guid, *good.*

Guid-e'en, *good even.*

Guidfather, *father-in-law.*

Guidwife, *the mistress of the house, the landlady.*

Guid-willie, *hearty.*

Gully, *a large knife.*

Gulravage, *riotous and hasty.*

Gumlie, *muddy, discoloured.*

Gumption, *understanding.*

Gusty, *tasteful.*

Gutcher, *grandfather, goodsire.*

Ha', *hall,*

Haddin, *holding, inheritance.*

Hae, *have.*

Haffets, *the temples.*

Hafflins, *partly; also, growing lads.*

Hafflins-wise, *almost half.*

Hag, *a pit in mosses and moors.*

Haggis, *a kind of pudding boiled in the stomach of an ox or a sheep.*

Hain, *to spare, to save.*

Hain'd, *spared.*

Hairst, *harvest.*

Haith, *faith!*

Haivers, *idle talk.*

Hald, *an abiding-place.*

Hale, *whole, entire.*

Haly, *holy.*

Hallan, *a partition-wall in a cottage, hall-end.*

Hallions, *clowns, roysterers.*

Hallowmas, *the 31st of October.*

Hame, *home.*

Han', *hand.*

Han' afore, *the foremost horse on the left hand in the plough.*

Han' ahin, *the hindmost horse on the left hand in the plough.*

Hand-breed, *a hand-breadth.*

Hand-waled, *carefully selected by hand.*

Handless, *without hands, useless, awkward.*

Hangit, *hanged.*

Hansel, *a gift for a particular season, or the first money on any particular occasion.*

Hap, *to wrap.* Winter hap, *winter clothing.*

Hap, *hop.*

Happer, *a hopper.*

Happing, *hopping.*

Hap-step-an'-lowp, *hop, step, and jump.*

Harkit, *hearkened.*

Harn, *coarse linen.*

Har'sts, *harvests.*

Hash, *a soft, useless fellow.*

Hash'd, *cut.*

Haslock, *the finest wool, being the lock that grows on the hals or throat.*

Hastit, *hasted.*

Haud, *to hold.*

Hauf, *the half.*

Haughs, *low-lying lands on the border of a river.*

Hauns, *hands.*

Haurl, *to drag.*

Haurlin, *peeling, dragging off.*

Hauver, *coarsely ground.*

Havins, *good manners.*

Hav'rel, *half-witted.*

Hawkie, *a cow, properly one with a white face.*

Healsome, *wholesome.*

Heapit, *heaped.*

Hearin', *hearing.*

Hearse, *hoarse.*

Hech, *an exclamation of surprise and grief.*

Hecht, *foretold, offered.*

Hechtin', *making to pant.*

Heckle, *a comb used in dressing hemp, flax, &c.*

Heels-o'er-gowdy, *head-over-heels.*

Heeze, *to elevate, to hoist.*

Heft, *haft.*

Hellim, *the helm.*

Hen-broo, *hen-broth.*

Herriet, *harried.*

Herryment, *plundering, devastation.*

Hersel, *herself.*

Het, *hot.*

Heugh, *a pit or ravine.*

Heuk, *a reaping-hook.*

Hich, *high.*

Hidin', *hiding.*

Hie, *high.*

Hilch, *to hobble.*

Hilchin, *halting.*

Hill-tap, *hill-top.*

Hiltie-skiltie, *helter-skelter.*

Himsel, *himself.*

Hiney, *honey.*

Hing, *to hang.*

Hirples, *walks as if crippled.*

Hissel, hirsel, *as many cattle or sheep as one person can attend.*

Histie, *dry, barren.*

Hitch, *a loop or knot.*

Hizzies, *young women.*

Hoast, *a cough.*

Hoddin, *jogging, plodding.*

Hoggie, *a young sheep one year old.*

Hog-score, *a line drawn across the rink in the game of curling.*

Hog-shouther, *a kind of horse-play by justling with the shoulder.*

Hol't, *holed, perforated.*

Hoodie-craw, *the hooded crow.*

Hool, *the outer skin or case.*

Hoolie ! *stop ! cautiously ! softly !*

Hoord, *hoard.*

Hoordet, *hoarded.*

Horn, *a spoon or a comb made of horn.*

Hornie, *Satan.*

Host or hoast, *a cough.*

Hostin, *coughing.*

Hotch'd, *fidgeted.*

Houghmagandie, *fornication.*

Houlets, *owls.*

Hov'd, *swelled.*

Howdie, *a midwife.*

Howe, *hollow.*

Howe-backit, *sunk in the back.*

Howes, *hollows.*

Howkit, *digged, dug up.*
Hoyse, *hoist.*
Hoy't, *urged.*
Hoyte, *to move clumsily.*
Hughoc, *Hugh.*
Hunder, *a hundred.*
Hunkers, *the hams.*
Huntit, *hunted.*
Hurcheon, *a hedgehog.*
Hurchin, *an urchin.*
Hurdies, *hips.*
Hurl, *to wheel or whirl.*
Hushion, *stocking-leg, worn on the arm.*
Hyte, *mad.*

Icker, *an ear of corn.*
Ier'oe, *a great-grandchild.*
Ilk, *each.*
Ilka, *every.*
Ill o't, *bad at it.*
Ill-willie, *ill-natured.*
Indentin, *indenturing.*
Ingine, *genius, ingenuity.*
Ingle-cheek, *the fireside.*
Ingle-lowe, *the household fire.*
I'se, *I shall or will.*
Isna, *is not.*
Ither, *other.*
Itsel, *itself.*

Jad, *a jade, a wild young woman.*
Janwar, *January.*
Jauk, *to dally, to trifle.*
Jaukin, *trifling, dallying.*
Jauner, *foolish talk.*
Jaups, *splashes.*
Ji!let, *a jilt.*
J:mp, *slender.*
Jimply, *neatly.*
Jink, *to dodge.*
Jinker, *that turns quickly.*
Jinkers, *gay, sprightly girls.*
Jinkin, *dodging.*
Jirkinet, *an outer jacket or jerkin worn by women.*
Jirt, *a jerk ; to squirt.*
Jo, *sweetheart, joy.*
Joctelegs, *clasp-knives.*
Joes, *lovers.*
Jorum, *the jug.*

Jouk, *to duck, to make obeisance.*
Jow, *to swing and ring.*
Jumpit, *jumped.*
Jundie, *to justle.*

Kaes, *daws.*
Kail, *broth.*
Kail-blade, *the leaf of the colewort.*
Kail-runt, *the stem of the colewort.*
Kain, *farm produce paid as rent.*
Kebars, *rafters.*
Kebbuck, *a cheese.*
Keckle, *to cackle, to laugh.*
Keekin'-glass, *a looking-glass.*
Keeks, *peeps.*
Keepit, *kept.*
Kelpies, *water-spirits.*
Ken, *know.*
Ken'les, *kindles.*
Kenn'd, *known.*
Kennin, *a little bit.*
Kent, *knew.*
Kep, *to catch anything when falling.*
Ket, *a fleece.*
Kiaugh, *anxiety, cark.*
Kilbagie, *the name of a certain kind of whisky.*
Kilt, *to tuck up.*
Kimmer, *a married woman, a gossip.*
Kin', *kind.*
King's-hood, *a part of the entrails of an ox.*
Kintra, *country*
Kintra cooser, *a country stallion.*
Kirn, *a churn.*
Kirns, *harvest-homes.*
Kirsen, *to christen.*
Kist, *a chest.*
Kitchen, *anything that eats with bread to serve for a relish.*
Kitchens, *seasons, makes palatable.*
Kittle, *to tickle ; ticklish, difficult.*
Kittlin, *a kitten.*
Kiutlin, *fondling.*
Knaggie, *like knags, or points of rock.*
Knappin-hammers, *hammers for breaking stones.*
Knowe, *a knoll.*
Knurlin, *a dwarf, knotted, gnarled.*
Kye, *cows.*
Kytes, *bellies.*
Kythe, *discover, appear.*

Laddie, *a lad.*
Lade, *a load.*
Laggen, *the angle between the side and bottom of a wooden dish.*
Laigh, *low.*
Laik, *lack.*
Lair, *lore.*
Lairing, *sticking in mire or mud.*
Laith, *loth.*
Laithfu', *bashful.*
Lallan, *lowland.*
Lampit, *limpet.*
Lan', *land, estate.*
Lane, *alone.*
Lanely, *lonely.*
Lang, *long.*
Lap, *did leap.*
Lave, *the rest.*
Lav'rocks, *larks.*
Lawin, *shot, reckoning, bill.*
Lawlan', *lowland.*
Lea'e, *leave.*
Leal, *true, loyal.*
Lea rig, *a grassy ridge.*
Lear, *lore, learning.*
Lee-lang, *live-long.*
Leesome, *or lo'esome, pleasant.*
Leeze me, *leif (or dear) is to me ; mine above everything else be.*
Leister, *a three-barbed instrument for sticking fish.*
Len', *lend.*
Leugh, *laughed.*
Leuk, *look, appearance.*
Libbet, *gelded.*
Licket, *beating.*
Licks, *a beating.*
Licin, *telling lies.*
Lien, *lain.*
Lift, *heaven, a large quantity.*
Lightly, *to underralue, to slight.*
Lilt, *sing.*
Limmer, *a woman of loose manners or morals.*
Limpit, *limped.*
Lin, *a waterfall.*
Linket, *tripped deftly.*
Linkin, *tripping.*
Linn, *a waterfall.*
Lint, *flax.*
Linties, *linnets.*
Lippened, *trusted.*

Loan, *lane.*
Lo'ed, *loved.*
Lon'on, *London.*
Loof, *palm of the hand.*
Loosome, *lovesome.*
Loot, *did let.*
Looves, *palms.*
Losh, *a petty oath.*
Lough, *a lake.*
Louns, *fellows, rascals.*
Loup, *to leap.*
Lowe, *flame.*
Lowan, *flaming.*
Lowin, *blazing.*
Lowpin, *leaping.*
Lowping, *leaping.*
Lowse, *to loosen.*
Luckie, *a designation applied to an elderly woman.*
Lug, *the ear.*
Lugget, *eared.*
Luggies, *small wooden dishes with straight handles.*
Luke, *look.*
Lum, *the-chimney.*
Lunardie, *a bonnet called after Lunardi, the aëronaut.*
Lunt, *a column of smoke.*
Luntin, *smoking.*
Luve, *love.*
Luvers, *lovers.*
Lyart, *grey.*
Lynin, *lining.*

Maf, *more.*
Mair, *more.*
Maist, *almost.*
Mak, *make.*
Majlie, *Molly.*
Mailins, *farms.*
Mang, *among.*
Manteels, *mantles.*
Mashlum, *mixed corn.*
Maskin-pat, *a tea-pot.*
Maukin, *a hare.*
Maun, *must.*
Maunna, *must not.*
Maut, *malt.*
Mavis, *the thrush.*
Mawin, *mowing.*
Mawn, *a basket ; mown.*
Meere, *a mare.*

Meikle, *as much.*
Melder, *corn sent to the mill to be ground.*
Mell, *to meddle.*
Melvie, *to soil with mud.*
Men', *mend.*
Mense, *good manners.*
Mess John, *the clergyman.*
Messin, *a dog of mixed breeds.*
Midden, *the dunghill.*
Midden-creels, *dunghill baskets.*
Midden-hole, *the dunghill.*
Mim, *prim.*
Mim-mou'd, *prim-mouthed.*
Min', *remembrance.*
Min', *mind.*
Minnie, *mother.*
Mirk, *night; murky.*
Misca'd, *abused.*
Misguidin', *misguiding.*
Mishanter, *misfortune, disaster.*
Mislear'd, *mischievous; ill-bred.*
Mist, *missed.*
Misteuk, *mistook.*
Mither, *mother.*
Mixtie-maxtie, *confusedly mixed.*
Moistify, *to make moist.*
Mony, *many.*
Mools, *the earth of graves.*
Moop, *to nibble, to keep company with.*
Moorlan', *moorland.*
Moss, *a morass.*
Mou', *mouth.*
Moudieworts, *moles.*
Muckle, *great, big, much.*
Muslin-kail, *thin broth*
Mutchkin, *an English pint.*
Mysel, *myself.*

Na', *not, no.*
Nae, *no.*
Naebody, *nobody.*
Naig, *a nag.*
Nane, *none.*
Nappy, *strong ale.*
Natch, *grip, hold.*
Neibors, *neighbours.*
Needna, *need not.*
Neist, *next.*
Neuk, *nook, corner.*
New-ca'd, *newly calved.*

Nick, *to break, to sever suddenly.*
Nickan, *cutting*
Nicket, *caught, cut off.*
Nick-nackets, *curiosities.*
Nicks, *notches.*
Niest, *next.*
Nieve-fu', *a fist-full.*
Nieves, *fists.*
Niffer, *exchange.*
Nits, *nuts.*
Nocht, *nothing.*
Norland, *Northland.*
Nowte, *cattle.*

O', *of.*
O'erlay, *an outside cravat, muffler.*
O'erword, *refrain.*
Ony, *any.*
Orra, *superfluous, extra.*
O't, *of it.*
Ought, *aught, anything.*
Oughtlins, *anything in the least.*
Ourie, *shivering, drooping.*
Oursel, *ourselves.*
Out-cast, *a quarrel.*
Outler, *un-housed, outlying.*
Owre, *over, too.*
Owsen, *oxen.*

Pack an' thick, *on intimate terms, closely familiar.*
Packs, *twelve stones.*
Paidle, *to paddle.*
Paidles, *wanders about without aim.*
Painch, *paunch, stomach.*
Paitricks, *partridges.*
Pangs, *crams.*
Parishen, *the parish.*
Parritch, *porridge.*
Parritch-pats, *porridge-pots.*
Pat, *put; a pot.*
Pattle, *a plough-spade.*
Paughty, *haughty, petulant.*
Paukie, *cunning, sly.*
Pay't, *paid.*
Pechan, *the stomach.*
Pechin', *panting.*
Penny wheep, *small beer.*
Pettle, *a plough-spade.*
Phraisin, *flattering, coaxing.*
Pickle, *a small quantity.*
Pit, *put.*

Placads, *public proclamations.*

Plack, *an old Scotch coin, the third part of a Scotch penny, twelve of which make an English penny.*

Plaiden, *plaiding.*

Plenished, *stocked.*

Pleugh, *plough.*

Pliskie, *a mischievous trick.*

Pliver, *a plover.*

Plumpit, *plumped.*

Pocks, *wallets or bags.*

Poind, *to seize or distrain.*

Poortith, *poverty.*

Pou, *to pull ; to gather.*

Pouk, *to pluck.*

Poupit, *the pulpit.*

Pouse, *push or thrust.*

Poussie, *a hare.*

Pouts, *chicks.*

Pouther'd, *powdered.*

Pouthery, *powdery.*

Pow, *the head, the poll.*

Pownie, *a pony.*

Powther, *powder.*

Pree, *to taste.*

Preen, *a pin.*

Prent, *print.*

Prie'd, *tasted.*

Prief, *proof.*

Priggin', *haggling.*

Primsie, *demure, prim.*

Propone, *to propose.*

Proveses, *provosts.*

Pu', *to pull.*

Puddock-stools, *toadstools.*

Puir, *poor.*

Pund, *pounds.*

Pyet, *the magpie.*

Pyke, *to pick.*

Pyles, *grains.*

Quaick, *quack.*

Quat, *quit, quitted.*

Quaukin', *quaking.*

Quean, *a young woman.*

Quey, *a young cow.*

Quo', *quoth.*

Rab, *Rob, Robert.*

Rad, *afraid.*

Rade, *rode.*

Ragweed, *the plant ragwort.*

Raibles, *rattles nonsense.*

Rair, *to roar.*

Raise, *rose.*

Raize, *to madden, to inflame.*

Ramblin, *rambling.*

Ramfeezl'd, *fatigued.*

Ramgunshock, *rugged.*

Ram-stam, *forward, precipitate.*

Randie, *quarrelsome.*

Randy, *a vixen.*

Ranting, *noisy, full of animal spirits.*

Rants, *jollifications.*

Rape, *a rope.*

Raploch, *coarse cloth.*

Rask, *a rush.*

Rash-buss, *a bush of rushes.*

Rattan, *a rat.*

Rattons, *rats.*

Raucle, *rough, rash, sturdy.*

Raught, *reached.*

Raw, *a row.*

Rax, *to stretch.*

Ream, *cream.*

Rebute, *a rebut, a repulse, a rebuke.*

Rede, *counsel.*

Red-wud, *stark mad.*

Reekin, *smoking.*

Reekit, *smoked, smoky.*

Reeks, *smokes.*

Reestit, *smoke-dried ; stood restive.*

Reif randies, *roysterers.*

Remead, *remedy.*

Remuve, *remove.*

Rew, *to take pity.*

Rickles, *stocks of grain.*

Rig, *a ridge.*

Riggin, *rafters.*

Rigwoodie, *withered, sapless.*

Rin, *run.*

Rink, *the course of the stones in curling.*

Rinnin, *running.*

Ripp, *a handful of unthrashed corn.*

Ripple, *weakness in the back and reins.*

Ripplin-kame, *a flax-comb.*

Riskit, *made a noise like the tearing of roots.*

Rive, *to burst or tear.*

Rock, *a distaff.*

Rockin, *a social gathering, the women spinning on the rock or distaff.*

Roon, *round.*
Roose, *to praise.*
Roosty, *rusty.*
Roun', *round.*
Roupet. *hoarse as with a cold.*
Routhie, *well filled, abundant.*
Rowes, *rolls.*
Rowte, *to low, to bellow.*
Rowth, *abundance.*
Rowtin, *lowing.*
Rozet, *rosin.*
Ruefu', *rueful.*
Rung, *a cudgel.*
Runkl'd, *wrinkled.*
Runts, *the stems of cabbage.*
Ryke, *reach.*

Sabs, *sobs.*
Sae, *so.*
Saft, *soft.*
Sair, *sore : to serre.*
Sairly, *sorely.*
Sair't, *serred.*
Sang, *song.*
Sannock or Sawnie, *Alexander.*
Sark, *a shirt.*
Sarkit, *provided in shirts.*
Saugh, *the willow.*
Saul, *soul.*
Saunt, *saints.*
Saut, *salt.*
Saw, *to sow.*
Sawmont, *a salmon.*
Sax, *six.*
Scaith, *hurt.*
Scaur, *to scare.*
Scaur, *frightened.*
Scaud, *to scald.*
Scawl, *a scold.*
Scho, *she.*
Schoolin', *schooling, teaching.*
Scones, *barley cakes.*
Sconner, *to loathe ; disgust.*
Scraichin, *screeching.*
Screed, *a tear, a rent; to repeat glibly.*
Scriechin', *screeching.*
Scrievin', *gliding easily.*
Scrimpit, *scanty.*
Scrimply, *sparingly.*
Scroggie, *covered with stunted shrubs.*
Sculdudd'ry, *fornication.*

Seizins, *investitures.*
Sel, *self.*
Sell't, *sold.*
Sen', *send.*
Set, *lot.*
Sets, *becomes, set off, starts.*
Settlin', *settling.*
Shachl't, *loose and ill-shaped.*
Shaird, *a shred.*
Shangan, *a cleft stick.*
Shanna, *shall not.*
Shaul, *shallow.*
Shaver, *a wag.*
Shavie, *a trick.*
Shaw, *show.*
Shaw'd, *showed.*
Shaws, *wooded dells.*
Sheep-shank, Wha thinks himsel nae sheep-shank bane, *who thinks himself no unimportant person.*
Sheers, *shears.*
Sheugh, *a trench or ditch.*
Sheuk, *shook.*
Shiel, *a shieling, a hut.*
Shill, *shrill.*
Shog, *a shock.*
Shools, *shovels.*
Shoon, *shoes.*
Shor'd, *threatened, offered.*
Shore, *to threaten or offer.*
Shouldna, *should not.*
Shouther, *shoulder.*
Shure, *did shear (corn).*
Sic, *such.*
Siker, *secure.*
Siclike, *suchlike.*
Sidelins, *sidelong.*
Siller, *money, silver.*
Simmer, *summer.*
Sin', *since.*
Sindry, *sundry.*
Singet, *singed.*
Singin', *singing.*
Sinn, *the sun.*
Sinny, *sunny.*
Sinsyne, *since then.*
Skaith, *hurt.*
Skaithing, *injuring.*
Skeigh, *high-mettled, disdainful, skittish.*
Skellum, *a worthless fellow.*
Skelp, *a slap ; to run with a slapping*

vigorous sound of the feet on the ground.

Skelpie-limmer, *a technical term in female scolding.*

Skinkin', *thin, liquid.*

Skinklin, *glittering,*

Skirl, *to shriek.*

Sklent, *to slope, to strike obliquely, to lie.*

Sklented, *slanted.*

Sklentin, *slanting.*

Skouth, *range, scope.*

Skreech, *to scream.*

Skriegh, *to scream.*

Skyrin, *parti-coloured.*

Skyte, *a glancing sliding stroke.*

Slade, *slid.*

Slae, *the sloe.*

Slaps, *gaps or breaches.*

Slaw, *slow.*

Slee, *sly, clever.*

Sleeest, *slyest.*

Sleekit, *sleek.*

Slidd'ry, *slippery.*

Sloken, *to quench, to allay thirst.*

Slypet, *slipped, fell over slowly.*

Sma', *small.*

Smeddum, *dust, mettle, sense.*

Smeek, *smoke.*

Smiddy, *a smithy.*

Smoor'd, *smothered.*

Smoutie, *smutty.*

Smytrie, *a number huddled together, a smatter.*

Snash, *abuse, impertinence.*

Snaw broo, *melted snow.*

Snawy, *snowy.*

Sned, *to lop, to cut off.*

Snell, *bitter, biting.*

Sneeshin-mill, *a snuff-box.*

Snick, *the latchet of a door.*

Snirtle, *to laugh slily.*

Snool, *to cringe, to sneak, to snub.*

Snoov'd, *went smoothly.*

Snowkit, *snuffed.*

Sodger, *a soldier.*

Soger, *a soldier.*

Sonsie, *jolly, comely, plump.*

Soom, *to swim.*

Soor, *sour.*

Sootie, *sooty.*

Sough, *a heavy sigh.*

Souk, *a suck.*

Soupe, *a spoonful, a small quantity of anything liquid.*

Souple, *supple.*

Souter, *a shoemaker.*

Sowps, *spoonfuls.*

Sowth, *to whistle over a tune.*

Sowther, *to solder, to make up.*

Spae, *to prophesy.*

Spails, *chips of wood.*

Spairges, *dashes or scatters about.*

Spairin, *sparing.*

Spak, *spake.*

Spate, *a flood.*

Spavie, *spavin (a disease).*

Spean, *to wean.*

Speel, *to climb.*

Speer, *to inquire.*

Spence, *the country parlour.*

Spier, *to ask, to inquire.*

Spleuchan, *a tobacco-pouch.*

Splore, *a frolic.*

Sprackled, *clambered.*

Sprattle, *to struggle.*

Spring, *a quick air in music, a Scottish reel.*

Spritty, *full of rushes or reed-grasses.*

Sprush, *spruce.*

Spunk, *fire, mettle.*

Spunkie, *full of spirit, mettlesome.*

Spunkies, *Wills-o'-the-wisp.*

Spurtle, *a stick with which porridge, broth, &c. are stirred.*

Squattle, *to sprawl.*

Stacher'd, *staggered, walked unsteadily.*

Stack, *stuck.*

Staig, *a horse two years old.*

Stan', *stand.*

Stanes, *stones.*

Stang, *to sting.*

Stank, *a pool of stagnant water.*

Stap, *to stop.*

Stark, *strong, hardy.*

Starns, *stars.*

Staukin, *stalking.*

Staw, *to steal, to surfeit.*

Stechin, *cramming.*

Steek, *to close.*

Steeks, *stitches.*

Steer, *to molest, to stir up.*

Steeve, *firm.*

Stells, *stills—commonly illicit.*
Sten, *a leap or bound.*
Stents, *assessments, dues.*
Steyest, *steepest.*
Stibble, *stubble.*
Stibble-rig, *the reaper in harvest who takes the lead, a stubble-ridge.*
Stick-an-stowe, *totally, altogether.*
Stilt, *halt.*
Stimpart, *an eighth part of a Winchester bushel, half a peck.*
Stirk, *a cow or bullock a year or two old.*
Stockins, *stockings.*
Stockit, *stocked.*
Stocks, *plants of cabbage.*
Stoitered, *staggered.*
Stoor, *strong, harsh, deep.*
Stoppit, *stopped.*
Stot, *an ox.*
Stoure, *dust, dust blown on the wind, battle or confusion.*
Stown, *stolen.*
Stownlins, *by stealth.*
Stowrie, *dusty.*
Stoyte, *to stumble.*
Strade, *strode.*
Strae, *a fair strae-death, a natural death in bed.*
Straik, *to stroke.*
Straikit, *stroked.*
Strak, *struck.*
Strang, *strong.*
Strappin, *strapping.*
Straught, *straight.*
Streekit, *stretched.*
Striddle, *to straddle.*
Stringin, *stringing.*
Stroan't, *pissed.*
Studdie, *a stithy.*
Stumpie, *dim. of stump, a short quill.*
Strunt, *spirituous liquor of any kind; to strut.*
Stuff, *corn.*
Sturt, *trouble, stir, disturbance.*
Sturtin, *frighted.*
Styme, *see a styme, see in the least.*
Sucker, *sugar.*
Sud, *should.*
Sugh, *a rushing sound.*

Sumphs, *stupid fellows.*
Sune, *soon.*
Suthron, *Southern, English.*
Swaird, *sward.*
Swall'd, *swelled.*
Swank, *thin, agile, vigorous.*
Swankies, *strapping young fellows.*
Swap, *an exchange.*
Swarf, *to swoon.*
Swat, *did sweat.*
Swatch, *sample.*
Swats, *new ale.*
Swearin', *swearing.*
Sweatin, *sweating.*
Swinge, *to lash.*
Swirl, *a curve.*
Swith, *swift, suddenly.*
Swither, *hesitation.*
Swoor, *swore.*
Sybow, *a thick-necked onion.*
Syne, *since, then.*

Tack, *possession, lease.*
Tackets, *hob-nails.*
Tae, *toe.* Three-tae'd, *three-toed.*
Taed, *a toad.*
Taen, *taken.*
Tairge, *to task severely.*
Tak, *to take.*
Tald, *told.*
Tane, *the one.*
Tangs, *tongs.*
Tapetless, *heedless, foolish, pithless.*
Tapmost, *topmost.*
Tappit hen, *a quart measure.*
Taps, *tops.*
T'apsalteerie, *topsy-turvy.*
Tarrow, *to murmur.*
Tarry-breeks, *a sailor.*
Tassie, *a goblet or cup.*
Tauld, *told.*
Tawie, *that allows itself peaceably to be handled.*
Tawpies, *foolish young persons.*
Tawted, *matted.*
Teats, *small quantities.*
Teen, *sorrow.*
Tell'd, *told.*
Tellin', *telling.*
Temper-pin, *the wooden pin used for tempering or regulating the motion of a spinning-wheel.*

Tent, *to take heed, mark.*
Tentie, *heedful,*
Teughly, *toughly.*
Teuk, *took.*
Thack, *thatch.*
Thae, *these.*
Thairm, *fiddlestrings, intestines.*
Theekit, *thatched, covered up.*
Thegither, *together.*
Themsels, *themselves.*
Thieveless, *without an object, trifling, impotent.*
Thigger, *beggar.*
Thir, *these.*
Thirl'd, *thrilled, bound.*
Thole, *to suffer, to endure.*
Thou's, *thou art.*
Thowes, *thaws.*
Thowless, *slack, lazy.*
Thrang, *busy; a crowd.*
Thrapple, *the throat.*
Thrave, *twenty-four sheaves of corn, making two shocks.*
Thraw, *to sprain or twist, to cross or contradict.*
Thrawin', *twisting.*
Thrawn, *twisted.*
Thraws, *throes,*
Threap, *to assert.*
Thretteen, *thirteen.*
Thretty, *thirty.*
Thrissle, *the thistle.*
Throwther, *mixed, pell-mell.*
Thuds, *that makes a loud intermittent noise, resounding blows.*
Thummart, *the polecat.*
Thumpit, *thumped.*
Thysel', *thyself.*
Tidins, *tidings.*
Till, *to.*
Till't, *to it.*
Timmer, *timber.*
Timmer-propt, *timber-propped.*
Tine, *to lose or be lost.*
Tint, *lost.*
Tint as win, *lost as won.*
Tinkler, *a tinker.*
Tips, *rams.*
Tippence, *twopence.*
Tirl, *to strip or uncover.*
Tirl'd, *rasped (knocked).*
Tirlin, *unroofing.*

Tither, *the other.*
Tittlin, *whispering and laughing.*
Tocher, *marriage-portion.*
Todlin', *walking unsteadily or softly like an infant.*
Tods, *foxes.*
Toom, *empty.*
Toop, *a ram.*
Toun, *a hamlet, a farm-house.*
Tout, *the blast of a horn or trumpet.*
Touzie, *rough, shaggy.*
Touzle, *to rumple.*
Tow, *a rope.*
Towmond, *a twelvemonth.*
Toy, *a fashion of female head-dress.*
Toyte, *to totter.*
Transmugrify'd, *metamorphosed.*
Trashtrie, *trash.*
Treadin', *treading.*
Trews, *trousers.*
Trickie, *tricksy.*
Trig, *spruce, neat.*
Trinkling, *trickling.*
Troggin, *wares sold by wandering merchants or cadgers.*
Troke, *to exchange, to deal with.*
Trottin', *trotting.*
Trow't, *believed.*
Trowth ! *in truth !*
Tulzie, *a quarrel.*
Tup, *a ram.*
Twa, *two.*
Twa-fauld, *twofold.*
Twa-threo, *two or three.*
Twal, *twelve.*
Twalt, *the twelfth.*
Twang, *twinge.*
Twined, *reft, separated from.*
Twins, *bereaves, takes away from.*
Twistle, *a twist.*
Tyko, *a vagrant dog.*
Tyne, *to lose.*
Tysday 'teen, *Tuesday at evening.*

Unchancy, *dangerous.*
Unco, *very, great, extreme, strange.*
Uncos, *strange things, news of the country-side.*
Unkenn'd, *unknown.*
Unsicker, *unsecure.*
Unskaith'd, *unhurt.*
Upo', *upon.*

Upon't, *upon it.*

Vap'rin, *vapouring.*
Vauntie, *proud, in high spirits.*
Vera, *very.*
Viewin, *viewing.*
Virls, *rings.*
Vittel, *victual, grain.*
Vittle, *victual.*
Vogie, *proud, well-pleased.*
Vow, *an interjection of admiration or surprise.*

Wa', *a wall.*
Wa'-flower, *the wallflower.*
Wab, *a web.*
Wabster, *a weaver.*
Wad, *would; a wager; to wed.*
Wad a haen, *would have had.*
Wadna, *would not.*
Wadset, *a mortgage.*
Wae, *sorrowful.*
Wae days, *woful days.*
Waefu', *woful.*
Waes me, *woe's me.*
Waesucks! *alas!*
Wae worth, *woe befall.*
Waft, *the cross thread that goes from the shuttle through the web.*
Waifs, *stray sheep.*
Wair't, *spend it.*
Wal'd, *chose.*
Wale, *choice.*
Walie, *ample, large.*
Wallop in a tow, *to hang one's self.*
Wame, *the belly.*
Wamefou, *bellyfull.*
Wan, *did win, earned.*
Wanchancie, *unlucky.*
Wanrestfu', *restless.*
War'd, *spent, bestowed.*
Ware, *to spend.*
Wark, *work.*
Wark-lume, *tool.*
Warks, *works.*
Warld, *world.*
Warlock, *a wizard.*
Warly, *worldly.*
Warran', *warrant.*
Warsle, *to wrestle.*
Warst, *worst.*
Warstl'd, *wrestled.*

Wasna, *was not.*
Wast, *west.*
Wastrie, *prodigality, riot.*
Wat, *wet; wot, know.*
Wat na, *wot not.*
Waterbrose, *meal and water.*
Wattle, *twisted wands.*
Wauble, *to wabble.*
Waught, *a big drink.*
Waukening, *awakening.*
Waukens, *wakens.*
Waukit, *thickened with toil.*
Waukrife, *wakeful.*
Wauks, *awakes.*
Waur, *to fight, to defeat; worse.*
Waur't, *worsted.*
Weans, *children.*
Weason, *the weasand.*
Wee, *little.*
   A wee, *a short period of time.*
   A wee a-back, *a small space behind.*
Weel, *well.*
Weel-gaun, *well-going.*
Weel-kent, *well known.*
Weet, *wet.*
We'se, *we shall or will.*
Westlin, *western.*
Wha, *who.*
Wha e'er, *whoever.*
Whaizle, *to wheeze.*
Whalpit, *whelped.*
Wham, *whom.*
Whan, *when.*
Whang, *a large slice.*
Whar, *where.*
Whare, *where.*
Wha's, *whose.*
Whase, *whose.*
Whatfor no? *for what reason not?*
Whatt, *did whet or cut.*
Whaup, *a curlew.*
Whaur'll, *where will.*
Whiddin, *running as a hare.*
Whigmaleeries, *crochets.*
Whingin', *crying, complaining, fretting.*
Whins, *furze bushes.*
Whirlygigums, *useless ornaments.*
Whisht, *peace.*
Whiskit, *whisked.*
Whissle, *whistle.*

Whistle, *the throat.*
Whitter, *a hearty draught of liquor.*

Yard, *a garden.*
Yaud, *a worn-out horse.*
Yealings, *coevals.*
Yell, *barren, giving no milk.*
Yerd, *yard.*
Yerket, *jerked, lashed.*

Yerl, *an earl.*
Ye'se, *you shall or will.*
Yestreen, *yesternight.*
Yetts, *gates.*
Yeukin, *itching.*
Yeuks, *itches.*
Yill, *ale.*
Yill-caup, *ale-mug.*

PENGUIN POPULAR CLASSICS

PENGUIN POPULAR CLASSICS

Published or forthcoming

PENGUIN POPULAR CLASSICS

Published or forthcoming

George Grossmith	The Diary of a Nobody
Brothers Grimm	Grimm's Fairy Tales
H. Rider Haggard	Allan Quatermain
	King Solomon's Mines
Thomas Hardy	Far from the Madding Crowd
	Jude the Obscure
	The Mayor of Casterbridge
	A Pair of Blue Eyes
	The Return of the Native
	Tess of the D'Urbervilles
	The Trumpet-Major
	Under the Greenwood Tree
	The Woodlanders
Nathaniel Hawthorne	The Scarlet Letter
Anthony Hope	The Prisoner of Zenda
Thomas Hughes	Tom Brown's Schooldays
Victor Hugo	The Hunchback of Notre-Dame
Henry James	The Ambassadors
	The American
	The Aspern Papers
	Daisy Miller
	The Europeans
	The Portrait of a Lady
	The Turn of the Screw
	Washington Square
M. R. James	Ghost Stories
Jerome K. Jerome	Three Men in a Boat
	Three Men on the Bummel
James Joyce	Dubliners
	A Portrait of the Artist as a Young Man
Charles Kingsley	The Water Babies
Rudyard Kipling	Captains Courageous
	The Jungle Books
	Just So Stories
	Kim
	Plain Tales from the Hills
	Puck of Pook's Hill

PENGUIN POPULAR CLASSICS

PENGUIN POPULAR CLASSICS

PENGUIN POPULAR POETRY

Published or forthcoming

The Selected Poems *of:*

Matthew Arnold
William Blake
Robert Browning
Robert Burns
Lord Byron
John Donne
Thomas Hardy
John Keats
Rudyard Kipling
Alexander Pope
Alfred Tennyson
William Wordsworth
William Yeats

and collections of:

Seventeenth-Century Poetry
Eighteenth-Century Poetry
Poetry of the Romantics
Victorian Poetry
Twentieth-Century Poetry
Scottish Folk and Fairy Tales